THE LAST OF THE FIRST

IAN W. SAINSBURY

Copyright © 2018 by Ian W. Sainsbury

All rights reserved.

No part of this book may be reproduced in any form or by any electronic or mechanical means, including information storage and retrieval systems, without written permission from the author, except for the use of brief quotations in a book review.

For my brother, Paul

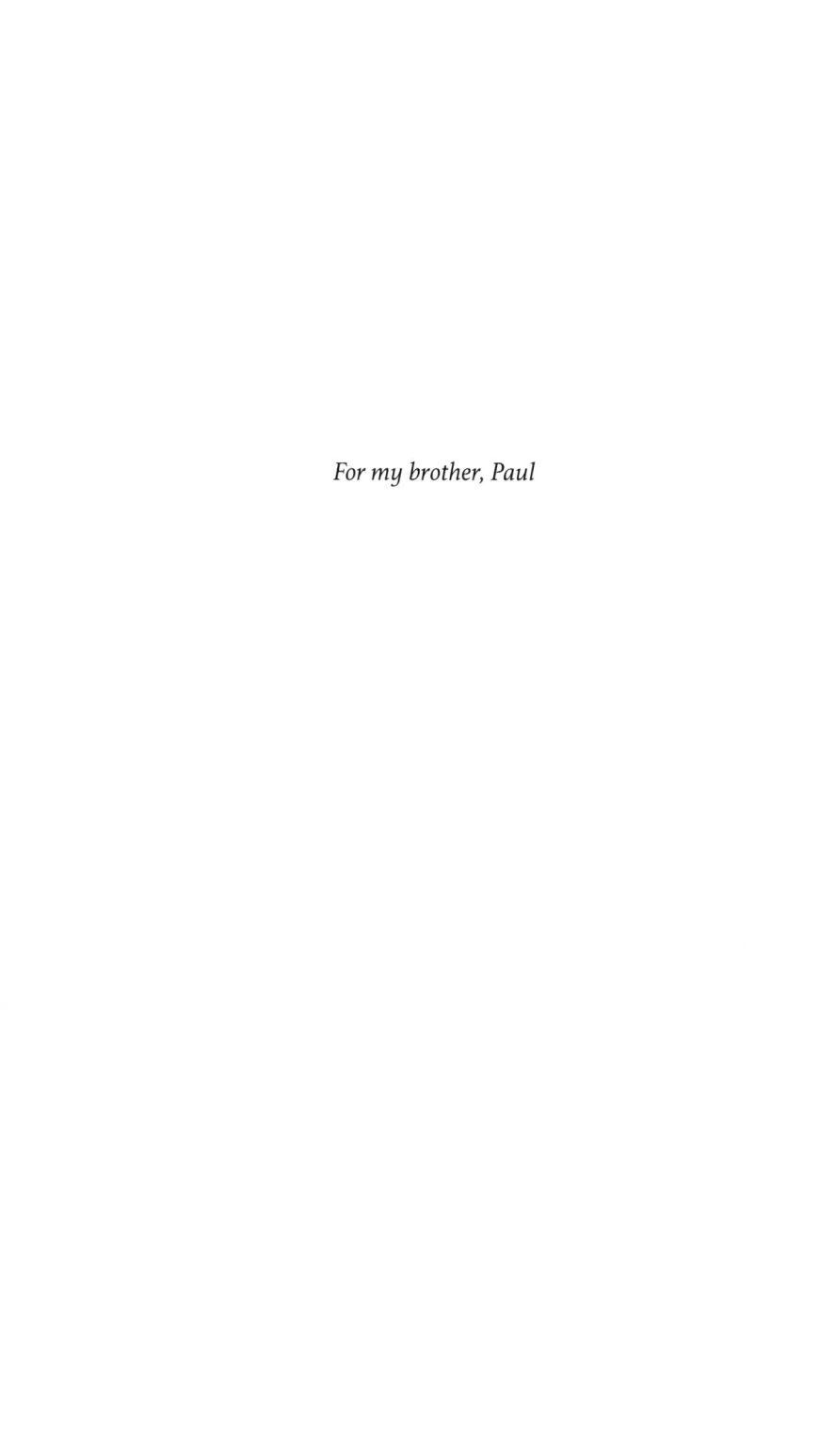

PREVIOUSLY IN THE HALFHERO SERIES... (A BRIEF CATCH UP WITH SPOILERS FROM BOOKS ONE AND TWO)

Abos is the world's first superbeing. Besides being strong, fast and bulletproof, she can return to a slime-like state when her current physical body dies. Which means she is not a *she* because her gender is dependent on the host body. Abos is no longer alone as she has found two more members of her species - Shuck and Susan.

While Abos brings the other superbeings back from their dormant states, her son Daniel has discovered a new purpose with fellow halfheroes Sara and Gabe, who, under the direction of United Nations representative, Saffi, bring in rogue halfheroes who have turned to crime. On a mission in Newcastle to take down drugs boss 'TripleDee' Davison, they are ambushed and drugged. They wake up in White Sands, New Mexico. Alongside every other halfhero alive, they are locked in a high-tech prison.

Abos searches for Daniel without success. But there's a new problem. Genius technology company owner, Titus Gorman, has found eight more of Abos's species. He has brainwashed them to be his protectors as he unleashes the Utopia Algorithm, a global cyber attack which redistributes all wealth. Gorman uses his superheroes—now known as titans—to commit murder and convince the US president to play ball.

When Shuck and Susan are fully grown, Abos takes them to America to search for the titans. The three superbeings can link their minds together. Onemind helps them with this searches they fly over swathes of America while mentally connected.

Meanwhile, Daniel, Sara, Gabe, and the other halfheroes break out of their prison, with the help of their own version of onemind. They head to Gorman's headquarters to confront him, only to find the eight titans waiting for them. In the ensuing fight, almost all the halfheroes are killed, Gabe included. Only Sara and TripleDee, who drive away, and Daniel, who is thrown over a cliff, and lies close to death, survive.

Abos, Shuck, and Susan find Daniel. While Shuck and Susan fight the titans, Abos takes his son to a nearby Albuquerque hospital, where he begins to heal. Abos goes back to find Gorman, only to discover Roger Sullivan, one of the scientists who knew him in Britain, is the real threat. Sullivan has killed Gorman, and he controls the titans. Susan and Shucks' bodies have been returned to dormancy and will be brainwashed in their new bodies. Abos suffers the same fate.

While recovering, Daniel finally meets Saffi for the first time. A tentative relationship develops. They mourn the loss of Gabe. TripleDee promises to fight alongside Daniel and Sara from now on, but he has a long way to go to earn their trust.

The situation is bleak. The titans now work for the American president, and Roger Sullivan is a national hero. Abos is male again and is being drugged and manipulated just as he was in the 1980s. It's Saffi who comes up with a plan...

During a Thanksgiving Day parade in New York City, the halfheroes divert the vehicles and the titans. Abos is confronted with a series of billboard images of home designed to break his conditioning. Daniel's favourite song —*Cars*, by Gary Numan—blasts out of a huge PA system. Abos remembers who he is and flies back to Great Britain.

Back in their farmhouse in Cornwall, Daniel, Abos, Saffi, Sara, and TripleDee are ready to accept a life on the run, when Sara has a better idea. She thinks they might be able to save the other titans from their mental enslavement. They all agree to give it a shot. Daniel has a secret he has yet to share. He has just found out his sperm was used anonymously for IVF treatments a generation ago. He is the father of a hundred and eight teenagers.

One superhero, three halfheroes and a human against eight titans and the military might of the United States Of America. Sara's plan had better be a good one.

<<<<>>>>

1

It was when the giant old man rose twenty feet into the air, his eyes liquid fire and his body wreathed in grey smoke that Tom first suspected he was dreaming.

Pretty much all of Tom's dreams started with sex, had sex in the middle, and ended with sex. He was sixteen years old. There was a girl in this dream—a cute girl—but fully dressed. Unusual.

That was how the dream had started. With the girl.

She was in a car. It was blue with a red passenger door. Tom was walking when it drew up alongside him, and the window whirred down.

The girl said nothing, but he knew, as she gave him a half-scared, half-excited smile, that she was asking him a question.

Are you going...?

Yes. Yes, he was. Tom was sure of that. He was going. Definitely. Where? Not a clue.

Then he was in the car. A second girl was driving, wearing 1950s-style sunglasses. She turned and smiled. Two girls smiling at him, but he hadn't tried picturing them naked. Bizarre.

The three of them didn't talk at all. Or maybe they did. It seemed to Tom that they must have had a long conversation because they were as comfortable together as old friends. No secrets.

Then they weren't in the car.

They were on a hill. It was high, giving a view across fields and villages so beautiful, it hardly seemed real.

He wasn't in Luton anymore.

The hill had a name, but he didn't know it yet. Tom and the girls climbed towards the summit, through purple heather and rough grass. Sheep ambled across their path.

Near the summit, Tom started to sense it. Half-scared, half-excited. For now, the excitement was stronger than the fear. Everything would be clear at the top. Everything would be right. Strange rock formations appeared as they got closer, like giant fingers pointing to heaven.

His friends were there. His family. His *people.*

When the sky darkened, the atmosphere changed and the word *scared* no longer did justice to the dread that sat in his belly like cold poison, then spread its spores throughout his body.

The others had arrived. They had come for Tom and his friends. The smoke-wreathed old man was there, too, with his terrible rage. And his power. A power that could crush bones, shred flesh. A power no one could stand against and survive.

Those awful eyes weren't looking at anyone in particular, but when Tom raised his head, he couldn't turn away. Other figures were moving somewhere in the air behind the old man, but Tom barely saw them.

The old man didn't look that old. No older than Tom's

dad, anyway. But dream-knowledge told Tom this being was ancient. And he was there to kill them. Although he and his friends had power of their own, Tom knew it wouldn't work. They weren't strong enough to stop him.

The old man raised his hands as if he were about to hurl an invisible boulder. There was nowhere to run, nothing Tom could do. He was going to die.

Tom woke up. After a few moments of disorientation, he clicked on his bedside lamp and looked at his watch. Five-fifteen. He slid out from under the duvet and went to the window. The dream was still with him, still half-real. More than that. Hard to believe it was a dream at all.

He twitched back the curtain. Still Luton. No sheep in sight.

Without thinking about what he was doing, Tom grabbed a canvas rucksack from his wardrobe and filled it with clothes, chargers, his Globlet, and headphones.

He paused at the top of the stairs. The bathroom was next to his parents' room. They might wake if he went in. No. He could buy toiletries on the way.

On the way to where exactly, Tom?

In the kitchen, he made himself a sandwich and put it in his rucksack along with a can of lemonade and a banana.

It wasn't until his fingers were on the handle of the back door that Tom had a moment of doubt.

I'm going to leave home, just like that? What about Mum and Dad? What about my eighteenth birthday party, and that girl I met at The Plough last week?

None of it mattered anymore. Well, it mattered, but it didn't matter as much as... whatever was happening to him, whatever had begun with the dream.

He scribbled a note and left it on the table.

Outside, the sun was already up, and the empty road

combined with the quiet made the scene less real than the dream that had woken him.

A car approached, the murmur of the engine the only sound in the sleeping street. Blue, with a red passenger door. Two girls. The car window whirred down, but Tom was already walking. He opened the rear door, threw his rucksack onto the back seat and slid in after it.

The car accelerated, turned right at the end of the street, and was gone.

2

"Whose stupid idea was this, anyway?" said Sara. Daniel had never seen her look nervous. She was checking the gas pipe again, scrolling through pages of notes on her Globlet as she mentally ticked off each element.

"Yours," said Daniel, stretching. Everyone reacted to stress differently. Daniel's brain handled pressure by focussing on something unrelated to the situation. This time, he was thinking of a Buster Keaton film he'd seen as a kid. He remembered a pit bull climbing up and down a ladder.

Must be hard to train a dog to do that.

Daniel walked over to Sara while she examined the seal on the pipe leading into the cabin. He took the Globlet out of her hands.

"Anything changed since last time you looked?"

"No, but—" Sara reached for the Globlet. Daniel put it behind his back.

That was a really amazing dog. I wonder if it was famous in its own right?

"But nothing. I've watched you check it all seven times. I've checked it myself twice. It'll work. What time do you make it?"

"Eight twenty."

"And the latest update said?"

"That they're due at Heathrow at eight-forty-two," said Sara.

Daniel put a hand on Sara's shoulder. "Great. No need to panic, then. You've turned the gas on, the seal is holding, there's nothing more you can do. I have a flask of tea in the van. Let's have a cuppa, shall we?"

Sara couldn't help but smile at the tone Daniel had adopted. He sounded like a parent trying to coax a three-year-old to eat broccoli. Daniel walked out of the warehouse, and she followed.

They paused at the door and looked back. The north Cornwall warehouse was perfect for their purposes, miles from the nearest town, abandoned over a decade ago. Most of the building's windows were broken, and grass was pushing up through gaps in the concrete floor.

In the centre of the empty space, brand new and incongruous, stood a large, windowless, single-room cabin, its walls constructed from thick corrugated steel. Designed to house oil platform workers in an emergency, it could—in theory—withstand an explosion powerful enough to level an office block. It was the size of a lorry trailer, positioned so that the door, on the shorter side of the rectangle, faced the warehouse entrance. The cabin was bright red.

"I'm still annoyed about the colour," said Sara.

"Don't worry. When they arrive, I can't imagine they'll discuss the colour scheme."

"*If* they get here."

"They'll get here, Sara. It's a brilliant plan."

She took a deep breath and puffed it out again with a long hiss.

"Okay," she said. "Tea it is."

A week earlier, Daniel and Sara had spent a day supervising the cabin's installation while avoiding awkward questions about its purpose.

Today, Saffi and TripleDee were coordinating the rest of the plan, waiting for them less than a mile away.

In an hour, it would be over, one way or another.

Daniel thought about how many parts of Sara's plan hinged on informed speculation, rather than facts. Then he decided not to think about it anymore.

I'm sure I saw a video of a dog who could drive a car once. Or was it an April Fool's joke?

"What are you thinking?" said Sara, as they walked to the van, noticing the look of concentration on his face.

"Oh," said Daniel. "Um. Just, er, you know, going over the plan, checking the details. Being thorough."

The car must have been an automatic. A dog couldn't operate a manual. Could it? Maybe if there were two dogs, and one was trained to use the gears —

"And have we thought of everything?" said Sara.

"What? Oh. Yup. Everything. Yeah."

"Good. I can't think of anything we've missed, but no one has tried what we're about to try."

They got into the van. Sara looked out of the window.

"A few clouds," she said. "Good. It might slow the investigation down."

"Sara?"

"Yes?"

"Didn't overdo it with the gas, did you?"

"Don't think so. Gave it my best guess."

"That's good. Wouldn't do to blow up bits of Cornwall."

"No."

They fell silent and sipped their tea as the minutes ticked away.

SAFFI AND TRIPLEDEE sat on the jetty. The plan had involved splitting up, as it made sense for Daniel and Sara to organise the trap in the warehouse. Which had left the former drug dealer, and former UN operations director, as uneasy partners for the past week.

"I'm just saying I feel like a spare part, pet, that's all."

Saffi's forehead crinkled as she reviewed TripleDee's words and tried to translate them. Her ear was tuned to the Geordie dialect now, but there were expressions that made no sense at all. And she'd never get used to being called *pet*. Although, to be fair, TripleDee used the word to refer to almost everyone.

"We wouldn't have the boat without you."

They looked at the white speedboat. TripleDee had found it after hanging around in the right pubs in Newquay for a few days. He had expressed a fondness for deals that involved a lack of paperwork and hinted that he would pay cash. Quite a lot of cash.

Within a week, he was the proud owner of a twin-engine beauty with no name, no external markings, and one previous owner who had suddenly taken a holiday in Spain.

"Aye, well," said TripleDee, "that's the sort of thing I'm good at."

He picked up a stone and sent it skipping across the waves.

"I just feel like I'm at the bottom of the food chain. Sara's okay, Daniel doesn't trust me, and I still don't know what you reckon. And it's been bastarding ages since I smacked someone in the face."

He sat down again. "I miss it a bit, that's the truth."

Saffi picked up her own stone and threw it.

"You're not used to being part of a team. It'll take time. I'm sure you'll be able to smack someone in the face soon."

"Ah, thanks, pet, I appreciate that. You're not as stuck up as I thought."

"Well," said Saffi, the corner of her mouth twitching. "Thank you very much."

As neither of them could come up with anything more in the way of conversation, they threw more stones and waited. And waited.

Saffi looked at her watch. Eight thirty-six.

"For fuck's sake," said TripleDee. "How much longer?"

"AIR FORCE One confirming final approach to runway two, landing in eleven minutes."

"Roger, Air Force One, and welcome to Great Britain."

It was the president of the United States' first visit to the UK since the reappearance—and subsequence disappearance—of The Deterrent the previous year. It had caused quite a stir in Britain, with many national newspapers trumpeting the return of their home-grown superhero. Initial celebrations turned to confusion, irritation, and hostility when The Deterrent said he had no plans to return to his home country. Worse still, the seven-foot leader of the titans claimed to have few memories of his years in Britain and declared he was now an American. Although his origins were still unknown, the British public, for two heady years in the eighties, had accepted him as their figurehead. He was Earth's only superhero, and the visible sign of Britain's return to the world's top table. A generation mourned his reported death, and that same generation reacted with anger when he resurfaced and switched allegiances. They felt betrayed, and they suspected dirty tricks from the US president, who laughed off any suggestions that he might share his team of superheroes. At a press conference the day before leaving for Britain, he answered a question from a UK journalist with a sentence subsequently looped on every news station.

"The titans are American, The Deterrent—who will be back soon, I'm sure—is American, and you guys have to live with that."

The president was neither a great public speaker nor a natural diplomat.

As the plane lowered its landing gear, the president saw crowds lining the perimeter of the airport. Tens of thousands had turned up. The presidential approach was quite a sight. Eight flying figures surrounded the descending 747 as it lined up with the runway.

The president handed his press secretary a tie and waited while she knotted it around his neck. She knew his eyes were on her cleavage.

"I always draw a crowd, Casey," said the president.

Casey was tempted, for a second, to show him the pictures on her phone of the placards the crowd were waving, the chants they were singing, and the unflattering masks many of them were wearing. Her favourite placard read, "You may have titans, but you're still a tit."

She resisted the temptation. Casey had steered him away from the subject of The Deterrent during the flight. The fact that the superhero had disappeared from the biggest parade in US history last year still made him furious. He was in a cheerful mood. Better to keep it that way.

"It might get bumpy when we land, Casey," said the leader of the free world. "Wanna sit on my lap?"

Casey smiled as if acknowledging his little joke and returned to her seat. She congratulated herself on managing, for about the thousandth time since she took the post, not to say, "fuck off." Her time would come.

Casey had only just pulled her seatbelt across her lap and snapped it into place when there was a bang, the plane lurched to one side, and alarms shrieked.

"What's happening?" she screamed as an oxygen mask dropped in front of her.

The president shouted, then fell silent. Casey wondered if he'd passed out. She looked at her boss. He was staring out of the window, his body rigid.

Outside the plane, The Deterrent stared back. The superhero pointed at the president and shot away from the plane, climbing out of sight.

The president regained the power of speech.

"Carter!"

An older man with a crew cut made his way down the aisle.

"Sir? Are you hurt?"

"No. But that asshole is here!"

"Sir?"

"The Deterrent! Send the titans after him. Now!"

3

Abos knew he could stay out of reach of the titans. Physically, there was nothing to choose between him and his pursuers. Mentally, it was a different story. His mind was his own, not dulled by a regime of drugs and hypnotic programming. Brainwashing techniques had improved since Station had practised it on Abos, but it still limited the subject's ability to think for his, or herself. Or *itself*, in this case.

The titans could follow orders, but they weren't good at improvising. They could work as a team, but they couldn't connect as onemind, the organic way Abos had linked with Shuck and Susan, the first two members of his species he had found.

The titans on the port side of Air Force One were taken by surprise when Abos dropped behind them and delivered a powerful kick to their backs, sending them spinning downwards. They responded faster than any human, but by the time they were back, Abos had given the 747 a firm slap. He made sure the president saw him.

Just as Sara had hoped, all eight of the titans were now

on his tail. Abos headed west. When he reached the Bristol Channel, he turned south at a speed that would have torn any aircraft apart. As it was, his clothes were ripped from his body by the force.

He kept the coastline on his left and looked ahead. Then he saw it. To the right and coming fast, Lundy Island. Using its lighthouse and the castle as a guide, he lined himself up with his destination, knowing he would be there in another thirty seconds.

Then it would be up to Daniel and Sara. If the plan didn't work, he'd shortly be rejoining the ranks of brainwashed superheroes, and his surviving children would spend the rest of their natural lives in prison.

DANIEL AND SARA stood by the van, partially hidden under some trees. It was Daniel's turn with the binoculars. He wished he'd bought a telescope. It was hard to use something designed for two functioning eyes. When he saw the titans, he thought there was something wrong with his depth perception because of their speed. When he opened his mouth to say something, Sara gripped his wrist.

Sara's voice was a whisper. "Am I dreaming, or are they—?"

"Yes," confirmed Daniel, as the first figure, wearing only a helmet, swooped through the open door of the warehouse, followed by eight giant naked versions of the incumbent American president. "Apparently so."

"That," said Sara, as she watched the parade of flying buttocks, "will haunt me for the rest of my life."

They stared at the warehouse door as the titans followed Abos into the red cabin within.

Daniel stopped breathing. Sara's nails dug into his wrist. Neither of them blinked. Daniel dropped the binoculars and sprinted towards the building.

ABOS RAN the length of the warehouse, pulled open the red door, and threw himself into the blast-proof cabin, picking up the item on the shelf at the back before turning to face his pursuers.

The titans came in after him without hesitation.

Inside the windowless room, all fixtures and fittings had been stripped out. When the last of the titans was inside, the door closed behind them, sealing the room. Daniel had done his part. Abos knew his son would now be running to safety.

Abos scooped two cigarette lighters from the floor. Daniel had insisted on two of them because of something he called Sod's Law.

Abos had died three times before. This time, it wouldn't just be him, it would be every known member of his species. If Sara's plan worked, it would mean freedom for all of them.

If the plan failed, it would mean extinction.

Abos placed his thumb on the jagged edge of the spark wheels.

"You can thank me later," he said, and flicked the lighter.

TRIPLEDEE AND SAFFI both looked up at the same moment when a dull, muffled boom sounded from the warehouse.

"Do you think...?" said TripleDee.

"I don't know. Could be."

Saffi pulled out her mobile phone. She was sure she would hear it ring, but this way, she would feel the vibration. She stared at it, willing it to ring. When TripleDee looked like he was about to speak, she held up her finger and shook her head.

She looked up towards the distant warehouse. At that precise moment, the screen of her phone lit up. Saffi dropped it, the phone bounced once on the wooden boards of the jetty, then headed towards the water. TripleDee's hand shot out and caught it.

Saffi fumbled to answer, forcing her shaking finger onto the right button.

"Daniel? Are you all right? And Sara? Thank God. Yes, yes. Call me as soon as you know."

TripleDee raised his eyebrows. "Well?"

THERE WAS a sound like a kick drum amplified through the world's biggest sub-bass speaker buried in a deep pit and covered in jelly. The air around the warehouse rippled. As Daniel got close enough to the van to see Sara's wide-eyed expression, he heard a whistling noise that grew in volume, followed by a sharp, loud crack.

Something smacked into Daniel's shoulder. He tasted dirt and spat. He was on the floor, flat on his face. Daniel groaned and rolled over, sat up and looked at the van. It had gone.

"What the—?"

After a second's panic, he located it, pushed back ten feet by the blast. The door opened, and Sara stepped out.

"Daniel? Are you okay?"

He stood up. "Nothing broken. I thought the cabin was supposed to contain the explosion."

"In theory," she said. "But it was designed to protect people from blasts outside. I couldn't predict what would happen if the explosion happened inside. Are you sure you're okay? What about your shoulder?"

Daniel twisted his head to look, peeling his T-shirt up.

"Ow," he said. His shoulder and part of his upper back were red. "Looks like a smacked arse. The shock-wave did that?"

"Uh-uh," said Sara, shaking her head. She pointed at a big oak tree. Embedded in its trunk was something that looked like a giant red axe head, splitting the tree to a depth of three feet.

Daniel moved closer, wondering what he was looking at. Then his brain connected the dots. It was the door to the blast-proof cabin. The force of the explosion, looking for any weakness in the structure, had found it and blown the door off, out of the warehouse and into the tree, clipping Daniel en route.

"Fuck me, that was close," he said.

"Too close," said Sara.

"Well, at least we know it worked," he said.

"I hope so. Only one way to find out."

The two of them walked towards the warehouse to see if, in fact, they had just spectacularly murdered their parent.

4

The Old Man, according to Matil's grandmother, had lived in the cave for as long as she could remember. His grandmother learned about him from *her* grandmother, who also described him as 'the Old Man.' If he was old back then, thought Matil, what did that make him now?

The villages of the Spiti valley were accustomed to hermits and truth seekers. As well as Indians and Tibetans, a few shiny-eyed, determined-looking westerners made their way to India's border with Tibet every year. Few expected the winters to be quite so hard, and the buses south were always busy a few weeks after the first snows. Spiritual retreats in Spiti suited only the hardiest individuals, a few of whom remained for a lifetime. Matil's grandmother said the Old Man liked it so much, he had stayed for two lifetimes.

The canvas bag bumped against Matil's side as he climbed the slope to the north of the village. Today he brought jam sandwiches, apples, and leftovers from last night's keu. It was good luck to feed the hermits, and most families close by took turns leaving items for the Old Man outside his cave. They placed food, clothes, toiletries, medicines, and books on a dead tree stump outside the cave's entrance. Since no one had seen the old man for over twenty years, the only evidence of his continued survival was the empty bowl returned to the stump.

Matil had sneaked out of bed one summer night and clambered up a nearby tree, hoping to get a glimpse of the legendary cave dweller. Everyone had bodily functions, and surely the Old Man wouldn't want to poo in his cave? Jagbil once said the hermit shit solid gold, and Matil spent a week searching the area for it until he caught Jagbil laughing with his friends.

What he had seen that night from the tree should have stopped them laughing, but no one believed Matil. He had settled in the upper branches with a good view of the cave mouth. There had been food and drink in a wooden box on the tree stump, and Matil had waited in silence, his eyes flicking from the black cave to the moonlit provisions.

A movement in the cave had brought him out of a doze. Some small sounds, footsteps perhaps. He had peered into the darkness, seeing nothing. Matil had looked back at the tree stump just in time to see the box vanish. No, not vanish. *Something* had emerged from the cave, scooped up the box and made the return journey in the time it took Matil to take one shocked breath.

Since then, whenever it was Matil's turn to take food, Jagbil would ask him if he was visiting his friend, The Flash? Jagbil, Matil had decided, was an idiot. He had also resolved not to spend more time than necessary near the cave. Whether or not anyone believed him, Matil knew the truth. Someone who could move that fast must be practising dark magic, not meditating and praying.

The Last Of The First

So when he placed the food on the tree stump and looked up to see the Old Man staring at him, Matil thought his heart would stop. His legs became heavy, his mouth dried up, and he stared at the hermit without a word on his lips or a thought in his head.

The Old Man lived up to his name. He was, without doubt, the most ancient person Matil had ever seen. His body, clothed in rough robes, was emaciated but strong, his legs polished mahogany, his arms sinewy and lean. It was his face that most clearly proclaimed his age. He still had teeth, yellow and stained, visible for a moment as he spat onto the dirt. He didn't so much have wrinkles as folds of skin that had developed their own set of wrinkles in the ridges and fissures scoring his features. His thin hair was the same white as the snow that covered the mountains during the long winters. His eyes, fixed on Matil, were buried deep within the geography of his face. They were the only part of the Old Man that looked young, but there was something wrong about them. Something that made Matil afraid. He remembered the stories his grandmother told him when he was small; stories of demons, of vengeful spirits.

The Old Man's eyes were yellow.

Matil remained frozen as the Old Man took a step towards him, then another. When the hermit spoke, it was with words that made no sense. His voice was like dead leaves in the wind. He spoke again, and Matil thought, this time, that he understood a word or two. The Old Man came closer, spoke again, and this time his words made sense.

"The year, boy. What year is this?"

In his terror, Matil couldn't remember. He was eleven years old, and he had been born in... no, was that right? He was too scared to think. Matil blurted out a year, not even sure if it was correct. The Old Man grunted and shook his head, whether in confusion or disgust, Matil wasn't sure.

The hermit examined Matil. He cocked his head to one side like a stray dog, but there was nothing endearing about the gesture. Matil's fear grew, becoming terror, his skin turning cold, his lips numb. With an effort of will that took all his strength, he wrenched his gaze away from those eyes and dug a foot into the dirt, turning to run.

His feet moved, but his body stayed where it was. With horror, he looked down to see he had risen from the ground. His feet were pedalling the air six inches from the earth.

When Matil looked back up, the Old Man was in front of him, his hot, fetid breath rank and foul. Up close, the hermit looked even older, his dark skin pitted with holes in among the gnarled folds of his face. Matil thought he saw the white bone of the man's skull through those holes. He wanted to gag, but his body was no longer his own to command.

The Old Man went to the tree stump, picked up the food and walked back towards the cave. For a moment, Matil was flooded with relief and joy. He was safe. Jagbil would never believe what had happened, but he would tell him anyway. And he would make them all swear never to come back up here again.

Then the Old Man glanced back over his shoulder and, still floating, Matil followed behind him like a child's balloon in a horror film, tears streaking his face as he passed out of the sunlight and into the darkness of the cave.

MATIL MUST HAVE SLEPT. During the few seconds before he opened his eyes, half-dreaming, he wasn't sure where he was. Maybe at school. It wouldn't be the first time he had dozed sitting up. Grandmother's house, perhaps. Sometimes, when she put down her sewing to rest her eyes, Matil would do the same. What a nightmare he had been having - thinking he was in the cave of the Old Man.

He heard the crackle of a fire.

Matil opened his eyes, and, with a calm certainty that temporarily overcame his fear, knew he was going to die.

The fire burned in the centre of a cave no bigger than the tiny yard in which Matil's family kept their donkey. The smoke snaked up to a hole in the rock ceiling. Matil had seen smoke curling from the mountain before, and had smelled the coriander and curry leaves the Old Man put in his tea. Not today, though. This smoke was acrid, the fire flaring and spitting as it burned. A shape flitted across Matil's vision. The Old Man. He paid Matil no attention, tossing a handful of books onto the fire.

The Old Man wore the saffron robes of a monk. As Matil watched, he threw his old clothes onto the fire. Then he walked away, into the darkness at the rear of the cave. Still floating, Matil followed. He tried struggling, but his body no longer obeyed him.

At the back of the cave, three tunnels led deeper into the mountain. The Old Man didn't hesitate, striding into the right-hand tunnel, bending a little to avoid scraping his head. Matil sank down until his toes nearly touched the floor, then bobbed along behind him.

For a second, hope flared in his heart. His family would miss him by nightfall. They knew he delivered food to the Old Man. They would enter the cave, discover the remains of the fire. More villagers would come to search the tunnels. They might find him. It was possible, wasn't it?

The Old Man turned to face him and held up his hand. His yellow eyes were fixed on something behind Matil.

First came a sound like stones sliding down a slope. Next, a deep, dull scrape of rock on rock. A heavy thud echoed around the tunnel, and the light from the cave they had left gave way to absolute darkness.

Matil smelled dust, tiny particles of grit irritating his nostrils.

The Old Man had blocked the tunnel. If anyone came after Matil, they could only explore the open tunnels.

No one would follow them here.

The Old Man walked for a long time in the darkness. Matil's mind entered a state he had never experienced before. He tried to think of his father, his mother and grandmother, but they slipped away from him, replaced by a slow, pulsing cloud of nothingness, a blank, empty space that swelled and receded with his breath.

All sense of time passing had dissipated by the time they stopped. For a while, Matil had been aware of a change in light, the sides of the tunnel gradually becoming visible. When the Old Man stepped into a chamber not dissimilar to the one they had left, it was lit by the moon, its glow reaching them from an entrance ten yards beyond. It wasn't only the light that was different; there was an odour, growing stronger. It smelled like rotting food.

In the cave, the Old Man removed his new robes, folding them before placing them on the cave floor.

Matil didn't want to see. He looked around the cave and discovered, in one corner, the source of the stench. It was piled high with raw food. The vegetables and leaves nearest the floor were rotting, but the top layer was fresher. The Old Man threw the apples Matil had brought onto the pile.

Matil watched the naked hermit stretch out onto the heap of stinking food. He shifted as if trying to get comfortable, and slimy green matter stuck to his ancient skin.

Then that horrible cratered countenance turned towards Matil, the yellow eyes met his, and a finger beckoned.

Matil's terror returned in a rush as he floated to hover over the Old Man, his body tilting and his face looking into that of the hermit's, inches away.

The Old Man reached up with his right hand. A dirty thumbnail, long and sharp. Matil couldn't move away as the nail scratched across his neck, before coming to rest next to the biggest vein in his throat. Matil looked into those yellow eyes one last time. There was nothing human there. A demon who wore a man's body but was no more human than the krait Matil had seen slinking in the woodpile.

There was no pain when the thumbnail sliced through his jugular, just an odd, loosening sensation in his throat, followed by warmth as his blood ran down his neck and onto the Old Man.

Even as his brain began the process of shutting down, Matil saw the change begin. Those terrible yellow eyes were clouding over. Matil's body fell on top of the hermit and slid down until his face was pressed against the papery skin of his chest.

Matil could feel the creature's heart beating. As his awareness stuttered and failed, the Old Man's heart slowed, fluttered, and stopped. There was a cracking noise as the ribs beneath Matil snapped and crumbled, the foul body losing coherence.

The demon is dead, thought Matil, as he succumbed to his own final sleep.

∼

It was dusk the same day when a figure appeared at the cave mouth and looked out across the valley. The tunnel

Matil and the Old Man had followed led to a ledge inaccessible to anything other than the shaheens that occasionally nested there.

The figure, dressed in the robes of a monk, looked out from the cliff face for a few seconds, then disappeared back into the darkness of the cave. Had anyone from Matil's village been there to see it, they might have remarked on the unusual height and strong physical condition of the monk. Looking more closely, they would have whispered to each other about an amazing resemblance to the missing boy. If Matil had been ten years older, surely he would have looked like this, they would have said, shaking their heads, puzzled and fearful.

But no one saw, and the figure did not re-emerge until the sun had dipped beneath the horizon and the night birds were calling.

He stepped out of the cave, his foot landing on nothing but the Himalayan air. He fell silently, the only sound his flapping robes as they twitched and snapped in the wind. In defiance of nature, his progress downward slowed ten yards from the tops of the trees, and when his bare feet hit the ground, it was with no more force than if he had jumped from the lowest branch of the nearest horse chestnut.

He walked. He was no demon, but the boy had been right to believe he wasn't human. This body was the latest to carry him. There had been many others. Some of his lives had been memorable. Most had not.

He walked because that was what he did. It was what he had always done.

He had been known by many names. The Old Man was among the least imaginative, but it wasn't the first time that label had been attached to him.

He walked south. He did not care where he was going, or

why he had chosen that direction. It made no difference to him. He knew he must walk, so he did.

According to the date the boy had mentioned, the Old Man had been in that cave for nearly two hundred years. He couldn't remember precisely when he had reached the remote village and retreated into isolation, but he knew he had been there too long.

As he walked, animals scurried out of his path, obeying a biological imperative they didn't understand.

The Old Man had a Purpose. It was the Purpose which kept him walking and prompted him to move on when he had been in one place too long. It was the Purpose which forced him to find a new body when necessary.

The problem was, the Old Man had forgotten what the Purpose was long, long ago. He only knew the Purpose was why he lived and that he must not rest until he had fulfilled it. He was sure that, when the moment arrived, the Purpose would be revealed to him, and he would know what to do.

And so he walked. And walked. And walked.

5

Apart from the missing door, the blast-proof cabin had survived, but it had changed shape. It now looked like more like a tube than a cuboid. The noise of the blast had been subtle enough it was unlikely anyone would have alerted the authorities. Even so, Daniel and Sara knew it would be best to work fast. They had just wiped out the titans, the most famous beings on the planet.

People would look for them. And they would look hard. Satellite imagery, security camera footage, and the statements of every eyewitness would be scrutinised.

They stopped near the opening where the door used to be. Daniel reached into a big laundry bag and handed Sara an oxygen mask, putting one on himself. Heat was still rippling out of the structure. Daniel stepped forward into the room. There was no smoke because nothing was burning, but the steel walls and floor were too hot to touch.

"It's bearable," he said, his voice muffled by the mask. "Come on in."

Sara joined Daniel just inside the doorway. They both

stared for a moment at the floor, then Sara let out a long breath of relief as she counted nine distinct puddles of slime.

The sight was surreal. Daniel experienced a momentary wave of dizziness as his brain fought against his gut, which was telling him he'd just murdered nine people, including his own parent.

"Abos and the titans," said Sara. "Sounds like a really shit band."

It wasn't the best joke, but they both succumbed to a fit of giggles.

"We—we—have to hurry," managed Sara.

Daniel went back to the laundry bag and brought out squares of plastic sheeting with eyelets and cord pre-threaded, designed to loop up into a sack. He laid them out on the warehouse floor and pulled two snow shovels from the bottom of the bag. He passed one to Sara before going back into the cabin and using his own to scrape the first green-blue puddle of slime away from the floor. The slime shifted as they worked as if it were alive. Which, Daniel reminded himself, it was.

"How long do we have?" he said.

Sara frowned. "We should go by the worst-case scenario. The titans might have radioed in their position at some point, and—even if they didn't—they'll have wearable tech that enables their position to be tracked. I'm assuming they have our location already."

"Which means?" Daniel said.

"Which means they'll be watching and waiting for now. They'll think their boys will have captured Abos. It's eight against one."

She scooped up the nearest puddle and walked back out

to the warehouse where Daniel was tying his first sack. He looked up.

"When will they move on us?"

"Once they realise something's wrong, which could happen any time. They'll want a satellite image, so they'll send the nearest RAF jet to take a closer look."

Daniel and Sara walked in and out of the cabin as they talked.

"Where's your driver?" said Sara.

"Texted him before we came in. He should be here any minute."

The plan was working so far, but every element had to go smoothly if they were to succeed. What the authorities did, or failed to do, over the next few days, was crucial to their success. There were four of them, and they needed to outwit the combined intelligence and military services of Britain and America. The survival of a species was at stake. And those puddles of slime weren't titans; they were Shuck, once a giant dog that terrorised East Anglia; Susan, who had been the mad monk Rasputin; Bastet, the cat goddess of Ancient Egypt; Boudicca, the Iceni warrior queen. The other four, according to Abos, probably came from cylinders identical to the one in which he was discovered. He had seen four such cylinders at Titus Gorman's headquarters in White Sands.

Six minutes later, they heard a diesel engine starting up, and a rhythmic beeping as the van reversed towards the warehouse. Sara ducked back into the cabin and stayed out of sight. Daniel jogged over, and as the van drew level, he banged on the rear. It stopped, and a short, wiry, sun-baked man wearing shorts and a faded Quiksilver shirt jumped down from the driver's seat. He squeezed between the back of the van and the warehouse door and fist-bumped Daniel.

"Good to go, Steve?"

Daniel nodded. "Yep. Here's the first payment." He put a roll of fifty-pound notes into the man's hand.

"That's five thousand, Jerry. The rest when you get to Edinburgh."

Jerry whistled, looking around the warehouse, then staring at the distorted shape of the blast-proof cabin. "Well, it's your money, Steve. I'm not going to ask."

"Best you don't," said Daniel. He opened the rear doors of the van, revealing nine old-fashioned milk cans.

"And you swear it ain't heroin or guns or nothing?"

"Jerry, I'll let you see exactly what it is before you go anywhere, okay?"

"Yeah," said Jerry, stuffing his hands in his pockets, "sounds fair."

Daniel looked at his watch and remembered Sara's worst-case scenario.

Four minutes and thirty-two seconds later, the anonymous white transit van left the warehouse, followed the winding B roads northeast, and headed towards Exeter and the M5.

Jerry held the steering wheel between his legs as he rolled himself a joint before lighting it and cranking down the window. It was another beautiful morning in Cornwall, and he had five grand in his pocket. He turned up the radio and laughed when he thought about what he was being paid to deliver five hundred miles away.

"What the fuck?" he said aloud and laughed even louder.

By mid-morning, Jerry's white van was the most wanted vehicle in the country.

∽

Daniel, Sara, Saffi and TripleDee were all in the speedboat when they heard the approaching jet.

Sara looked at her watch. It was eight twenty-five.

"That was tight. Five minutes earlier, and they might have seen us."

TripleDee had already untied them from the moorings, and they were drifting away from the jetty. He went to start the engine, but Saffi stopped him.

"The jet will have thermal imaging equipment," she said. "It rained last night, so moisture on the boat's awning should help keep us invisible, but if you start those engines, they'll light up beautifully on the pilot's screens. It's a flyby. Wait for it to pass overhead again, then go."

TripleDee took his hand away from the ignition as she spoke.

"What exactly did you do at the UN?" he said.

"I would tell you, but I'd have to kill you," she said. TripleDee laughed, then stopped. Saffi was the only human there, the others being halfheroes. But he had met no one with her aura of quiet authority. Sara might be the brains of the team, but Saffi exuded a sense of experience, and, when she spoke, everyone listened.

They all heard it then. The jet had returned, lower this time, the noise making conversation impossible as it passed. When the roar had become a whine, then a hum, Saffi turned to TripleDee.

"Okay, Trip, how fast can this thing go?"

He turned the ignition, pushed the throttle all the way forward, and the twin engines pushed the prow up as the boat powered through the water, heading out into the open sea.

Saffi directed TripleDee as they headed southwest,

following the line of the coast. While they could still see land, Daniel called out landmarks as they passed them, consulting a map on his phone.

"Padstow."

"Newquay."

"St Ives."

"Land's End."

"And on our right, ladies and gentlemen, the famous Scilly Isles. Twinned with the Sensible Isles in the Caribbean."

No one laughed. Sara chewed her nails. Daniel pulled her hand away from her mouth.

"I didn't think people did that for real when they were nervous."

"I'm not nervous," said Sara, in a voice an octave higher than normal.

Daniel couldn't think of anything reassuring to say, so he shut up and watched the Scilly Isles recede as the surrounding waves deepened and broadened, becoming rolling, tilting hills of water.

"Ah," he said, and threw up over the side.

Saffi rubbed his back, which is the universal treatment for violent vomiting, crossing all borders, and equally useless everywhere.

After another twenty minutes, she tapped TripleDee's arm.

"This is it. Cut the engines."

The silence that descended after the thrash of the propellors was almost surreal. Daniel noticed other sounds; the splash of the waves against the hull, the creak of fibreglass and wood, the distant cries of seabirds. After a few seconds, he decided the slow rock and tilt of the boat at rest was even worse than when it was moving, and he brought up the rest of his breakfast.

"Urggghhh," he said. "What now?"

Saffi handed him a bottle of water, then checked the coordinates on her GPS device.

"We wait for our ride to show up," she said.

6

Air Commodore Fiona Bardock was on the ground at the location of the incident a few minutes before ten thirty that morning.

Four years earlier, at thirty-three, she had resigned her commission, married her partner, and turned her back on what all her peers assumed would be a swift climb up the ranks. The British government allowed her to do so and gave her a pension of unprecedented generosity, on the understanding that she would make herself available for any national emergency or international incident which required her expertise.

After Jake had brought her tea in her studio, and re-tuned the radio to a news channel, she put down her paintbrush and listened to the unfolding story. The attack on Air Force One, the rumoured return of The Deterrent, and his subsequent pursuit by the titans was reported in an excited, breathless fashion she hadn't heard on Radio Four since a minor royal had been filmed in a strip club.

Fiona changed into combat gear, the only clue to her rank the subtle blue and yellow epaulette on her shoulders.

"Mmm," Jake said when she walked into the kitchen, "you know how much I like it when you wear your uniform."

"Down, boy," she said. "I have work to do."

He buttered a piece of toast and covered it with a thick layer of crunchy peanut butter.

"Protein," he said, putting it into her hand as she picked up the pre-packed rucksack that lived in the porch.

"Thanks," she said, taking a big bite, then smearing a peanutty kiss onto his lips. "I'll call you."

"Any idea when...?"

She shook her head. "As soon as I find The Deterrent and eight titans."

Fiona's hand was on the door of the car when Jake called after her.

"Maybe they won't need you. They must have other investigators. Have they even asked yet?"

She blew him a kiss and got into the Range Rover. Just before she closed the door, her phone rang. She held it up and waggled it at Jake before pushing it onto the hands-free cradle and starting the engine.

He waved as she bounced away over the potholes dotting the mile-long lane that led from their cottage to the main road.

"Once a soldier, always a bloody soldier," he said.

∾

THE PRESIDENT HAD SKIPPED the motorcade from Heathrow, heading straight to central London by helicopter instead. MI5 had set up an operations area for his team in its Thames-side headquarters. A senior MI5 officer led the way. By the time the president and his staff were shown into the suite of rooms, the US Director of Intelligence was on one video conference screen. A second screen showed a woman the president half-recognised. He sat down at the head of the table and beckoned to Casey.

"Who the hell is that old woman? She keeping the seat warm until her boss gets there?" he said, jerking his head towards the screen.

"My name is Roberta Grayling, Mister President," said the woman on the screen. "I'm director of Airforce Intelligence, Surveillance and Reconnaissance."

"Shit," said the president to Casey, "can she hear me?"

There was an awkward moment of silence before the woman spoke again. "The line is open, sir."

The president grunted and turned to the other screen. "Chuckie, what have you got for me?"

Director Of Intelligence Charles T Winters had once broken a man's nose who had called him Chuckie.

"Sir, at this stage we are reliant on satellite and drone imagery until we get intel from British forces on the ground. They are on the way to the location pinpointed by the RAF. If I can hand over to—"

"You sure they found the right place? What about the tracking devices?"

"All signals from the titans' trackers stopped transmitting at eight hundred and forty-four hours, sir. The British have sent their best operative in to head up the investigation."

"Good. Make sure he reports to me."

"*She*, sir. Air Commodore Fiona Bardock. Sir, Director Grayling has the intel from the RAF flyby."

"Who?"

Roberta Grayling coughed, and the president looked at her.

"Mister President, you should be able to see the thermal image on the screen now."

Casey pointed at the largest screen on the far wall, which showed a black-and-white photograph taken from the jet that morning. The warehouse was the only sizeable building for miles around. The aftermath of the explosion showed as a splash of bright white in an otherwise grey picture.

"What am I looking at?"

Grayling tapped some keys and a cropped image, showing only the warehouse itself filled the screen.

"Sir, the bright white patch in the centre shows a source of heat. This warehouse is listed as unoccupied. If you look at this second image, taken by the same jet forty-three seconds after the first, you'll notice a slight change in colour."

The president could detect no such change. He grunted again. He had found the grunt to be the single most useful sound he could make since taking office. Whenever he wasn't sure what was going on or couldn't answer a question, the grunt was a useful stalling tactic. If he followed the grunt with a pause during which he squinted at his questioner, he found they would often answer their own question.

"The colour change indicates that the area has cooled during the preceding forty-three seconds. Such rapid cooling suggests an event involving intense heat now returning to ambient temperature."

"An event involving intense heat?" Couldn't she speak English?

"A flash fire or an explosion. Whatever it was, it happened at the same moment the trackers went offline."

"Are you saying someone has blown up the titans?"

The Last Of The First

"It's a possibility, sir, yes."

"Jesus. When will this Air Commodore woman get there?"

The Director of National Intelligence answered him. "Sir, she should be there now. MI5 can patch you through."

The tall, thin man who had shown them in—*what was his name? Jones? James?*—had put on a headset and was speaking into it. He nodded at the president.

"Air Commodore Bardock is on comms now, sir."

∼

FIONA BARDOCK REACHED the warehouse ten minutes after an army squad had secured the perimeter. The officer in charge waited as she jogged from the helicopter, then handed her a headset.

"Ma'am, I'm Corporal Gregg. I have the president of the United States for you."

She made no move to put on the headset.

"Gregg, has anyone touched anything?"

"No, ma'am."

"Stop calling me ma'am. Call me Bardock."

She saw the moment of recognition on his face. Bardock was a legend in military circles. Her promotion to Air Commodore, shortly before her resignation, was unprecedented within the Royal Air Force Special Investigations Branch. It occurred just weeks after the capture of the world's most wanted terrorist. It didn't take a genius to connect the dots.

Yes, ma'am, er, sir, um, Bardock."

"That's better." She still held the headset. Gregg pointed at it.

"Um, hadn't you better..? The president?"

Fiona scanned the area in front of the warehouse and started walking. Gregg jogged to catch up.

She stopped at the warehouse door. Without going in, she walked back towards the trees at the edge of the car park.

"Where's the van?" she said. Gregg shook his head in confusion, then looked at the headset.

"The president, ma'am, Bardock."

Fiona removed her beret and jammed the headset onto her head.

"Sir?" she said.

The voice at the other end was instantly recognisable and unmistakably angry.

"Well, you took your sweet ass time, Ms Bardock."

"It's Mrs Bardock. My husband took my name. Please call me Bardock. How can I help you, sir?"

"You can give me a goddamned update, that's what you can do. *Bardock*."

"An update, sir?"

"Yes."

"No."

"What did you say?"

"I said no, sir."

There was an odd sound through the headset. Fiona thought it might have been a grunt. She crouched down and looked at the pattern of tyre treads where the concrete began. She spoke as she walked back to the warehouse door.

"Sir, I can't give you an update as I've just got here. The next hour is crucial in the search for relevant evidence. If I am to stand a chance of finding your missing titans, I need to work, and to work, I need to be left alone. I will be in touch when I have something to update you with. Goodbye, sir."

She handed the headset back to a slack-jawed Gregg.

"We're looking for a long wheelbase Transit," she said. "It was parked back there overnight, under the trees. According to the Met Office, it rained yesterday and part of last night, but it's been dry since around 5am. The tyre marks are fresh, and they're strongest where it came out onto the car park. It turned and reversed up to the doors. Look at the tread marks."

Gregg did as instructed.

"The left rear has a bald patch. You can see it here as it reversed. There it is again, faintly, leading towards the road. Wanli 215s. Not the cheapest tyre, but at the budget end of the market. And this set has seen better days. I think they'd struggle to get through an MOT. Where did the jet scramble from?"

"Ma- er, Bardock, sir?"

"Which RAF base was the jet from?"

"Brize Norton."

"Good. Get me the images from the flyby. The pilot approached from the east, so I want the images captured in the ten miles leading up to the warehouse. Not just the thermal images, get the standard photographs as well. We need to find that van."

∽

"Hello? Hello? Bardock?"

The president looked around the room. Casey was studiously tapping something into her Globlet, and the live feeds from the Pentagon showed two deadpan faces. The president glared at the tall Brit, whom he suspected of smirking.

"You—Jones. Did she hang up on me?"

The tall man approached. "It's Jameson, sir. Er, Air Commodore Bardock is the most successful military investigator since our records began. She has unorthodox methods, but you will find no one more capable."

"Excuse me? Did you say Bardock?" The interruption came from Roberta Grayling.

"Yes, ma'am," said Jameson.

"Mr President, Bardock is the best in the world at what she does. She has worked with our intelligence community on a few occasions, and she has proved indispensable. Charles?"

The Director Of National Intelligence nodded. "She's the best. She just takes some getting used to."

The president of the United States grunted again.

"Jameson, get me some coffee."

Jameson, Deputy Director General of MI5, smiled and left the room. He paused outside his office, where his assistant kept a jug of freshly roasted coffee at all times, then changed his mind and went to the awful machine in the canteen instead.

7

When Saffi had told him they'd be sitting in the middle of one of the busiest shipping lanes in the British Isles, Daniel had pictured the M25 at rush hour, eight lanes nose to tail, never getting beyond walking pace.

The reality was different. Turning a full three hundred and sixty degrees, he counted twenty-seven vessels, but even the nearest—a fishing trawler—was too far away for him to make out the name on its side. He spotted a huge red prow in the distance pointed towards them.

"That it?"

Sara picked up the binoculars and took a long look at the approaching ship.

"*MV Liberace*," she read aloud as she focussed on the side of the hull. "Yes, that's it. Undo a few buttons on your shirt, roll up your trouser leg and stick your thumb out."

"Liberace?" said TripleDee, "Dinna tell me they named a ship after that piano-playing poofter?"

Sara lowered the binoculars and waited. Eventually, TripleDee remembered she was gay.

"Not that there's anything wrong with that, pet, I mean, I wasn't saying that, no, not at all. It's just, you know, that's what we used to call him when I was at school. I know better now. I'm not homophobic or nothing. It's just a funny name for a big old ship like that, isn't it? Isn't it? No, I suppose not, they could call it anything, why not that, eh? Yeah, now I think about it, it's a good name for a big, fuck off ship like that. I like it. *MV Liberace*. Yeah. Got a real ring to it, hasn't it? *Liberace*. Nice. Yeah."

Sara winked at Daniel, who grinned at her, hanging onto the steering wheel as his newly emptied stomach hit him with a wave of nausea and dizziness.

"Um," he said, pointing, "are you sure they've seen us? That looks a bit close."

They all turned to look at the huge ship bearing down on them. It looked unnatural, the containers on its deck sitting as high above their speedboat as if they were the upper floors of a tower block. Two cranes stood even higher. The windows of the bridge were just visible beyond the stacked containers, but it was impossible to see anyone inside as the sun bounced off the glass.

"Is it even slowing down?" said Saffi, standing beside Daniel.

Sara's phone beeped once with an incoming message. She tapped on the screen.

"They see us, and they have slowed a little in preparation. There are sixteen crew on board, but only the captain, the chief officer, and the second and third officers know about us. The rest of the crew are performing an emergency pirate drill, which involves locking down key sections of the ship and hiding in a safe room. They are out of the way for the next twenty-five minutes. There's no margin of error. This has to work first time."

As the prow got closer, blotting out their view of the sky, everyone was quiet. Despite knowing the captain had noted their position, they still tensed as the distance between the enormous vessel and their own tiny craft grew ever shorter, the rumble of its immense engines drowning out the cries of the distant gulls.

When the *Liberace* was three hundred yards away, Sara told TripleDee to start the speedboat's engine, turn, and set them on an identical course to the approaching ship. At one hundred yards, he moved the speedboat wide of the red prow and watched as it came alongside, matching its speed as closely as he could, the smaller boat skipping across the wake. On the deck, a crane designed to load containers swung out, and a wooden pallet hanging from an iron hook lowered towards them. By the time it reached the level of the boat, it was swinging wildly. Sara raised a hand, and it stopped. When she lowered her hand, the pallet matched her action, and Daniel and TripleDee manoeuvred it into position until it was straddling the back of the small boat.

They loaded bags and personal possessions, then climbed on. Daniel was hanging back until last, but TripleDee put a hand on his shoulder.

"Daniel, you look like shit, pal," he said. "I think I saw your spleen come out the last time you puked. You go ahead. I'll take care of this."

Daniel didn't argue. Once he was on the pallet, Sara threw a rope to the Geordie below.

"Loop it under your arms," she called.

Triple Dee put the rope around himself. "Okay," he shouted, "Ready?"

"Ready," confirmed Sara.

TripleDee knelt in the bottom of the speedboat, raised his fists over his head, and brought them down with all his enhanced strength. The bottom of the hull splintered like matchwood and water gushed in. He stood and kicked down with his heel. That was enough to cause the first hole to widen. The entire hull cracked and, within a second, TripleDee was up to his knees in water.

"Shit! Pull me up!"

Sara waved at the distant crane, and the winch above reversed its engine. Triple Dee hung underneath them, giving some colourful descriptions of how cold and wet parts of his anatomy were. Below him, only a cluster of bubbles gave any clue as to the location of the sinking speedboat.

The captain of the *Liberace* was waiting for them. He watched as TripleDee took off the rope. The pallet reached the deck seconds later.

"Welcome aboard. I am Captain Andreas. I will be your only contact. You were very clear about the need for discretion."

"Agreed," said Sara. "And thank you."

Captain Andreas tilted his head in answer. The money they had promised him, half of which was already in his account, would—even after paying his officers a generous bonus for their silence—allow him to retire a decade earlier than he had thought possible. The olive groves of Crete were calling, and he looked forward to getting fat and old there.

He led his unorthodox visitors to the stack of six hundred containers that made up the bulk of the *Liberace*'s cargo. He stopped in front of a container at the bottom of a stack of seven, and removed the large padlock on the door.

"I will lock you in," he said. "Any member of the crew seeing it unlocked would check otherwise. You understand, yes?"

Daniel fixed the captain with a baleful stare. "We can get out if we need to. You know that, right?"

Captain Andreas swallowed. Daniel was the biggest man he had ever seen. He glanced over at the second man, who had punched a hole in the bottom of a boat with his bare hands. He nodded.

"Uh, there are torches just inside the door. I have connected a generator inside. You'll need these keys."

Sara took the keyring. "Thank you, Captain. I'll let you get back to your crew."

She led the way into the dark container. Each of them carried some bags and joined her. When they turned, Captain Andreas was silhouetted in the doorway. It was the last time they would see any natural light for four days. If everything went according to plan.

The captain closed the door, and left them in darkness.

Sara clicked on the torch and shone it around the container. It was empty apart from three more torches in the corner. Saffi, Daniel and TripleDee picked them up.

Sara opened a door at the far end, revealing a similar door leading to the container beyond it. She unlocked it. Inside, Daniel could hear the faint hum of the generator. Sara was shining the torch onto the side of the container. She leaned over, there was a click, and lights flickered on overhead.

They were standing in a dormitory, four beds laid out, a locker next to each. Two areas at the far end had been partitioned off. TripleDee walked over and peered into each.

"Showers and a shitter," he said. "Very nice. Extraction fan, too. Good thinking. I had chilli sauce on that kebab last night, and me ring's on fire."

"Lovely," said Sara. "Shall we?"

Daniel took Saffi's hand as they followed Sara and

TripleDee into the next container. Saffi squeezed his hand, leaned up and kissed him.

The next container was a living area. There was a large table, a galley kitchen, and a desk with a powerful computer. Daniel tapped the spacebar, and the screen lit up with the familiar Glob homepage. Even after its late founder had been denounced as a traitor, the world had decided it was too familiar with the words Glob, globbing, Globule, and Globlet to change, even if Titus Gorman had held the world's financial system to ransom. Among many of his users, Gorman's actions had raised him to the status of a folk hero.

"Wifi," said Daniel. "Spectacular." He typed in a few words and a news site opened. DOW JONES PLUMMETS AS US REACTS TO LOSS OF TITANS. PRESIDENT INSISTS THEY WILL BE BACK AND 'GREATER THAN EVER.' BIGGEST MANHUNT IN HISTORY UNDERWAY.

"Right," said Daniel. "Better hope this works, then."

He walked up to the door at the end of the third container and opened it. They had bought four containers, each loaded onto the *Liberace* according to their instructions. So far, everything looked good in the first three. But if the fourth container didn't contain the items they had specified, and overpaid for, the plan would fall apart faster than a self-assembly wardrobe.

He felt around the wall of the container until he found the switch. The lights flickered on revealing the fourth forty-foot container. Daniel stepped inside. Saffi was next, then Sara. TripleDee was the last to enter, looking at his mobile phone. "What's the password?" he said. "I thought, since we've got a few days, I might binge on Jason Statham films." He looked up from the screen, taking in the contents of the last container. "Oh, thank fuck for that," he said.

"Come and help with the bags," said Daniel, stepping back into the next container. "If we're the subjects of the biggest manhunt in history, we'd better get started, don't you think?"

8

Three hours after leaving Luton, the blue car with the red door left the motorway, following minor roads through countryside unlike any Tom had ever seen. It was flat around Luton. Now, Tom stared out at a blanket of greens, yellows, and browns undulating around the narrow strip of road. Unfamiliar town names came and went. Kidderminster, Tenbury Wells, Ludlow, Craven Arms.

He looked at the two girls again. He knew their names were Kate and Shannon although neither of them had spoken. Names were unnecessary. 'Kate' and 'Shannon' were arbitrary labels.

Tom. Even his own name sounded alien. He pictured the letters. T, O, M. Tom Evans. Written on his water bottle at primary school in permanent marker, then in exercise books and at the top of test papers. Now, this method of identification and separation had lost much of its meaning. Names came from his old life where there were fences between people. There were no fences between Tom and the girls. He was still him, but he was also them.

What the hell does that even mean?

He looked at sheep grazing in the fields, watched a tractor climb a distant hill. He thought about his mum and dad. Phil and Melissa. Their names were still necessary. Tom didn't have the same connection to them as he did with the girls. He would call them soon, let them know he was okay.

Tom's thoughts drifted around the confines of the small car, as did theirs. Kate was from Ealing, Shannon from Barnet. He knew they had both felt changes begin over the last months, both dreamed dreams they couldn't remember. And then they'd dreamed one they couldn't forget.

They'd both woken up in the early hours knowing it was time. Time to leave. Time to arrive.

The car stopped once, at a small town at the foot of a range of hills. They ate sandwiches in a tiny courtyard garden at the back of a cafe. It was busy with tourists and walkers, some of whom whispered comments to each other about the teenagers sitting at the corner table. Their silence was unusual, although they looked happy enough. It wasn't until they had paid their bill and left that a woman nudged her own teenage daughter, plucked the mobile phone out of her fingers and said, "Did you see that? Not a single electronic device between them."

"Weirdos," said the girl, and snatched back her phone.

Tom and the girls went to an outdoor equipment shop on the main street. They picked out a large tent, sleeping bags, portable stoves, plates and cutlery. The manager, seeing the growing pile of equipment, devoted three-quarters of an hour to them, making sure they had everything they needed for a camping trip. It had been a slow day in the shop, and when the till rang up a bill of nearly two thousand pounds, the manager beamed at his young customers.

Tom handed over his bank card. The manager slid it into

the payment device, then stopped. It seemed only fair to offer them a discount. That this was the first time in his life he had offered money off did not strike him as odd until later.

"Now," he said, "let's see what we can do. That tent retails at four hundred and fifty, but it's not very good."

He walked over to the shop floor, picked up the tent and returned it to the shelf. He moved further back into the shop, returning with a large green bag.

"This is what I use," he said. "It's not a famous brand, but it's well made, light, weatherproof, and easy to assemble."

The manager rubbed his chin for a moment.

"One seventy seems about right. How does that sound?"

It sounded good. By the time the manager had done the same for all their purchases, he had reduced a one thousand, nine hundred and eighty-nine-pound bill to seven hundred.

Kate, Shannon and Tom picked up the gear and, with the manager's help, loaded it into the car.

"Do you need any maps?" he said, then answered his own question. "Yes, of course. Hang on."

He returned with an Ordnance Survey map, opened and folded to the right page. Tom told him where they were going and the manager used a yellow highlighter to outline a route across the hills.

"This should see you there by tea time. Great to meet you all. Good luck."

He watched the car drive away, then opened his laptop. He would need to order new stock. The storeroom would have to be cleared to make space for it. There would be more teenagers coming, and they'd need equipment. It was going to be a busy afternoon.

After dinner that evening, when his wife had gone over

the day's incomings and outgoings, he was flummoxed by her angry tone.

"Why, Jonathon? Why on earth did you let them take all that equipment at trade price? And why have you ordered that gear? The season's all but over. What the hell were you thinking?"

He couldn't give her the real reason. She wouldn't understand. He knew the young people in his shop that day were only the first. He had to be ready to help the rest. And he'd given them the discount because, during the time they'd been in his shop, he'd felt decades of weariness, worry, and cynicism lift from his shoulders like someone helping him out of a rain-sodden overcoat. He'd stood at the back door of the shop after they'd left, a cup of tea in his hands, looking at the Long Mynd rising behind the town, a few hikers visible in the heather, and he'd been at peace. The world was beautiful. How could he have forgotten something so simple and so obvious?

Now, as he looked at his wife, arms folded, lips tightly shut, an echo of that feeling returned to him. He jumped out of his seat, pulled her out of hers and whirled her around like a girl, before pulling her close and kissing her on the mouth, over and over. She resisted at first, then kissed him back, giggling in shocked pleasure.

"Jonathon Henry Nicholas Parker," she gasped, between kisses, "are you on drugs?"

∿

Tom, Kate and Shannon left the car in the town, swapped their trainers for walking boots and their ripped jeans and hoodies for more practical walking clothes. They did this in a carpark. Five or six cars slowed down as they passed the three teenagers stripping down to their underwear without a shred of modesty or embarrassment.

They distributed the camping equipment between three rucksacks, shouldered them and walked through the town towards the hills. They crossed a cattle grid onto a narrow road. Above them, gliders dipped their wings into the thermals and circled up into the wispy clouds.

They looked much like the other walkers they encountered, most of whom volunteered a greeting as they passed.

Near the summit of the Long Mynd, the ground levelled off. Tom's legs already ached, although they had many more miles to walk. He knew he would feel the effects over the next couple of days. They paused for half an hour to watch the gliders take off, pulled by a winch across the rough, tufted grass before rising as if on invisible rails. They passed around bottles of water and ate a few dried dates and figs. Then the three walkers moved on, following a path that led, after a short climb, to the highest point of the hill. For the first time, they could see their destination.

Tom felt a thrill of fear and excitement pass through him. Although it was still seven miles away, he knew he was looking at the hill from his dream. As they set off towards it, the name from the map came into his mind. Not just the name of the range of hills they were heading towards—the Stiperstones—but the specific landmark he'd seen in his dream.

The Devil's Chair.

9

It took Jerry a while—he was pretty stoned by that time—but after five miles heading north on the M5, he noticed something strange about the surrounding traffic.

The M5 was always busy—it was the only major road out of the southwest towards Bristol, London, or the north—and a large proportion of the vehicles were commercial. Articulated lorries, rigid seven-and-a-half-tonners, and every size of van plied their trade along the southwest artery. Seven-year-old white long wheelbase Transits such as Jerry's were a common sight. Just... not *this* common.

Ahead of him on the motorway, he counted twelve vans similar to his own. He looked to his right. There was a white Transit in the middle lane. He checked his mirrors. Five, no, six more behind him. Jerry reached into the glove-box and took out one of his emergency pre-rolled joints.

He had been mistaken. The other vans weren't similar, they were identical. He'd had an argument with a bollard two months ago in a Newquay car park, leaving a dent and a scrape above the near-side rear wheel arch.

Every van he could see had the same dent and scratch. Every one. Jerry thought about not lighting the joint for a second, then shook his head and did it anyway. He accelerated to seventy-eight miles an hour. The van *could* go faster, but would shake so violently that the joint would fall out of his mouth. There was a burn on his leg to prove it. Jerry looked at the number plate of the first van he got close to. Just like his, it was covered in mud, obscuring the letters and numbers.

He slowed and allowed three more white Transits to overtake. Each number plate was unreadable.

At every junction, Jerry watched one or two of the vans leave the motorway and, as he passed the slip road, another one or two join. He thought again about his cargo. If someone was going to all this trouble and expense to protect what he was transporting, they must be smoking something a hell of a lot stronger than the weed fat Barry had sold him.

∾

BARDOCK LOOKED up from the Globlet.

"Long wheelbase Ford Transit, white, heading west," she said, and handed the device to Gregg. "We only have this image from the Typhoon, so we cannot assume the van is heading for the M5, although that's likely. It may have stopped somewhere and offloaded its contents. We don't even know yet that it's carrying the payload we're looking for."

Gregg had been there five minutes earlier when the explosive experts presented their initial verbal report. A gas explosion had occurred inside the blast-proof building in the middle of the empty warehouse. The blast was powerful enough to blow the door off the structure, sending it across the carpark and into a tree. Anyone inside the cabin would have been killed, but there was no evidence to suggest a death had occurred. No bones, no ash. Nothing. Gregg was bemused.

"Sir, Bardock? What payload? If the titans weren't inside when it exploded, where are they? Are you saying they all got into the van voluntarily?"

Bardock reminded Gregg of his duties under the Official Secrets Act, then briefed him on the encrypted report on her Globlet.

Gregg took a moment to process the update. "So we could be looking for containers? Something that can transport liquid?"

Bardock was impressed by how quickly Gregg adapted to new information. He'd just learned that the superbeings they were looking for returned to a slime-like dormant state when their bodies died. Instead of expressing incredulity, or asking questions, he had focussed on what was important.

"Correct," she said. "It's possible that the van is local. Get your team on the phones and into the nearest villages and towns. Give them the description of the vehicle and locate any white vans that match it. Tell the drivers to report to their local police station. Contact the Highways Agency and the Transport Police. We want Highways monitoring their cameras and passing on the details of every van that matches the description to the traffic police. They need to pull over and check every white van within the radius we give them."

She turned away and started to walk around the perimeter of the warehouse. She called back over her shoulder.

"Do it now. The longer that van's out there, the bigger

the area we have to check. It's likely that the van will be empty, but it's best to be thorough."

She walked away. Gregg stared for a moment, processing her last comment, then jogged towards his waiting officers.

Bardock walked anti-clockwise around the exterior of the warehouse. She took her time, pausing after every step to check for footprints.

Her earpiece buzzed, and she swore, then stopped walking.

"Mr President?"

"No. Jameson, MI5 Assistant Director. The president has requested that I liaise with you. What do you have?"

"We have details of a white van that left the warehouse after the explosion. We are trying to identify the vehicle and its driver as quickly as possible."

Jameson waited, but Bardock said nothing more.

"Look, Bardock, we've worked together before. I know you don't like to speculate, but please, be honest with me. Do you think we'll find the van?"

"The van? Yes, we'll find it."

"What is it you're not telling me?"

"It's too easy," she said. "Whoever planned this has money and enough intelligence to cover their tracks. They rented the warehouse under a false name, transferring money from a bank account which no longer exists. They bought a blast-proof cabin and had it installed. They knew how to destroy the bodies of the titans and—most telling of all—they are working with The Deterrent. We're supposed to believe they loaded the titans into the back of a white van and sent them on their way?"

Jameson consulted the three screens in the situation room. One of them was flashing up reports from the traffic police and CCTV operators watching the M5.

"Maybe so," he said. "The latest reports suggest the M5 has more white vans over one thirty-mile stretch than has ever been seen before. Every few minutes, a few of them leave the motorway and more get on. All the number plates are obscured. We will close the motorway at junction twenty-four and block the exits and entrances at twenty-five and twenty-six. That'll give us a twenty-mile stretch of stationary traffic. We'll be able to check every white van matching the description."

"And what about the ones who've left the motorway?"

"We'll find all of them, eventually."

Bardock fell silent again. Jameson cracked first. "What?" he said. "Still not convinced?"

"No," she said, walking to the rear of the warehouse. The smell of the sea was unmistakable as she rounded the corner of the building. "It's too obvious. I'll know more when I finish examining the site."

Jameson had worked with Bardock long enough to recognise a dismissal when he heard one. There weren't many people the Assistant Director of MI5 would allow to treat him this way, but Bardock was a special case. His wasn't the only career boosted by shutting up and listening whenever Fiona Bardock spoke.

"I'll leave you to it," he said. "Report back with your findings."

Bardock didn't reply, just clicked off the comms and looked at the back door of the warehouse. Padlocked. Big, old and rusting, as if it hadn't been opened for years.

She took a pace back and looked around the door. Clumps of weeds, long grass, and nettles had grown against the back of the building, filling the area between the warehouse and the trees behind. The grass was bent back in places, the nettles snapped. Someone had passed this way.

She walked back and inspected the padlock more closely. The fact that it was old and rusty meant nothing. It could have been brought here and placed on the door that morning. If so, it was a simple, subtle, piece of misdirection. She closed her eyes and pictured the door from inside of the warehouse. There was no need to go back and look - she could review her mental images.

She opened her eyes and nodded to herself with satisfaction. There had been a slight scrape in the dust by the door - an arc suggesting it had been opened.

She turned her back on the warehouse and followed the trail through the trees towards the sea.

10

The Old Man reached a main road at dawn on the third day after leaving his cave. When he emerged from the trees and stepped onto the edge of the dusty highway, he stopped and stared.

Things had changed over the centuries.

No longer were the roads the province of people, donkeys, and horses. The noisy, foul-smelling carriages that passed him now were faster, and there were many more of them. They moved slowly compared to the speeds he could reach, but they could cross distances much more quickly than the transport he remembered.

The Old Man had not survived as long as he had without mastering the crafts of observation and mimicry. When he found a location where the bigger vehicles stopped temporarily, he retreated from the roadside, sat cross-legged in the shade of a tree and, eyes half-shut in an attitude of meditation, watched the comings and goings for many hours.

Some vehicles had two wheels, some four. The largest had six, eight, ten, or twelve. Many featured glass apertures along each side. These last stopped regularly at the side of the road, disgorging people from inside their white, blue or yellow shells. Others, waiting, swapped places with those who disembarked. Money changed hands. The Old Man observed that the front of these gaudy metal carriages carried names of places, some of which he recognised. One he knew to be a city although its name had changed a little. He would learn more if he went there.

As the day became darker towards evening, the Old Man joined the line of people. Vehicles with New Delhi painted on their noses appeared regularly.

As he approached the group, he relied on centuries of instinct to single out the right candidate. A middle-aged man, his suit worn and patched, a battered briefcase by his side. The Old Man stopped, placed both hands together and bowed.

"I am hungry," he said.

The man smiled at the young monk in front of him. "Follow me, brother, and we will see what can be done."

He led the Old Man to a roadside stall and bought him chapatis and daal, with lassi to wash it down. The Old Man thanked him.

"You are waiting for the bus?" said the man in the suit. The Old Man admitted it. "And where is Buddha sending you?"

"New Delhi," said the Old Man. "But I have no money."

The man shook his head. "My father always told me it was lucky to meet a monk. He said if we helped a monk, our generosity would be repaid many times over. If I give you my last rupees, will I be repaid many times over?"

The Old Man didn't respond other than bowing again. The traveller put a wad of crumpled notes into his hands. "Think of me when you achieve enlightenment, eh?"

The bus—as they called the metal vehicles—reeked of body odour, food, and strange acrid substances he could not identify. As night fell, his fellow passengers slept, but the Old Man watched the scenery flash by, and when he caught sight of his destination, he thought at first that he was dreaming.

A haze hung over the city. Like a fog, but not a fog, it wavered and shimmered, making the Old Man distrust his eyes. The city that flickered behind the haze was vast, a dense canopy of buildings, squashed together shoulder to shoulder, jostling for room. Some buildings were taller than any he had ever seen. Nothing familiar, all was strange, frenetic and busy. As the bus passed the city limits and all signs of the natural world disappeared, the stench and noise of hundreds of similar vehicles packed around them was an assault on the Old Man's senses.

He looked around him in something close to panic, but the other passengers remained unperturbed. Most were awake now, eating, drinking, and talking, as if nothing untoward were occurring. To them, all of... this... was normal. Unremarkable. The Old Man deepened his breathing, ignoring the foul taste in his nostrils and mouth. He waited for calm to come as he experienced a wave of disgust at the people packed into this metal tube, and all of those who lived in the hellhole around them. He fought an urge to destroy, to rip apart this bus, to scream his rage at the pits they had dug to plant their foul structures; no doubt burning the grass, cutting down the trees, and driving away the animals and birds. When they weren't squatting in their buildings, they were pumping out clouds of choking smoke to travel from one place to another, adding more fumes to the stench of dust, sweat and shit.

He breathed and closed his eyes.

When the Old Man opened his eyes again, the driver of the bus was pushing his shoulder.

"Kashmiri Gate," he said. "Last stop."

The Old Man left the bus. When he saw that he was surrounded by other buses and more people than he had ever seen in one place, he held his breath and walked towards daylight and open space. Anyone in his path was thrust aside before he reached them. He left consternation, anger, and pain in his wake as people picked themselves up from the floor and looked around for the source of the aggression. No one believed it could have been the young monk who strode among them, head and shoulders above everyone else.

After an hour of walking, turning down one street then another, his head lowered, the Old Man heard birdsong and stopped in his tracks. Across the street a sign announced a 'park.' Behind it was a glorious green area with trees, grass, and water.

Changing course, he walked out into the road. Although oblivious to the screech of brakes, the shouted warnings, and the blaring of horns as motorists avoided hitting him, he had no choice but to acknowledge the pickup truck that speared him at thirty-six miles per hour, throwing him into the tailgate of a lorry.

Both vehicles stopped. The driver of the pickup jumped down. There had been a blur of saffron robes before the sickening impact and he was calculating how the killing of a monk might affect his next incarnation. He'd probably come back as a dung beetle.

The pickup driver came face-to-face with a man in a blue jacket. The logo on his pocket matched that on the side of his lorry. The man bent down to inspect a dent in his tailgate. He pointed back at the pickup, which was more severely affected. Behind a V-shaped dent, the bonnet had been pushed up and smoke curled from the damaged radiator.

Both drivers turned towards the park to see the young monk strolling among the trees. They looked at each other, at their vehicles, then back at the unconcerned victim of the accident. Without a word, they got back behind their respective wheels and drove away.

11

Saffi found Daniel in the fourth container. Speakers all around the forty-foot space made sure it was never silent, and the constant murmur of voices covered the monotonous drone of the *Liberace*'s engines. Hours of downloaded educational podcasts and TED talks were being fed to the occupants of each of the nine bathtubs lined up against one wall.

He turned as she approached and put his arm out, drawing her close.

"I'm not sure there's any point in it," he said. "The podcasts, I mean."

Twenty-four hours had passed since Daniel, Saffi, Sara, and TripleDee had brought the titans and Abos onboard. They were somewhere between Ireland and America. So far, everything had been quiet. No dramas. No boarding parties. No jets, no helicopters.

"It can't do any harm, though, can it?" said Saffi. She listened more closely to the nearest speaker. "Although I'm not sure what good Sherlock Holmes stories will do them."

"Hey, knock it off. That was my choice. *When you've elimi-*

nated the impossible, whatever remains, however improbable, must be the truth. Class. Come on."

"Well, yes, but what about Jane Austen? George Eliot? Dickens?"

Daniel pulled a face. "Boring."

"Boring?! Dickens? We need to talk."

"Count yourself lucky," said Daniel. "Sara stopped me including Monty Python and classic Doctor Who episodes."

He smiled at her, and she tutted, then grabbed his face and kissed him. The kiss lasted longer than he expected, and Saffi's hands began to move over his body before she pulled away, flushed.

"It's not easy sleeping in a dormitory and having no privacy anywhere," she said.

"It'll only be a few days," he said. "Unless they track us down first, in which case, we won't ever see each other again."

He looked down into the nearest bath tub. The body growing there was recognisably human already, and about the size of a six-year-old. The blood they'd brought from the latest raid Abos had made on the London hospital's stock had been distributed randomly. They had no way of knowing what gender each of them would be, and no way of telling which embryonic form was Abos.

"Ow," said Daniel, as he registered a punch from Saffi, which hadn't hurt in the slightest.

"Prat," she said. "Don't say things like that."

"Sorry," he said, bringing her hand to his lips and kissing it. "You almost swore then."

"You drove me to it."

"What about talking dirty? Think you could give that a go?"

"Daniel Harbin, get your mind out of the gutter for five minutes, would you?"

They walked the length of the room, checking on each tub. There was nothing they could do but wait. Sara was dealing with the stress by burying her nose in her ebook reader. TripleDee was, as he had threatened, bingeing on Jason Statham films.

Daniel took a deep breath. There was one issue he and Saffi hadn't discussed since he'd first told her, a month earlier.

"Um," he began, then stopped. Hard to know how best to broach the subject of the one hundred and eight children he had only recently discovered he had fathered. Or, rather, that his sperm had fathered, when it had been used to help one hundred and eight childless couples become parents.

"Your hundreds of children?" prompted Saffi, knowing where he was heading.

"Er, yeah. Although it's only a hundred and eight children."

"*Only?*"

Daniel coughed then turned to look at Saffi. She was smiling and shaking her head.

"I'm teasing," she said. "I've been thinking about it, too. It must have been a big shock for you. To go from being childless, to have a vasectomy, then to find out... well, I can understand why you've needed time to get used to the idea."

"Thank you."

They had reached the end of the container. Daniel leaned over the phone that was playing the podcasts. He had five minutes before episode one of *The Hitchhiker's Guide To The Galaxy* began.

"It's not even as if they're children anymore," he said, steering her away from the phone and back along the line of baths. "The youngest of them, according to Palindrome's report, turned seventeen last month. The oldest will be nineteen just after Christmas. They're grown up."

Palindrome, the anonymous contact who was queen of the internet in Daniel's view, had uncovered evidence of Station's—or, rather, Daniel's—sperm donation.

"Really?" Saffi squeezed his hand. "Were you grown up at seventeen? Or nineteen?"

At that age, Daniel had been transforming from an awkward, socially inept teenager with a weight problem to an awkward, socially inept teenager with superpowers.

"Nah," he said. "I bet you were, though. Probably taking a management course or something."

Saffi went quiet for a moment. Daniel reviewed what he knew about her. She had been a teenager studying in England when her father had been killed in the Middle East.

Shit. Idiot.

"Um, anyway, what I'm saying is that they don't need me swanning in, saying, *hi I'm your real dad, did any weird powers kick in when you grew pubes?*"

Saffi had a habit of not speaking until she was sure of the best way of expressing her thoughts. Daniel was determined to learn to do the same. One day. Eventually.

"Many halfheroes did not survive adolescence, did they?" she said.

He shook his head. "I know what you're thinking, Saff, but Palindrome ran searches on every name. All the kids are alive, and there are no hints of any special abilities."

"Oh, well thank God they're healthy. But how would you know if they had any powers? They would hide them, yes, just as you did?"

"I guess so. But their parents *wanted* them. They would

know if something was wrong. These babies must have seemed like miracles to them. It was different for me. My mum treated the cat better than she treated me. I was an embarrassment. She hated herself, and she hated me."

"I'm sorry, Daniel."

"Don't be. But the parents of these kids... well, they love them, right? They will notice if something's wrong. Even if most of the kids hid what was happening, others would talk to their parents. I don't think they have any abilities, Saff. I hope not."

They were at the door to the living area container. Saffi put a hand to Daniel's cheek.

"Do you want to see them?"

"Part of me does, I suppose. But most of me... no. I don't want to mess anything up for their mums and dads. That wouldn't be fair. I don't know if the kids have been told anything. What right do I have to walk in and... no. No. I've never been their dad. They've got dads. Proper dads. I'm just glad they're okay, they're loved, you know?"

"Yes," said Saffi. "I know."

"And you think it's all right? If I don't want to meet them?"

She put her head on his shoulder. "I think it's a decision no one else can make for you, Daniel. And if you think it's the right decision, I will support you."

He rubbed her back as they held each other. It was the right decision. It would be selfish to do anything else. Yes. It was the right decision.

So why did he feel like shit?

12

Bardock stood on the jetty for the second time in twenty-four hours. The search for the van had led to the biggest tailback ever seen on the M4, but no arrest had been made. The target must have been one of the vehicles peeling off onto the A and B roads. Which made their job that much harder. The first few hours had been crucial, and they'd blown it.

Jerry Sotterly. Handyman, surfer, small-time dope dealer. The team on the phones to local towns had made a list of vans matching the description and got in touch with all of their owners. All but one: Jerry.

Bardock walked the wooden boards and examined the mooring posts again. There were no clues as to the identity of the boat she was convinced was there when the titans arrived. The thermal images and photographs from the flyby had missed the jetty, so she had nothing solid on which to base her hunch. Nothing apart from that mark on the floor where the door at the rear of the warehouse had been opened, and the broken and bent vegetation suggesting at least two people's progress through the woods since the last rainfall thirty hours ago.

And the feeling in her gut that she was right. That feeling had never let her down. It was her body's way of letting her know that her subconscious had assembled information and built a hypothesis.

For her, Jerry Sotterly was only a distraction. No one else, from the president down, could see this, and she wouldn't waste time trying to persuade them. They had a target, and the boys at the top liked a target. But Jerry was all wrong, and by the time they found out, the titans could be anywhere.

Jerry lived in a village four miles from the warehouse. He was well-known and his van was a familiar sight in the area. His drug-dealing activities were minor - he bought for his own use and sold some to his mates. His last words to his girlfriend yesterday, before setting off, had been, "Pack a bag. When I get home, we'll fly somewhere hot."

Hardly the words of a master criminal. Every other aspect of this crime had been planned by someone thinking a dozen moves ahead. Jerry didn't fit into that picture at all.

She looked at the depth of the water lapping around the jetty. Bardock was no sailor, but any boat moored here would have to be small. A small boat meant a small fuel tank, limiting the distance it could travel.

She picked up her radio.

"Gregg?" she said. "Get onto the local harbours. I want a list of places a small boat could reach from—"

Gregg cut through her instructions. "Ma'am, er, Bardock, sir, they've got him."

"Got who?"

"Sotterly. And they've recovered the titans."

"On my way."

Bardock tucked the radio back into her pocket and started the climb through the trees back to the warehouse.

Recovered the titans? I doubt it.

∼

JERRY SOTTERLY WAS GOING through the most terrifying day of his life.

He'd followed the massive bloke's instructions to the letter. Steve had said to get off the M4 after a few junctions and use smaller roads. He'd done that, and found a garage with a jet wash to give the van a good clean, including the number plates, which belonged to Jerry's girlfriend's car. That was the only crime they could accuse him of. That's what he kept telling himself when the shit, an incredible amount of heavily armed serious shit, hit the fan.

Jerry followed the minor roads all day, always choosing an alternative route over the quickest, finding himself driving through picturesque villages. He had a phone full of dub tracks, enough dope to get him through a week, the sun was shining, and there was another five grand due when he got home. Even the first five grand would cover the holiday he'd planned.

He avoided London, driving east until he could head north through Kent, joining the M25 to pass under the Thames through the Dartford Tunnel before getting back onto smaller roads and heading north.

Jerry slept in the van the first night, in a lay-by outside Peterborough. He set his alarm for four o'clock.

The roads were deserted when he set off again. He watched the dawn bleeding warm, rich colours back into the fields and hedgerows, and he smiled. A beautiful day and no mistake. He saved his first joint to accompany the coffee and bacon butty he enjoyed at a truck stop at 6am.

Steve had said he could get to the meeting point any time that day. Someone would meet him. His destination was a car park on an industrial estate just outside Edinburgh. Even allowing for his circuitous route, he would be there by lunchtime.

He never made it to Edinburgh.

A police motorcyclist radioed in his number plate as the road Jerry was following cut alongside the A1 for a few miles. The number plate wasn't registered to the van, but that wasn't unusual. Anonymous white vans had long been a favourite with burglars. The fact that the number plate belonged to a Nissan Micra bought in Newquay raised some flags. When the owner of the Micra was confirmed as Linzi Harperton, who shared an address with one Jerry Sotterly, the traffic police headquarter's computer did the digital equivalent of jumping up and down, letting off firecrackers and yelling, "WE GOT HIM!"

Jerry was forty miles south of Edinburgh when he heard the first helicopter. His third joint of the day was on the go and he was taking long draws on it in between bites of a flapjack and swigs from a bottle of ginger beer.

He only became concerned about the first helicopter when it was joined by a second. Even then, he wasn't overly worried. They were coming closer, sure, but the odds they were after him were astronomical. Even the mild paranoia of a habitual dope smoker wouldn't allow him to believe anyone would send helicopters after Jerry Sotterly.

The sound of a third helicopter made him narrow his eyes, lean forward, and peer through the insect-splattered windscreen. The first two choppers sounded normal, a distant *fubaduba fubaduba fubaduba*. This was different. It

The Last Of The First

was much lower in pitch, with a repetitive thumping note to its approach, which Jerry heard as *muthafucka muthafucka muthafucka*.

He was craning his neck to look out of his window when he turned a corner and nearly ran straight into the roadblock.

Jerry had only ever seen a roadblock on TV. They looked like they meant business in the movies: cars, vans, and lorries blocking the whole carriageway, a dozen armed officers staring down the telescopic sights of nasty-looking weapons. There would be a grizzled alcoholic detective with woman trouble and a grudge standing at the front, a big pistol in one hand, the other held up, palm out. Jerry had always enjoyed those scenes. So clichéd. So Hollywood. He suspected a real roadblock in Britain would be two fat blokes in high-vis vests, a Ford Mondeo parked across the road and a plastic triangle saying *Police: Stop*.

The high-vis jacket was the only detail Jerry got right.

It took a long 1.96 seconds for his brain to react to the situation and send an urgent message to both his feet, which responded by stamping on the brakes so hard that all four wheels locked. The van slid to a stop in a cloud of smoke.

Fifteen yards ahead of his stalled vehicle was a roadblock Hollywood would have rejected as over-the-top. Three forty-foot artic lorries in a row blocked not just the road, but the pavement on one side and a hawthorn hedge on the other. Blue and white striped barriers came next. Crouched behind them were thirty armed officers in helmets and bulletproof vests. The dark, big guns they carried, and the practised, professional way in which they were aiming them at Jerry were bowel-looseningly terrifying.

A plain-clothes officer wore the high-vis vest, but she wasn't grizzled and—judging by the way the handgun she was pointing at Jerry's face didn't wobble a millimetre—wasn't an alcoholic either.

"Jerry Sotterly," she shouted. "Get out of the van. Keep your hands where we can see them."

His brain was still slow to respond. The words *Jerry* and *Sotterly* seemed familiar, particularly when used in that order, but he couldn't process why. Then the un-grizzled non-alcoholic officer screamed, "Do it now!" and his body bypassed his brain entirely. His hand pulled open the door, his legs shuffled him along the seat until he half-stepped, half-fell out of the van, and he lay down on his front.

"Ow," he said, as his forgotten joint squashed against his face and burned his cheek. He raised his head and spat it away. That was when he saw the *muthafuka* helicopter. It was a massive, long, military green job with two rotors thudding away. Four ropes hung down from it, and figures with guns strapped to their backs were abseiling down.

"What the fuck?" gasped Jerry. He heard running footsteps. A vehicle behind his van screeched to a halt, a door was flung open, and more heavy boots approached. A pair of shoes approached from the front and one of them ground out his discarded joint. He looked up to see the pistol-carrying officer. She was still pointing the gun at his head. It was all very unfriendly.

"Look," he said, "I've got five joints in the glove compartment, and there's an ounce of resin in my pocket. It's for personal use only, I swear."

"Don't try to be funny," said gun-woman.

Jerry frowned, his brain still on a temporary leave of absence. He hadn't been trying to be funny. Then he heard the back doors of the van being opened, and he remembered.

It's a misunderstanding. They'll have a look inside and they'll let me go. They'll have to. It's nothing dodgy. They might think I'm weird, but they can't arrest me for that.

He heard a metallic sound.

They're unscrewing the milk cans. Great! They'll know it's all a mistake.

"It's all a mistake," he said to the gun-woman. He tried his most charming smile. He had always had a way with the ladies. Her eyes flicked down.

"Say one more word, and I'll kick you in the face."

Oh.

"Target confirmed, repeat confirmed."

The shout came from the back of the van. The voice was American. Jerry wondered what had been in that last joint. Perhaps this *was* a movie after all.

"How many?" This from a second American voice.

After a pause, the first voice shouted back. "Nine. That's all the titans plus The Deterrent. We got 'em all, sir."

"We'll chopper them back to London, then they can be flown back home. I'll inform the president. Good work, soldier."

The woman standing over Jerry muttered something. It sounded a lot like, "Yeah, and take all the credit, why don't you? You wouldn't have found it at all if not for the police and MI5, you arrogant prick."

"The police and MI fuuuuth," said Jerry, as gun-woman delivered on her threat and kicked him in the face. He rolled onto his side, tasting blood.

"Get him on board," said gun-woman. Two big blokes grabbed an arm each and dragged him towards the big helicopter.

"But, but..." he said, in between spitting gobs of blood onto the road. "Ith all a mithttake. Ith all a big mithtake..."

13

The Old Man opened his eyes to find morning and afternoon had already passed. The low, warm, yellow light of dusk rippled through the leaves of the tree whose trunk he had leaned against while he slept. Even dusk was wrong here, the light sicklier, the evening song of the birds half-drowned by coughs and splutters from the metal carriages on the nearby roads. They were moving slower than the pedestrians alongside them, many of whom wore masks to avoid the worst of the fumes.

What was the point? Was this progress? The last time he had been in a city, it had reeked of human and animal smells. They were still here but overlaid with hideous artificial odours.

A wrenching twist of memory, buried deep, surfaced so unexpectedly that he cried aloud.

He remembered.

He remembered walking.

He remembered walking in front of a line of animals at dusk. The narrow path wound down the mountainside and brought him to a small group of huts. The village. His village.

The air tasted of honey and figs, the breeze was cool, and the goats were docile, sleepy, their bleats sporadic. He was a big man, considered a giant by the villagers, but out here, with the mountains looming around him, he felt small, insignificant, and... for the first time he could remember... almost at peace. The thousands of lives behind him, the thousands to come; he could forget them for hours at a stretch up here.

The animals made their way into the small pen, and the Old Man ducked through the doorway of his dwelling. His love, Khryseis, looked up as he entered. She was holding their son. Over countless lifetimes, he had avoided fathering children. It had been easy for millennia when those whose bodies he wore were little more than animals. It had become more difficult when he found he could form relationships with depth and meaning. He had connected with these new people. He had half-convinced himself that his Purpose, long-forgotten, would never be fulfilled. That it might be better if he were to become—as far as he was able—part of the society which had accepted him.

He stopped in the doorway when he realised Khryseis and his boy were not alone. Three men rose to their feet. One of them he knew - Meurius, the leader of their small community. He had welcomed the Old Man after he had proved his worth by ridding them of a wolf-pack. The Old Man had given the skin of the biggest wolf to Meurius as a gift. He was wearing it now.

"Tros," said Meurius. Tros was the name of the man whose blood had provided him with this body a decade before.

"Meurius."

The leader of the village held the Old Man's gaze for a few moments, then dropped his eyes. He gestured towards the strangers. Well dressed, armed. One carried himself with authority. The other—a big, bearded man—looked like an experienced soldier. Tall, but still a head shorter than the Old Man. The smaller one spoke.

"My name is Stolos. I come here seeking you, Tros. Your bravery and strength are unparalleled, and word has spread of your power. We have heard of you in Athens."

The Old Man stood as still as an oak, as silent as a stone. Stolos smiled without humour.

"Even here, even in the mountains, you know that war is coming. We need men of your strength, Tros. If half of what we have heard is true, you will find fame and glory as a champion of the Greek forces. You can protect our country and our people. You will bring honour to your village."

The Old Man knew it was over. It was time to leave again. But, this time, he would abandon a wife and a child. He felt a wound forming in the core of his being.

"I seek neither glory nor honour," he said. "I wish to be left alone."

Stolos exchanged a look with his silent companion. The big man barked a command. The Old Man heard movement outside, the muffled clink of sheathed weapons. He turned his head and saw six men in the fading light. Battle-hardened soldiers, grim-faced, hands on hilts. Stolos spoke again.

"Greece needs you, Tros. When your country calls, you must answer."

"I answer to no country."

The tension in the confined space was fast reaching the point where violence would be inevitable. The Old Man stepped forward, his eyes on Khryseis and his son. When the big soldier half-drew his sword, Stolos placed a hand on his arm.

The Old Man brought his lips close to the ear of his woman. "Leave this place," he whispered. When she began to speak, he interrupted. "Say nothing. Remember me as I was. When you have a chance, find a new home for yourself and the babe. When you are ready, find a new man. I will not return."

He kissed her and stepped back, looking at Meurius.

"How much did they pay you?" he asked.

The leader stuttered a little in his lie. "Wh—what do you mean? How dare you accuse—aargh!"

He fell and clutched his leg. The Old Man's kick had been so fast that no one reacted until Meurius was on the floor, clutching his shattered knee. The limp he would suffer for the rest of his life would remind him of this betrayal.

The big soldier drew his short sword and pointed it at the Old Man's throat.

"Out," he said.

The Old Man looked at the sleeping baby on Khryseis's hip, then, for the last time, he looked into her eyes. What had he been thinking? Swearing to himself that he would never forget her, but knowing he would, he stepped out of the hut and walked towards the mountain.

The soldiers outside hesitated for a moment, then unsheathed their weapons and followed. He broke into a jog, making certain his pursuers didn't lose sight of him. He looked over his shoulder. Stolos and the big soldier were following.

The Old Man led them east, uphill. He knew the terrain, the half-hidden paths. He had to slow down twice to make sure they could keep up.

The pursuit lasted twenty minutes. Long enough to be well out of sight of the village. The Old Man stopped at the gorge, his back to a cliff edge that plunged hundreds of feet into the valley.

When the big, bearded soldier rounded the corner and saw where the Old Man had made his stand, he smiled.

"I wouldn't have put you down as a coward," he said, breathing hard. He undid the leather belt holding his sheath and let it, and his sword, fall to the stony ground. He adopted a fighting stance and advanced. "You are coming with us, Tros. Willingly, as a volunteer in the Greek army, if you wish, but this *is the last time we will offer. Turn us down again, and your corpse will serve as an example to other traitors."*

The Old Man watched him advance. The six soldiers and Stolos behind him were relaxed and confident. They must have seen the bearded soldier fight before and were sure he would prevail against this giant peasant.

The Old Man had neither the time nor the inclination for niceties. His grief at leaving his woman and child had already flared into brutal anger.

He walked towards his challenger with his arms by his sides, offering no defence. Only his yellow eyes, blazing with hard fury, gave any clue as to his intentions.

The bearded man, when he moved, was fast, fluid, and well-practised. His first strike—a hard jab at the base of the ribs—was intended to prevent his opponent from drawing breath. A cracked rib cage weakened attackers. It was an intelligent opening, and, for a big man, the soldier's attack was fast.

The Old Man turned aside, and the intended blow missed by inches. Despite having his balance unexpectedly upset, the soldier followed through with a leg sweep intended to bring Tros to the ground. Again, a smart move. The Old Man jumped over the bearded man's leg and took a pace to the side, waiting.

When the soldier resumed his fighting pose again, a seed of doubt had crept into his expression. His next attack was far less nuanced; a flurry of punches aimed at the head and torso.

This time, the Old Man didn't move aside. He looked beyond his attacker and stared at Storos while his champion rained blows on him, any of which would have felled a normal opponent. Storos paled as he watched.

The bearded soldier soon tired and stepped back to survey the damage. His eyes showed real fear for the first time as he registered the lack of injury on the yellow-eyed giant. When the Old Man laughed at him, he reacted with fury, scrambling back for his sword, unsheathing it and jabbing upwards into his enemy's belly.

It was like stabbing a rock. He dropped the sword in pain and shock and looked up to see an enormous hand reaching for him.

The Old Man picked up his opponent by his neck, still looking at Storos. Then he closed his fist and, with a series of brittle snaps, every bone in the man's neck snapped. His head lolled backwards, coming to rest between his shoulders, his blood-filled eyes staring unseeingly at the waiting soldiers.

"Kill him!" screamed Stolos.

The soldiers charged with the confidence brought on by their numerical advantage. As they drew close, the Old Man moved his hand across his body as if waving away an insect. All six men were swept off their feet and into the air.

Stolos dropped to his knees as he watched his soldiers rise, carried away from the safety of the mountain pass and over the gorge, before falling to their deaths below. Their screams echoed for half a minute. He collapsed face down into the dirt and prayed to the gods. He tried to move, but his legs would not obey his commands. And what was that awful smell? He dragged himself onto his side, and with a terrible realisation discovered the source of the stench. His bowels had opened. He began to cry.

The Old Man walked to the edge of the cliff, stooped, and picked up two heavy stones. He bowed his head and spoke softly. Stolos heard gentleness and sorrow in his tone. Perhaps he would survive this day.

"Goodbye, Khryseis," said the Old Man, kissing the first stone before lobbing it underarm into the gorge. A stream ran through the valley. He saw the splash half a second before its sound reached his ears.

He kissed the second stone. "Goodbye, Heracles." He watched it fall beside the first, then turned towards Stolos. The man began to babble.

"Tros, thank you for sparing me. There is so much I can do for you. No need to be our champion. I can see now that I made a mistake. Why, you could challenge the gods themselves. I could get you anything you wanted. Riches, women, an army of servants to attend you. Anything, anything! I am a respected man, I have great influence in Athens, I... why do you not speak? I have a family also, Tros, a wife, children, think of them, think of them."

His voice failed him as the giant man bent and lifted him as easily as a gourd of water. The analogy, as he was about to discover, was not entirely inaccurate.

"I need you," said the man, tracing a long nail along Stolos's neck.

"Oh, thank the gods, yes, you're right, yes, you need me, you need me, thank you, thank you." He stopped speaking as his voice failed, his throat full of liquid. A bitter taste, thick and metallic. They were at the edge of the cliff now. Tros wrapped his arms around Stolos as he choked and spluttered.

The Old Man came in close. "I need your blood," he said.

Stolos screamed, but it came out as a wet, flapping hiss of air.

The Old Man leaned backwards. Together, they fell into the gorge.

∼

THE OLD MAN let his eyes focus on the scene around him. The memory had taken him by surprise. Flashes of previous lives rose unbidden at times, echoes of long-forgotten emotions. He didn't remember being Tros. He remembered remembering being Tros, and even that memory was centuries old.

Now he was hungry and thirsty. He looked to the side and found that passers-by, thinking him meditating, had left gifts. There were two bottles of water, and a foil package containing six gol gappas: spiced potatoes and chickpeas in crispy shells. They were still warm. He ate them without ceremony, washing them down with the water.

A day had passed while he had sat beneath the tree. The stream of traffic surrounding the park was heavier than ever as workers made their way home. The air in the park tasted better away from the stinking streets, but the Old Man could still feel his nostrils and throat clog with alien particles; filthy, gritty, and poisonous.

He had to get out of the city. This had been a mistake. Whatever his Purpose was, he would not find it in this place, where everything was unbalanced, where nature had been suppressed.

The Old Man stood and stretched his long limbs. It was time to leave India. He would head to the coast and find passage to somewhere less crowded. The country had changed beyond recognition during the generations he had spent squatting in the cave. He had never stayed in one place for so long before. His compulsion to move on had diminished in power during those years. His sense of identity had diminished, too. He would wander again, recover himself step by step.

And he would do it on his own two feet. Although he could fly, he had stopped doing so centuries ago unless it was unavoidable. Flying meant missing the details. He looked down at his bare feet, flexing his toes in the close-cut grass. Time to go.

As he left the park, he paused, watching an excited crowd around a street vendor's stall. He moved closer and saw a miracle. In the top left corner of the stall, hanging from a hook and swaying, was a glowing box containing moving pictures, as if tiny humans and animals were contained within.

Controlling his breathing, the Old Man stepped closer. Finding the device troubling and unsettling, he looked at the jabbering crowd surrounding the stall, listening to what they were saying. None of them were shocked or amazed by the magic box. They treated it as if it were something they saw every day. From the snippets of conversation he heard, it seemed the box brought them information. Information that was, somehow, up-to-date. The events they were discussing had happened recently. Days ago? Hours? Minutes, even? And the pictures showed events taking place thousands of miles away from New Delhi.

In the gabble of the crowd, he heard mention of America and Great Britain, but other words were unfamiliar, although they cropped up again and again. *Titans. The Deterrent.*

Steeling himself against the nauseating effects of the glowing box, the Old Man looked up and watched the moving pictures.

A bus of sorts, but winged like a bird, flew towards a city. Surrounding it were flying men, their faces concealed by helmets.

The picture changed to a woman speaking while words appeared beneath her. He turned away again as dizziness took hold.

When he looked back, he saw a picture of the sky with distant figures flying at great speed.

Could humans fly now?

He grabbed the nearest person and spun them around. A middle-aged woman faced him, her lips curled to deliver an angry comment. When she saw his robes she hesitated, then put her hands together and dipped her head. The Old Man barely saw her.

"Who are these flying men?" he said. "Where are they from? Can everyone fly now?"

She laughed in surprise, then clapped a hand over her mouth as if trying not to be disrespectful.

"No, no, only the titans can fly. And The Deterrent, of course. They all disappeared yesterday, so they might be dead now. The Deterrent came here once, you know. To New Delhi. I was a young woman then. There were floods in Uttar Pradesh. He rescued thousands. The Deterrent. He met the Prime Minister. I went to see. He was quite a peach that boy. Big, too. As big as you!"

As if aware she might have said something inappropriate, she reddened.

"Where?" said the Old Man. "Where are they? These pictures? The... titans."

"Are you joking with me? You have never heard of them?"

"Where?"

Something in his tone brought her up short, and she looked frightened at the intensity of this huge young monk.

"In England, UK, Great Britain, London. They're Americans now, you know, but they were on a trip with the president. They - hey!"

The Old Man had turned and was walking away. She called after him.

"You are serious? You've never heard of The Deterrent? Were you brought up in a cave? Oh..."

The woman's voice dried to a hoarse whisper as the monk reached the road and, with a speed that registered as an orange and saffron blur against the whitewashed buildings behind, flew up into the darkening sky.

14

The president of the United States arrived back home a day earlier than scheduled. A press release preceded him, drafted by Casey on Air Force One as they crossed the Atlantic.

The press release spoke of the reappearance of The Deterrent, suggesting he had been working through some 'personal issues.' The other titans had pursued him at Heathrow, and, in an undisclosed location, had persuaded him he needed treatment. A quote from the Chief Medical Officer was already being re-posted on most news feeds where he suggested that The Deterrent was suffering Post Traumatic Stress Disorder from the years he'd spent in Britain.

All of which gave the president the perfect opportunity to do one of his favourite things when he got back home: sweep through the assembled press without comment, a determined, strong, presidential look on his face. A look that said, *no time to talk now. I have superheroes to save, and a nation to run.* At least, that was how he thought he looked when he practised the facial expression in front of the mirror.

He was greeted by a few of his most senior staff at the airport as they prepared to transfer the milk cans containing the titans to a Pentagon facility. The Chief Medical Officer was one of those waiting, and the president had an uncharacteristic moment of self-doubt, when the most senior doctor in the country saw his expression and asked him if he needed a prescription for constipation.

The scientists gathered at the hi-tech Pentagon facility were an unusual mix. Biologists, geneticists, chemists, pharmacologists, and neurologists rubbed shoulders with psychologists, psychiatrists, counsellors, and one of the country's foremost proponents of neuroscience-linguistic programming. The word 'charlatans' was sometimes muttered at the water cooler.

The biologists, geneticists, chemists, pharmacologists, and neurologists confined their opinions to the water cooler because none of them wanted to miss the chance to study a new species. Not that their study had yielded any conclusions. Like the British team over half a century earlier, they found the titans' physiology unrevealing. Although they *knew* these beings weren't human, any samples taken of skin, blood, or saliva, revealed nothing out of the ordinary. They were as much in the dark as they had been when Roger Sullivan first assembled the team.

A photograph of Sullivan receiving his medal from the president was the only decoration in the main laboratory. When he'd suffered a second heart attack—fatal, this time—a month after the New York parade, the rest of the scientific team had been delighted. Sullivan, according to a geneticist with a gift for expressing the consensus, had been "a third-rate scientist and a first-rate asshole."

Curwan, a neurologist, had taken over as team leader. It didn't matter who was in charge as there was one team member who knew far more about the creatures than anyone else. It was Mike Ainsleigh they went to for help, it was Ainsleigh who remembered every experiment carried out on The Deterrent between his discovery in 1969 and his disappearance in 1981. Ainsleigh was a conundrum. There from the beginning, he preferred to work alone. He could only be approached by one person at a time, or he would refuse to speak, and he seemed to hate himself for helping them. There were rumours he was only there because the alternative was prison.

When the armoured vehicle arrived, and the squad of soldiers escorted the trolley containing nine milk cans to the gleaming white and chrome laboratory, Ainsleigh was waiting along with everyone else. He stood at the back, hunched over, his eyes downcast, chewing the ends of his long grey hair and muttering. He shuffled forwards while the soldiers unscrewed the cans.

One side of the lab was a gigantic window looking through to a room containing a dozen large containers. Each container was two-thirds full with fresh vegetables, fruit, and vitamin-enriched pastes developed by the team. Nine blood drips stood ready. The blood didn't come from the president this time. Polls showed the public found it distasteful that all the superheroes had looked like giant versions of their leader. They suspected him of vanity. Torn between having superhero versions of himself flying around or being more popular, the president conceded and ordered that blood should henceforth be donated by intelligent, athletic men and women from Ivy League colleges.

The titans would be studied again before new bodies

were grown. There had been few opportunities to examine the species in its dormant, slime-like state.

As the soldiers left, the scientists stepped in, reaching into the cans with swabs and taking tiny samples to smear across slides and examine under electron microscopes.

There were a few grunts of surprise from the first scientists to reach the cans. The consistency seemed different, the colour a little more green. There was even a distinct odour which had never been present before.

Mike Ainsleigh shuffled forwards as the first geneticist departed with his sample, taking the man's place by the milk can. He tied his hair back into a ponytail and leaned over, frowning. After a few seconds, he took a long, deep sniff. A few of the team looked up in surprise at the strange, strangled noise he made then. It sounded a lot like a suppressed giggle.

Ainsleigh stood up straight and looked around the room at the assembled group of top scientists, smiling at the banks of cameras and microphones recording everything. He held up his hand and extended his forefinger, waving it in the air as if he were about to perform a magic trick. Then, to everyone's horror, and before anyone could stop him, he stuck his hand in the can, scooped a big blob of titan slime onto his finger, and stuck it into his mouth.

One of the chemists screamed. Curwan looked as if he might throw up.

Mike swallowed, said, "yum," then started laughing. He hooted with mirth, putting both hands on his knees and howling as tears streamed down his unshaven cheeks.

It took him twenty minutes to regain some self-control and tell Curwan what was so funny.

∾

BARDOCK SPOKE to her husband from bed in her hotel. She had been ordered to gather any evidence, send what they had to MI5, then stand down. She had ignored that order.

"I can do what I like, Jake," she said. " I'm retired. They can't order me to do anything."

"Come home then, Fiona." He was the only person she would tolerate calling her Fiona. Even her mother called her Bardock. Early in their relationship, Jake had tried 'Fi' on for size, and she'd walked out of the room and not spoken to him for the rest of the day. As she'd been straddling him at the time, he didn't make the same mistake twice.

"Well, I could come home, but I'd only have to come back again, so what's the point?"

"You're not making sense, Fiona. They've wrapped up the operation."

She changed channels on the TV. The news was full of the president's brisk walk through the press corps on his return to Washington. He had an odd expression on his face.

"I think the president might suffer from haemorrhoids," she said.

"What?"

"Never mind. Washington is five hours behind us."

"Er, yes. So?"

"Well, the president and his milk cans—"

"His *what*?"

"Oh, they didn't release that detail. Not surprised. Anyhow, they arrived at ten past nine this evening our time. They'll be transferred to the Pentagon, where their scientific team will be waiting. I reckon that'll take an hour. Maybe another half an hour to run the first tests. All done by about ten forty-five our time. It's five to eleven now. Which is why

I'm calling you from the room phone rather than my mobile."

"You've lost me, Fiona. Not for the first time. What does any of that have to do with which phone you used to call me?"

"I want to leave my mobile free for when Jameson calls. Should be any minute."

"Unless you're wrong and you're paying for a hotel in the back arse of nowhere when you could be in bed with me."

Bardock's phone rang. Jake sighed.

"Do you ever get tired of being right?" he said.

"Not yet," she said. "I love you. Speak later."

Jake was the only person she'd ever said "I love you" to. Her mother had told her she was incapable of love, and her father had disappeared before she was born. Bardock had negotiated the adult world of sexual encounters with some enthusiasm but had avoided relationships. Her own company had proved sufficient. Jake had been a surprise.

She picked up her mobile phone.

"Sir? Yes, still here. I thought it was as well to stay nearby. Oh? As a matter of fact, yes, I have. Gregg and his team ran a search for boat sales and rentals. I also had them check every harbour and jetty."

She listened as Jameson updated her orders. "Yes, sir, I could do with extra resources. Excellent. Have someone call me if they find something. I'll be back at the warehouse at five tomorrow morning. Sir? What was in the milk cans when they tested them? I beg your pardon? Say again? It's hard to understand you, sir. Are you laughing? Thank you, sir. What's that? No, I never get tired of it. Good night."

She laid back on the pillow, turned out her light and, in the darkness, burst into laughter.

"Mushy peas?" Gregg looked at Bardock as if he suspected she were joking. Her expression was unreadable.

"That's right. Each milk can contained five litres of mushy peas. Is there something wrong with you, Gregg?"

"No, ma—Bardock," said Gregg, his face reddening and contorting. He snorted, tried to turn it into a cough and ended up hiccoughing violently.

"Well then, pull yourself together and get back to work on finding this boat. We have a description of the most likely candidate now, correct?"

"Yes—*hup*—we do. It was—*hup*—bought in Newquay six days ago. The owner took a holiday straight after the—*hup*—straight aft—*hup*—straight after the sale, so we—*hup*."

"Gregg, I'm taking you off this case and recommending you be demoted to the rank of private with immediate effect."

Gregg' eyes widened, and he took an involuntary step backwards.

"You can't do that, I mean, why? Why would you do that? I'm working hard on this, it was me who found the boat, I stayed around when you told me the titans weren't in the cans—"

Bardock held up a hand. He stopped talking.

"Well," she said. "I always thought it was an old wives' tale. You live and learn."

"What?" Gregg was pale.

"Curing hiccoughs by giving someone a shock."

"You mean I'm not—?"

"No. You're doing a good job. Keep it up."

Gregg opened his mouth, then closed it again, looking

very much like a guppy. A woman in combat fatigues ran up and handed him a piece of paper.

"We found him, sir, the boat owner. In a villa near Madrid. He said he could describe the man who bought the boat, so we got him straight over to the Spanish police. They've done a Photofit. It's on the second sheet."

"Good work." As the woman jogged away, Gregg turned so that Bardock could read what he was reading.

"Very tall, built like a rugby player, strong Geordie accent."

He flipped the page over, revealing a Photofit of a man in his late thirties or early forties, a cap pulled over a shaved head which looked tattooed.

Gregg pulled a face. "Not much to go on, is it?"

Bardock took the sheet of paper from him and studied the face for a moment.

"Dave Davie Davison," she said. "Newcastle drug dealer and gang boss. Nasty piece of work. Reputed to be a halfhero. Known by most people as TripleDee."

"How the fuck," began Gregg. He flushed and tried again. "Sorry, I mean, how on earth, ma'am, sir, er, Bardock?"

"Oh. A case last year."

The case had been intriguing but frustrating. She had been brought in when a spate of disappearances occurred among suspected, or confirmed, halfheroes. She had spent a month chasing leads. Whatever had happened to them, their tracks had been covered beautifully. It was as if they had vanished off the face of the planet.

She tapped her finger on the photofit. "Well, well," she said. "A missing halfhero mixed up in the disappearance of the titans. Curiouser and curiouser. Gregg?"

"Bardock?"

She handed back the picture. "Get onto those teams

looking for the boat and push them harder. Meanwhile, have someone bring me a map of this stretch of coast, and everything within a hundred miles accessible by water."

She felt an itching sensation about an inch into her skull alongside her left ear. She knew she had missed something. And she would not rest until she'd worked out what it was.

15

Daniel checked on the bathtubs for the fifth time that morning. One of the half-formed bodies was growing much faster than the others, and he wanted to be there when it woke up. When *he* woke up. The facial features were that of an Asian man, his black hair growing so fast Daniel thought he could see it happening in real time. The face even had the beginnings of stubble.

Daniel opened an ebook on his phone and sat next to the tub. He was just getting lost in the story when the body next to him sat up, coughed wetly and smiled.

"Hello Daniel," said the Asian man.

Daniel almost dropped his phone. "Abos?"

"Yes. It is good to see you." He climbed out of the tub and stretched. For the first time in a male body, Abos was about an inch shorter than Daniel, but still well over six feet. The blood must have come from a very short man, as whenever Abos grew a new body, bulk, strength and height were always added to the original DNA template.

Daniel went to a locker in the corner of the container

and brought back underwear, trainers, cotton tracksuit bottoms, a T-shirt, and a hoodie.

"Hungry?" he said, as Abos got dressed.

"Yes," said Abos. They paused in front of a mirror. "It is good not to look like The Deterrent anymore. But I think I would have preferred to be female again."

"I'll bear it in mind next time you get reduced to a puddle of slime," said Daniel, smiling.

"The others will wake today," said Abos, walking around the containers. "The process is faster now. I have grown more new bodies than the others. My knowledge helps them in onemind."

"That's good," said Daniel, "because I don't know how long we have before they find us. Come on through."

In the living-space container, Abos was hugged immediately by Sara and Saffi when they realised who he was. TripleDee hung back until they had released him, then stepped up and delivered a quick bear hug of his own.

"I don't mind admitting, you're a sight for sore eyes, man. Even if you look like Jackie Chan on steroids."

Daniel steered Abos over to the computer desk. Headlines scrolled down the screen.

GONE AGAIN: WHERE ARE THE TITANS?

PRESIDENT COMMITS MORE RESOURCES TO THE HUNT FOR SUPERHEROES

ARE THE TITANS DEAD?

TITANS ACTUALLY SECRET NAZIS FROM THE FUTURE.

"Who writes this shit?" said TripleDee.

"That's the thing with twenty-four-hour news," said Sara. "Even on a slow day, they still have to pump out new content every minute."

"How long before the others are conscious?" said Saffi.

Daniel answered her. "Abos said it would be today. They grow bodies faster now. Something to do with the onemind thing they do."

"Good," said Saffi, "because now they know the van was a decoy, they'll throw everything at finding us. The reputation of the US and UK intelligence communities is at stake, and the president doesn't like to look incompetent."

"Like he needs any help," said TripleDee.

Abos was silent.

Sara crossed her arms and shook her head. "This is the worst bit," she said. "The waiting. Until the bodies are grown, we're sitting ducks."

"You always said this would be the hardest time," Saffi reminded her. "But this is a fantastic hiding place. Hardly anyone knows we're here. The captain was the only one who saw us board, and there's no way he could know we had nine superheroes in our backpacks. It's a brilliant plan, Sara."

Sara half-smiled. "Thanks. I'll be a lot happier when the titans have woken up."

"Not titans."

They all looked at Abos. He had turned in his seat and was looking at them, golden eyes shining out from his strange new face.

"What do you mean?" said Daniel.

"They're not titans."

"I get you," said TripleDee. "That was what they were when they had been brainwashed by the Americans. Now they're free. I thought about changing me name too, you know, cause TripleDee was, like, the name of a badass crime boss and I've, like, moved on, haven't I, so I thought mebbe I should go back to being Dave, or even David, but then I thought that sounded a bit gay, no offence, Sara, and I'm just too used too... I'm going to stop talking now, okay? Okay."

Saffi felt a strange sensation in the atmosphere as if the air was charged with static electricity.

"Do you feel that?" she said. "Anyone?" She looked at the others. Their expressions were nearly identical, faces relaxed, breathing deeply, eyes unfocussed. Daniel turned towards her.

"Abos is showing us the onemind." His voice was soft and full of wonder. "Can't you see it?"

Saffi looked around. "I don't see anything." Watching the others, she tried to relax, slowing her own breathing. It wasn't the first time in her life she had been excluded, but this was different. It wasn't that she didn't belong. She *couldn't* belong.

I'm the only human being here, she thought. She looked at Daniel, aware that his breathing had synchronised with that of the others. It was at that moment, as a chasm opened between them, that she realised she loved Daniel Harbin.

"Are you linked with them?" she said. "Are you linked with the titans?"

"Not titans," Daniel said. "They are The First."

∾

IT TOOK Bardock ten minutes to identify the source of the itch in her skull telling her she'd missed something. She stared at the maps brought into the warehouse, then called for the local harbour master. An overweight man of about seventy, dressed as if he expected to be photographed for the cover of *Pipe-Smoking Retired Bearded Sea Captain* magazine rolled out of a taxi ten minutes later. He had a gift for using twelve words when one would do.

Bardock pointed at the area of water southwest of the Cornish coast. "Is that a shipping lane?"

"Ah, well, if that's where I think it is, young lady, then, well, I'd have to say that yes, you'd be correct to say so. Busy, too. I remember when I was just a boy, my old dad once—"

"What kind of ships?"

"What's that? Say again? I don't hear quite as well as I used to. Still, can't complain, that Bert Trannick at the sweet shop's got shingles again, so he has, and that's no fun when—"

"The ships. What kind of ships use that stretch of water?"

"Well, now, let me have a little think. Container ships, cargo ships, the odd trawler. Thing is, you don't see the trawlers there quite so much these days. Still a few, but what with quotas and cheap frozen muck in the supermarkets, a whole way of life is dying. I was talking to Jack about it in the Three Boars Sunday gone. I said—"

He stopped and looked at the finger Fiona Bardock had placed on his chest. Then he saw her face and swallowed.

"Shut up and listen," she said, in a voice which had once made a terrorist cry. "I will ask you questions. I want to hear a yes or a no. Nothing else. Do you understand?"

The harbour master nodded rapidly. "Yes," he said.

"Am I right in thinking cargo or container ships are the main source of traffic in that shipping lane?"

"Yes."

"If a smaller boat were to pull alongside one of those cargo ships at sea, would it be possible for them to board?"

The harbour master's lips worked for a few seconds, as he tried desperately to bite back all the information he wanted to impart. "Yes," he said, then opened his mouth to expand, "but—"

Bardock had already turned her back on him.

"Gregg," she called, "get over here and ask him how a small boat can transfer its occupants to a cargo ship. Try to get it done in under twenty minutes."

She pulled out her phone and called Jameson's direct line. He answered on the second ring.

"Jameson."

"Two things. Can you get in touch with every ship that was in the water anywhere near Cornwall yesterday and offer a massive reward to anyone who thinks their ship might have picked up passengers at sea?"

"Of course. What else?"

"Can you put me in touch with the nearest American military vessel in the Atlantic?"

~

Daniel was in two places at once. He was on the container ship *Liberace*, somewhere between Ireland and America. There was a metal floor underneath his feet. He was inside a forty-foot container nestled in a stack of similar containers. Sara, TripleDee, Abos, and Saffi were with him. In this place, it was Saffi he looked at, Saffi he reached out to. It was Saffi's hand he held. He drew her close, and she put her arms around him.

In the other place, Saffi wasn't there. She couldn't follow him. Onboard the ship, he held her tighter as his consciousness left her far behind.

Daniel was an observer in the other place. It was as passive an experience as watching a film, but he was *there*. Daniel saw the other place through eyes that weren't his own. They couldn't be. For a start, there were two of them. He had to adjust to the strange sensation of seeing the world through a pair of eyes. But he wasn't afraid. He knew the others were with him. And Abos was guiding them.

He was inside a mountain, standing in an enormous artificial cave. A vast screen showed the view outside. He wore layers of a synthetic material designed to maximise his body heat, minimising the energy needed to keep the caves warm. It was still cold.

The mountain's natural caves had been requisitioned, enlarged, and linked by tunnels a decade earlier. Only a few hundred individuals remained there now. The last communication from the only other outpost had been received over a month ago.

The screen showed a landscape becoming less hospitable by the day. Daniel could see three trees - the only three in sight big enough to be visible through the crust of snow and ice. They were dead, as were the birds that had once made nests in their branches.

He walked down the curving ramp leading to the chamber containing machinery on which the last remaining chance of survival depended. Survival of a sort, anyway. They had rushed their experiments of late, cutting corners as conditions worsened. What should have taken twenty years, they had tried to achieve in two. There would be no time for checks. It would take weeks to effect the changes in physiology necessary for survival, with no guarantee of success. They might end up dead, or worse, mindless monsters. They might emerge too soon, and crawl out to die on the crust of ice covering their empty, frozen cities.

He reached the chamber. The others were there, robed in furs as he was, hoods and cloth coverings obscuring their features. Only their golden eyes were visible.

It was the end of times. Their planet was changing, just as the scientists had predicted. Billions had refused to listen, accusing the scientists of scaremongering. Billions refused to listen, and billions died.

The scientists made their own plans during the last decades. They had long been capable of building craft that could carry them through the inhospitable reaches of space, but they knew the journey to find a new home might take hundreds, or even thousands, of generations. They assembled the ships in orbit around the planet. When the giant craft were ready, shuttles began moving thirty-thousand individuals aboard, a tiny fraction of the planet's population.

Years before the climate changes came to pass, the massive engines of the leviathans lit up, and those left behind looked up into the night sky with scorn, amusement, pity, horror, or regret, as the explorers left them behind. Those on board the fleeing ships watched their home recede knowing they would die on those vessels, never setting foot on land again. It would be their ancestors who would take that step, starting anew on the first planet that could support life. When, or if, they found one, could they be sure their descendants wouldn't selfishly ravage the new planet? Even those not prone to cynicism wondered if their great-grandchildren's great-grandchildren would avoid the catastrophic mistakes of their ancestors.

Left behind, the scientists turned back to the other project that might yet save their species. They worked tirelessly as the days grew shorter, and colder, and the nights became so bitter that their bodies could not survive outside for more than a few minutes.

They had evolved from the simplest of organisms over billions of years, becoming an intelligent species with its own societal structures, its own art and culture, its own discoveries, inventions, and intellectual constructs. But they had made a misjudgement, had failed to see the inevitable consequences of the impending planetary changes until it was too late.

Even as the greatest minds among them worked to prepare one last chance for some to survive, they knew they were unlikely to succeed. And, even if they did, their civilisation would be lost forever. Time would do its work over millennia. Towers would crumble into dust, great works of art and literature would vanish, and no one would be left to mourn the loss. The planet would endure, but no trace of their achievements, of their presence even, would remain.

No one would remember the First unless they remembered themselves.

He walked forward into the chamber, lay down where he was directed and waited for death, or—possibly—rebirth.

∽

DANIEL WAS first to re-adapt to his surroundings as onemind dissolved. His sense of the cold chamber in the unfamiliar world faded, and he was aware of Saffi's face looking up at him, her mouth moving, panic in her eyes.

Sound returned all at once, and he heard the roar of jet engines outside, the rhythmic thock of helicopter rotors. He looked at Saffi in confusion.

We're in the middle of the Atlantic. How can there be a helicopter outside?

Then Saffi's words penetrated the last of the fog lifting from his mind.

"It's the US Navy, Daniel. They're threatening to board us."

16

Bardock stood on the bridge of the *USS Smithwatson*, one of the newest Nimitz-class nuclear aircraft carriers in the American fleet. She looked across at the tired, rust-flecked hull of the *MV Liberace,* which had now come to a stop. They had delivered an ultimatum and given them five minutes to respond. There were three minutes left.

She handed the binoculars back to Admiral Conley.

"How difficult would it be to board?" she said.

He shrugged. "Not difficult at all. We drop troops off by helicopter, use fighters to provide covering fire. Or we torpedo the prow and wait until they're in the lifeboats. Then we can just pick them up."

"I like your thinking, sir. But my orders are that the lives of the titans cannot be risked."

Conley shrugged again. The situation contained elements he'd never encountered before in a long and distinguished career. He wasn't overly impressed by the instructions he'd received from the Chairman of the Joint Chiefs of Staff telling him to take orders from the British woman. Matters had got even worse ten minutes later when the Commander-in-Chief had called with orders of his own. "If you can't get them back, sink the ship. No survivors. If I—or, rather, America—can't have superheroes, no one will."

Conley looked at Bardock.

"I heard they can fly," he said. "It's not as if they're gonna drown, right?"

On a satellite phone during the flight to the *Smithwatson*, Bardock had been briefed by Curwan, one of the Pentagon scientists. She knew about the titans' dormant state. Now she needed to know more, and what Curwan told her during that call, or—rather—what he didn't tell her, made her uncomfortable. According to Curwan, if the right conditions were available, the titans could grow fresh bodies in seventy-two hours. Which gave her twenty hours to act if the regrowth process had begun immediately on boarding the container ship.

Bardock had asked Curwan the obvious question.

"If they grow new bodies, won't they fly back to America?"

The scientist had clammed up. He had not explained his opinion that the titans would be less than enthusiastic to resume their duties. Instead, he had insisted Bardock recapture them while they were still dormant or—if she were too late for that—before their new bodies were fully grown. A scientific team was on its way to the *Smithwatson*. Curwan claimed they would bring the equipment necessary to ensure the titans would continue to be true patriots. Whatever that meant.

Bardock had spent the rest of the flight mulling over the implications of the conversation, putting the new information together with what she already knew about The Deterrent. There was another piece to this puzzle: the fact that halfheroes were involved. Jerry Sotterly's description of 'Steve', the man he had dealt with when he had loaded his van with milk cans, didn't match TripleDee, but it did closely match someone else on a classified database. Daniel Harbin, the first child of The Deterrent. His file had been full of holes that suggested redactions at senior level. He was presumed dead. Presumed.

The Deterrent was the father of the halfheroes. And it had been The Deterrent who had led the titans into the trap. For the first time since taking the case, Bardock allowed herself to speculate about motive, rather than letting the facts guide her. Why would The Deterrent want to cause harm to other members of his species? Why did he desert the titans in New York? And how were his children involved?

With thirty seconds left until the deadline expired, the radio buzzed. Admiral Conley picked up his headset.

"Bardock," he said, handing over the radio and picking up a second headset, "they want to negotiate. You're the officer in charge of this operation."

She took the headset.

"Who am I speaking to?" she said.

"That's hardly important." It was a female voice, British, possibly Midlands.

"My name is Air Commodore Bardock. You are suspected of killing, or kidnapping the titans. We are about to board the *Liberace*. Come out on deck where we can see you. Unarmed."

"Let's not waste time playing games, Air Commodore Bardock."

"Just Bardock."

"Bardock, then. Yes, we have the titans. They are in a container on this ship. They are in their dormant state - I will assume you know what that means. I'd have no compunction about throwing them overboard if you come anywhere near us. They'd sink. And we are five thousand metres above the bottom of the Atlantic. They'd be lost forever. If it had crossed your mind to torpedo us, consider the consequences."

"This is not a negotiation," said Bardock. "You have stolen the property of the United States. I am speaking to you from the *USS Smithwatson*, a nuclear aircraft carrier with the capacity to blow your ship out of the water in a dozen different ways."

"Property?" the female voice sounded genuinely angry. Interesting. The woman's outrage on the titans' behalf belied her threat to throw them overboard. "*Property*? They are sentient, they are intelligent—they are nobody's property, Bardock. Here's a suggestion. Why not let them make their own decision about whether they want to be the president's poster boys. How does that sound?"

"Yes. I agree. Once you've returned them."

"Okay. We'll hand them over in forty-eight hours."

Bardock said nothing. Forty-eight hours fitted with what Curwan had told Bardock about the time-scale needed for the titans to regrow bodies. She couldn't give them forty-eight hours. Despite her claim, this woman was playing games. Their source on the *Liberace* had mentioned two men and two women. TripleDee and Harbin accounted for the men. Bardock was convinced she was talking to the brains behind the whole operation. Who else would lead the negotiations? But who was she? Another halfhero?

At that moment, something occurred which convinced Bardock the woman she was speaking to was The Deterrent's daughter. According to the reports Bardock had read, some halfheroes could influence other people mentally, manipulating another person's thoughts. Bardock had paid little heed to that idea as it seemed so outlandish. Now, she wished she'd spent more time studying those reports. A voice had just spoken in her mind.

I should give them the time they need. The situation is delicate. If we try to board, there are too many unknowns, and we risk losing the titans.

Bardock took the headset away from her ear and looked at Admiral Conley.

"Did you hear something?" she said.

He shook his head. "What kind of thing?"

"It doesn't matter." Bardock didn't put the headset back on immediately. She waited. Sure enough, after a few seconds, the voice returned. It was a familiar voice. It was her own voice.

I should give them the time they asked for. That's the right decision.

Bardock's mind was, as anyone who had ever worked with her would confirm, unusual. Her reputation had been made on the back of cases where she had reasoned her way to conclusions which astounded those around her. When she had explained the chain of logic she had followed, everything made perfect sense, but it was clear to her superiors that her gift was rare, if not unique. She could observe a crime scene with a level of attention others had grown out of before primary school. Bardock saw the scene as it was - seeing everything, without imposing filters. She could hold every detail in her mind. Such an ability might have been debilitating, rendering her unable to function, but Bardock's toddler-like attention was combined with a degree of concentration rarely found outside world-class athletes. Once she had stored every detail internally, she could zoom into any part of a scene and apply her incisive reasoning before zooming out again to see how her conclusions affected the rest of the picture.

As a child, her unusual manner, combined with clumsy social skills, had set her apart. After a period of illness in her teens, which her mother insisted was psychosomatic, she was sent to a psychiatrist. After a series of tests, he offered a diagnosis which gave her mother a label she could apply to her troublesome daughter. Bardock didn't have much time for labels.

Her unique mind turned out to be anything but a handicap when she joined the military. It had saved her own life, and others, many times. And right now, it was handing her an advantage.

Bardock watched the alien thoughts arise in her mind with a kind of stunned fascination. This woman—this *halfhero*—talking to her from the *Liberace*, was trying to manipulate her mind. If it had been anyone else, she might have succeeded.

Bardock thought fast. If she refused to go along with the woman's demands, she would reveal that she was impervious to her power. Better to play along, make her think it had worked. That way, they wouldn't be expecting the attack when it came.

She pushed the headset to her ear and spoke into the mic.

"Okay. We'll give you some time."

"You will?"

The voice sounded surprised. Maybe she'd sensed resistance from Bardock when she was planting thoughts in her head. Bardock decided to give her something else to worry about.

"Not forty-eight hours," she said. "It's now sixteen

hundred hours. You have until six tomorrow morning. Fourteen hours."

There was no reply. Bardock wondered who the woman was talking to, what they were discussing. Then the line clicked open again.

"Very well. Six o'clock."

Bardock put the headset on the desk. The admiral gave her a look.

"I hope you know what you're doing," he said.

Bardock had no intention of keeping her word. If the halfhero believed she had successfully influenced Bardock's thoughts, she would be unprepared for what was coming next.

She turned to Admiral Conley.

"Navy Seals on board?"

"Yes."

"Good. I'll need a squad. We'll board in an hour."

∽

ON THE *LIBERACE*, Sara handed the radio back to an ashen Captain Andreas. His eyes flicked from her to Daniel and TripleDee.

Daniel put his face a few inches from the captain's sweaty brow.

"I see that the president of the United States has offered a ten million dollar reward for information leading to the recovery of the titans. I already know you're a man who can be bought. Did you sell us out?"

Andreas shook his head. As his entire body was already shaking, it made him look like a nodding dog on the dashboard of a car.

"N-n-no, not m-me, no, of c-c-course not. We have a d-deal."

"Yes. Or, rather, we *had* a deal. Now get on the PA system and assemble your crew."

Andreas slid gratefully away from the man looming over him and sat at the console on the bridge. He took a few calming breaths before speaking into the microphone.

"Attention all crew. This is your captain. B-brief immediately in the assembling room. That is, Room assembly in the immediate brief. Er, all crew. Briefing room. Now."

Twenty minutes later, Captain Andreas and his crew were locked into the 'Citadel,' their secure hiding place in the event pirates boarded the vessel. As well as food, drink, and a ventilation system, there was a radio in there. Until Daniel punched it and it fell apart in a shower of tiny components.

Before leaving, Daniel opened the weapons locker, removed the six machine guns inside and bent three of the barrels out of shape with his bare hands, snapping the others in half over his knee.

"Don't try anything silly," he advised as he left, and they all agreed that they wouldn't.

∼

BACK ON THE bridge of the *Liberace*, Daniel found the others waiting for him.

"I still can't get me head around the whole First stuff," said TripleDee. "I mean, we were *there*, right? What planet were we on? When was that? Why couldn't Saffi see it??"

Sara put a finger up to her lips.

"I'm as interested to find out as you are," she said, "but we have more pressing problems. I don't know how successful I was at *nudging* that Bardock woman. She resisted. And she was different, her mind was different. It was as if she knew I was there. It's never happened before. I can't tell you if I influenced her."

"Well, she gave us until tomorrow morning," said Daniel. "It must have worked, right?"

Sara shook her head. "I don't want to rely on it. Abos. How much time before they're ready?"

"It will be faster now," said Abos. "A few hours. Onemind has formed while they are growing. The link is established. Their brains are developing more quickly. We all share resources. That is how I know what I am. Who we are."

"The First?" said Saffi. Daniel had promised to describe his experience.

"Yes, The First. The onemind is unlocking our species memory. We are not just individuals. When we are onemind, each of us contributes towards a larger consciousness. Onemind provides memories, but there is much missing. There are only nine of us. There should be thousands."

"Thousands?" said Daniel. "There are thousands of you?"

"I do not think so. Not anymore. Many have been lost."

"Look," said Sara, "I know this is incredible stuff, but we might all be in prison, or dead, within the next few hours, so please shut up."

Even Abos looked surprised. Sara pointed at him. "Is there any way of speeding up the growth process?"

"No. But they will be ready before the deadline tomorrow morning."

"Okay," she said. "I hope that will be enough. Our trump card is you, Abos. They don't know you're conscious. Could you take them on - if we backed you up?"

Abos looked out at the massive aircraft carrier.

"Yes," he said. "I think so. But they are heavily armed. I do not wish to provoke a conflict which could lead to the destruction of this ship. People will die. And until the others are fully grown, they are vulnerable. Better to wait. With our full strength, we can get away without loss of life."

"That's settled, then," said Sara. "Let's get something to eat. We need to rest. Someone should stay here on the bridge to keep watch. Saff, why don't you take the first shift? Daniel, you relieve her at seven."

Everyone sniggered apart from Abos.

Sara rolled her eyes. "Oh, grow up."

Abos raised his hand as if he were in a classroom. "I will rest now for two hours. Then I will watch. I will not need any more sleep."

"I'll stay with Saffi now," said Daniel.

The others left in silence. Neither Saffi nor Daniel spoke for a few minutes. Then Daniel told Saffi everything he'd seen when Abos had shown them the onemind memory.

"Their planet was dying?"

"Yes," said Daniel. "I guess so. At least, it was getting too cold for them to survive. But the memory was incomplete."

Saffi looked at the sky. "And somewhere out there is the rest of his species."

"If the ships got through. If they found another planet where they could start again."

"Well," she said at last, "at least that answers one question. There is intelligent alien life out there."

17

When the Old Man arrived in London, it was mid-afternoon. It had been decades since he'd flown for any distance. He was hungry. Starving, in fact. And confused. After so many lifetimes alone, to learn that others may have survived, that his people were returning...

It must all be connected to his Purpose, but he had lived so long he no longer knew what would happen when they returned. When he found them, it would become clear. It must become clear.

The air above London was thick, and he felt his throat clogging with particles of burned fuel as he descended. His anger grew as he came closer. The city was vast and, just as had been the case in New Delhi, the earth was covered with stone, brick, and glass. Here and there were green patches, where humans had allowed nature to remain, in a controlled, repressed form.

He coughed and spat black dirt. So much had changed, and, so far, none of it was for the better.

Below him was an open space between the buildings. He headed towards it.

The usual crowd of tourists were feeding the pigeons in Trafalgar Square, throwing overpriced seed, posing for photos as the birds perched on their arms and heads. The stone lions at the base of Nelson's Column looked on.

A tour guide gathered her group around her before continuing a well-rehearsed spiel.

"We're now in front of the famous fourth plinth. The other three plinths have held statues since they were first built. The two at this end are larger because they were intended to display equestrian statues. Indeed, as you have just seen, the third plinth shows King George the Fourth on his horse. Unfortunately, the money ran out for the fourth plinth in eighteen forty-one, and the planned statue of William the Fourth was never erected. Since nineteen ninety-nine, the plinth has been home to various modern pieces, even—once—for ordinary members of the public, who applied for a slot via a website and could do whatever they liked while they were up there. My favourite was the lady who described the sexual inadequacies of her ex-husband in great detail. She was funny."

"Where's the big cock?" A middle-aged woman with a Nigerian accent was waving her handbag. "My sister told me there was a giant cock."

The tour guide was unruffled. "Well, it's true that the fourth plinth displayed a bright blue cockerel for a while, but that was a few years ago."

"Oh, bloody hell," said the woman. "I have brought my camera and everything. And now you tell me I can't see the big cock."

"I'm afraid not, madam," said the tour guide. "We all understand your disappointment. As you can see, the plinth is vacant. The planned sculpture of our future king kissing The Deterrent was deemed a little too controversial. Still, I'm sure we'll have exciting news regarding its replacement any time now."

"A tall Buddhist with golden eyes," said a small man with an ice cream.

"Well, that's an interesting idea, sir. You could always suggest it to the commissioning body." The tour guide laughed at her own joke. No one else did. She had lost their attention somehow. No one in the group was looking her way at all. They were all gawping at the empty plinth. She turned. There was a tall Buddhist monk in orange and saffron robes standing on the plinth. And he had golden eyes. Like The Deterrent and the titans.

"Where the hell did he come from?"

She hadn't addressed the question to anyone in particular, but the short man with the ice cream answered. "He dropped out of the sky." There were nods of agreement from others in the group, and dozens of other tourists were hurrying over.

Various voices spoke at once.

"Is he a titan?"

"They don't have Asian titans, do they? Just white ones."

"I thought they all looked like the president, only fit and good looking."

"I don't think he's a titan."

"Who is he? Miss, who is he? Miss? Miss?"

The tour guide realised the question was being addressed to her.

"He's one of those street magicians, I believe," she said. "You know, hidden cameras and the like. I'm afraid they're popping up all over the place."

Some of the group looked around for cameras while a few of them burst into applause.

"Please don't encourage him," said the tour guide, wrinkling her nose as if smelling something bad. "They usually don't have a licence, they get in everyone's way, it's all very annoying. Just ignore him."

The monk jumped down from the plinth, walked up to the group and plucked the ice cream from the small man's fingers, devouring it in one bite before striding away.

"Rude," said the man.

"They're all the same, bloody magicians," said the tour guide.

"Are there any other big cocks we can look at?" said the Nigerian woman.

∼

THE OLD MAN needed more food, fast. He had made an uncharacteristic error, flying across continents without making sure he had taken on enough energy. The ice cream helped a little, but the short boost was gone too quickly. He stumbled as he reached the edge of the square, then sat down.

The pigeons around him fluttered away, then returned as he lay down on his back, dizzy and nauseous. He turned on his side and watched them eat seeds from the dirty concrete. Reaching across, he scraped seeds towards him, picked them up with shaking fingers, and transferred them to his mouth. He repeated the process a few more times, snatching as much as he could from under the pecking beaks of the indignant pigeons.

"That's gross, man. Really."

He looked up and saw a boy of eight or nine years watching him with fascination.

"I mean, you're eatin' off the floor an' everything. S'gusting. You missed a bit. By your ear."

The Old Man shifted and scooped up the seeds the boy was pointing at. He didn't understand much of what the child was saying. The language had changed beyond recognition during the centuries since he'd last been in Britain.

"You gotta 'spect youssself, man. Ain no one gonna 'spect you if you don 'spect youssself. D'ya get me, tho'?"

The Old Man wasn't sure if the boy was speaking English at all. With an effort, he pushed himself up into a half-sitting position. His head hurt, and his vision was getting blurry. Not good.

A pigeon waddled past with the insouciant manner unique to the feathered denizens of Trafalgar Square. The Old Man's hand shot out and grabbed it. Still assuming it was under no threat, the bird didn't voice any protest, just waited placidly to be returned to the ground, where it could have a nice shit and eat more seeds.

The Old Man bit its head off and drank its blood before flipping the body over, ripping it apart and wrenching its bloody breast apart with his teeth.

The boy watched, his face slowly breaking into a smile.

"Oh, man," he whispered, "that is dope." He reached into his pocket and fished out his phone, pointing the camera towards the Old Man as he grabbed a second pigeon and eviscerated it.

"Badass," breathed the boy, his face a picture of admiration.

The Old Man looked up at him, blood covering his mouth and chin. The phone was an unfamiliar device, but the boy was pointing it towards him. Possibly a weapon. He waved his little finger, and it blew apart in a cloud of glass and plastic.

The boy looked at his bloody hands and the remains of his phone.

"The fuck?" he said, then dropped the last few pieces, tilted his head up to the sky, and wailed, "DAAAAAAAAAAAADDDDDD!"

A big man appeared at the crying boy's side. He carried a large sandwich in one hand. After a flurry of dialogue back and forth, which the Old Man did not try to follow, the newcomer stepped forward, his shadow falling across the robed monk. The Old Man was sucking clean the ribs of a third pigeon. He was already feeling much stronger.

"My boy says you busted his phone, Buddha boy. What are you gonna do about it?"

The Old Man may not have understood the words, but the tone was clear. He ignored the provocation until the smell of the sandwich wafted his way. Then he put the third headless corpse down and stood up to his full height. The boy's father, with a heroic effort of will, didn't flinch when the monk, his face smeared with blood, stared down at him with emotionless yellow eyes.

"Um. Just saying, yeah, you broke his phone. You should buy him a new one. You hearing me? You owe my boy a phone."

With inhuman speed, the Old Man snatched the sandwich from the boy's father. He took a big bite and chewed, still looking at the man. Then his other hand shot out and pulled a wallet from the man's pocket. He opened it, took out the banknotes, then let it fall to the floor.

"Dad! Dad! He took your money! And your sandwich! Kick his arse, Dad! Kick his arse! Dad! Where are we going? Why don't you beat him up? Dad, owww!"

The Old Man turned his back and walked away. He was still hungry. And he needed to learn the language. Which meant a new body.

He walked down the first side street he found, avoiding the wider thoroughfares, which were as busy with vehicles as New Delhi's had been.

Outside a large window, he paused. People were eating, sitting at white tablecloth-covered tables, talking and laughing. As new people came to the door, a well-dressed man greeted them and showed them to a table. Wracking his brains for the few words he could remember, the Old Man entered. The well-dressed man approached, stopped, and looked at the tall, dirty monk with blood smeared around his mouth. The rest of the room fell silent.

"I require... repast. Food, if you please," said the Old Man.

The well-dressed man shook his head, his voice low and urgent. "I'm sorry, sir, we are too busy, we have no tables available."

The Old Man couldn't understand what he was saying. He held up the banknotes and pointed at a vacant table. "If you please," he repeated. "Food now."

The Maitre d' had been confronted with awkward situations before, but a Buddhist monk was a first. He walked the man to the door, one arm on his elbow, trying not to breathe through his nose. For a second, the robed figure didn't move - it was like trying to push a block of stone. Then the monk acquiesced, leaving the restaurant without further incident.

The Maitre d' didn't like the look the man gave him with those weird eyes of his, though, not one little bit.

∾

The Last Of The First

SIX HOURS PASSED before the Old Man went back to the restaurant. He had eaten well enough, taking food from people as they walked the streets holding sandwiches, fried meats, vegetables, and various sweet morsels. A few had protested, but one look at the Old Man had dissuaded them from pursuing the matter.

The restaurant was nearly empty when he got back. When he had been ejected earlier in the day, he had checked the alley running along the side of the building, finding a large metal container used to hold uneaten food, much of which was rotting. Perfect for his purposes.

He checked the front of the building. The Maitre d' was supervising the cleaning of the room by a servant. The Old Man moved to a shadowed doorway along the alley and waited.

The servant emerged first and hurried away. A few minutes later, the back door opened again, and the well-dressed man came out. He turned to lock up.

The Old Man looked both ways before crossing the alley. All was quiet. He lifted his hand as he walked, and the Maitre d' grunted as his body was pushed against the door by an invisible force.

The Old Man twisted his hand in the air when he was two paces away and caught the body as it fell, the neck cleanly snapped.

Holding the corpse by bunching up its shirt and jacket in front of the ribs, he jumped eight feet, landing in the stinking container and pulling the lid down after him. He took the blood he needed from the wrists and, as it poured onto his skin, he stopped breathing and willed the process to be as fast as possible.

The sun was rising when he climbed out of the container and put on the well-dressed man's clothes. He was bigger than his victim as always. The dark suit jacket wouldn't fasten around his chest, and the trousers finished three inches above his shoes. Such ill-fitting clothes would draw attention.

Crossing three roads, he made his way back to a shop he had seen the previous afternoon. He went in through the rear door, the lock splintering as he pushed it open. An alarm shrieked into life, and he looked around in shock until he found its source and silenced it.

He located suitable clothing, dressed and looked at himself in the mirror. He was Caucasian now, bearded and tall. It was satisfactory.

By the time the Old Man had walked to Regent Street, the pavements were already busy with commuters. He took a coffee from one of them and a cup full of thin porridge from another, then made his way to Euston Square Gardens.

On a bench under a silver birch tree, he listened to the complex, musical song of a blackbird in the branches above. Some sounds echoed through the centuries unchanged.

The Old Man looked at the timepiece on his wrist. It was 6:55. He had checked the opening hours of his destination the previous day but decided against going in until he had an English-speaking body.

Two and a half hours to wait. He let himself lapse into a low-energy state, his pulse slowing and his thoughts ceasing. He did all this despite his excitement. There were others like him. He had almost forgotten there would be others. That knowledge had been lost along with his Purpose. Today, he would banish some of his ignorance by visiting the biggest repository of information in the country.

The Old Man was going to the library.

18

Abos stretched out on his bed and closed his eyes, his breathing deepening. No one else could sleep. TripleDee, after an hour of turning from one side to the other, walked through to the middle container and started watching Blade Runner. Ten minutes later, Sara came in.

"Harrison Ford," said TripleDee. "Is he human, or one of them?"

"Long time since I've watched it," said Sara. "It's supposed to be ambiguous, isn't it?"

"I always thought it was obvious."

"Really? So which is he?"

The radio beside the computer crackled into life. "Guys, this is Saffi. They're coming now. Wake Abos and get up here!"

By the time Abos, TripleDee, and Sara had joined Abos on the bridge, ten boats were three-quarters of the way between the *Smithwatson* and the *Liberace*. Two helicopters were flanking the container ship, and Daniel was watching them through the binoculars.

"A dozen in each boat, maybe ten on each helicopter," he said, handing the binoculars to Sara. "Abos?"

Abos looked at the approaching boats. His body grew still.

"I need you," he said.

Daniel looked at him. Somehow, Abos carried his unique *Abosness* from body to body. The Asian man standing beside him looked to be in his late twenties, but Daniel had no problem accepting him as his father.

"What can I do?" he said, then realised Abos hadn't been speaking to him. Daniel could sense onemind forming, but —this time—he wasn't invited.

Behind them, on the main deck of the *Liberace*, the top layer of forty-foot containers was moving. Like the teeth of a giant zip opening, the containers in the centre tilted and moved away from each other. Over six hundred containers peeled apart and toppled outwards, plummeting into the ocean with a series of crashes that made the ship roll. The Seals' smaller boats rocked from side to side as the heavy wake reached them. Daniel could see them taking evasive action, turning from the *Liberace* and powering away for a short distance, to avoid being hit by the falling cargo.

When the carnage was over, only the bottom layer of containers remained on deck. As the sound of the splashes receded, Daniel heard both helicopters' engines rise in pitch, like instruments obeying a conductor. When he turned back to Abos, he'd gone.

Daniel and the others ran outside. Abos hovered fifty feet above them, arms outstretched. The whine of the helicopters was louder, and the pitch of the note they emitted was still rising. The helicopters blades slowed. As a cloud blocked the evening sun, Daniel could see into the cockpit, and he glimpsed the pilot fighting the joystick and flicking switches.

Then the rotor blades stopped, the whine turned into a grinding shriek, and something gave way with a rapid series of bangs, followed by silence. Daniel looked from one helicopter to the other as they hung in the air.

The Seals onboard responded. Grappling ropes appeared from the belly of each static chopper. Dark silhouettes emerged, weapons slung across their shoulders. As the first of them began the descent, the helicopter moved again. Not under its own power this time. Arms still outstretched, fingers splayed, Abos made a gentle pushing motion towards the choppers and they tilted, tails angled towards the water, then flew back towards the aircraft carrier.

One of the crew of the second helicopter, perhaps frustrated by this demonstration of their impotency, opened fire with a large machine gun. Bullets sprayed up the side of the *Liberace* and across the deck, heading towards the halfheroes and Saffi. Abos lowered his hands, and the helicopters dropped out of the sky. The machine gun continued to fire, and the bullets strafed across the prow of the lead boat. Daniel saw two soldiers cut down, one falling into the waves.

The helicopters slowed as they fell until they came to rest on the surface of the water.

There was a moment of quiet. A cliché popped into Daniel's mind.

"The calm before the storm," he said.

Events soon proved him right as a shitstorm of unforeseen proportions began which not everyone on the *Liberace* would survive.

∽

On the bridge of the *Smithwatson*, Admiral Conley watched the situation spiral out of his control. He didn't like having teams of Seals operating under their own orders. He didn't like bringing his vessel into a situation where there were so many unknown factors at play. He didn't like these flying clowns, whatever the hell they were. He didn't like handing over part of his command to some Brit he'd never heard of. And, most of all, although he'd never say it aloud, he didn't like the fact that an incompetent in the White House could send the men and women under his command into danger.

Despite all of this, Admiral Conley was a military man, and a patriot who knew his place in the chain of command.

The moment the helicopters fell from the sky, he ordered the torpedo crews to prepare their payloads and stand ready.

Bardock was still on his bridge. "What are you doing?" she said. "That ship is civilian, and you have no way of knowing how those... titan... things will react if you fire on them."

While she was speaking, the choppers touched down on the water, and their occupants scrambled out to safety.

"They could have killed them," she said. "Are you even looking? They spared their lives."

Conley ignored her. "Prepare to fire," he said. His orders had been clear. If the titans showed any sign of aggression towards them, he was to attack.

"Wait," she said. "No. No. They're not attacking us. Look. For God's sake, look!"

The Seals swam to safety as the helicopters vanished, leaving a trail of bubbles. Conley focussed his binoculars on the lead boat. Looked like one fatality, one injury. Both caused by friendly fire. He took the microphone away from his mouth, thinking, his expression grim.

Bardock knew to say nothing more.

~

DANIEL WATCHED the boats come closer. They moved slowly this time, and none of the Seals raised their weapons. The lead boat had turned back, taking the corpse and the wounded man back to the *Smithwatson*.

Abos shut his eyes. A loud metallic tearing sound came from the deck of the ship, and Daniel turned in time to see the top of a container peel itself back like the lid of a sardine tin. Figures emerged from the opening, floating up into the sky.

From the boats, fingers pointed, and shouts from the Seals carried across the water. They were close enough now that Daniel could hear individual words, such as, "titans," "bulletproof," and, "shit."

The figures that rose from the ship may once have been the titans, Shuck and Susan among them, but they were unrecognisable. Some were only semi-formed, their bodies hairless. They drifted up in front of the stunned Seals.

As a teenager, in a semi-hypnotised state of boredom and mild arousal, Daniel had once spent an afternoon watching a broadcast of synchronised swimming. It was this he remembered now as the First, moving in perfect harmony, formed a horseshoe behind Abos. There was a prickling sensation at the base of Daniel's skull, an un-scratchable itch.

"You feel that?" said Sara, as they looked up.

"Aye," said TripleDee.

"Yes," said Daniel.

They didn't need to say anything else. Abos was the dominant mind. He had taken control of the First. Their minds were linked to Abos as strongly as human limbs are linked to the brain. When the brain gives the signal, the limbs respond.

Saffi squeezed Daniel's arm to get his attention.

"Are you okay? Are you with me? Daniel?"

"Sorry," he said, blinking. "It's the onemind. Even the weak connection we have with it can be overwhelming. Abos is protecting the First. Until they are fully grown, they are vulnerable."

"Then they have to leave," said Saffi. Her voice was urgent. She turned Daniel to face her and looked into his eyes. "Tell him. Tell Abos. Tell him to leave, get the others to safety until they are strong enough to protect themselves. Worse case scenario here, the Americans lock us up. Abos and the others can rescue us later."

She pointed at the huge aircraft carrier dwarfing the *Liberace*. "It's not as if the navy will torpedo an unarmed cargo ship, is it?"

"You're right," said Daniel. "Sara, we need to talk to Abos."

Sara and TripleDee were looking up at the figures above them, their eyes unfocussed, their bodies still. Sara's head dropped, and she looked at Daniel.

"He knows," she said. "He heard Saffi through us."

Beside her, TripleDee nodded his head.

"He agrees. They're leaving."

∽

Bardock pointed her binoculars at the figures on the *Liberace*, then tilted them up towards the titans.

She had seen two men and two women on the deck.

TripleDee was easy to spot. She tentatively identified the second male as Daniel Harbin although his file had mentioned nothing about a missing eye. The two women were unknown. One was tall and strikingly attractive. The other was shorter, dark hair, possibly of Middle-Eastern extraction.

She was about to comment on the flying figures, most of whom were naked, when they moved so fast it looked like an optical illusion. One second they were over the container ship, the next they were hovering above the *Smithwatson*.

On the aircraft carrier's deck, fighter crews prepared the jets for takeoff. Six Super-Hornets were ready to go, their pilots strapped into their cockpits and awaiting orders. No one was sure if they were under attack.

The siren that blared out across the *Smithwatson* suggested they were.

Admiral Conley watched his crew follow emergency procedures. His options were limited. The titans were so close now that missiles would be useless. At this range, he had the Sea-whiz, or Close-In-Weapon-Systems, and the handheld weapons carried by the crew.

Bardock knew the admiral wasn't about to share his orders with her, but she hoped he knew better than to start a fight with the creatures hovering above his ship.

She had done her job, followed a logical chain of reasoning, deduced cause from effect. She had located the missing titans. This was the result. The most powerful beings in the world were hanging above her head while she stood on the bridge of a warship so full of armaments it was a floating bomb.

Perhaps she should have stayed at home and finished her painting instead.

The titans were unrecognisable. Bardock's briefing had warned that their appearance could change, but she hadn't expected this. The lead figure was an Asian male. He was the only one who was clothed. Three of the others were male, the rest female. One male, and two of the females, had partially formed bodies, larger than any human, but with dough-like embryonic faces. When they moved, they moved together.

"What the hell are they doing?" said Conley.

As if in answer to his question, the lead titan raised his right arm. Every other figure behind him did the same.

Bardock winced at a noise so loud it was painful. On the deck, pilots scrambled out of their planes while the ground crew ran forward. Every aircraft now looked deformed. The right-hand wing of each had been snapped off and lay on the deck beside them.

Not a single plane had escaped. The *Smithwatson* was now an aircraft carrier only in name.

Admiral Conley issued his orders. His vessel was under attack.

"Open fire."

A short burst of gunfire was followed by an unnatural silence. The sailors on deck pointed their weapons upwards in confusion.

The *Smithwatson* carried two automatic defence systems - the Sea-Whiz and the Seasparrow, both driven by powerful supercomputers and able to react faster than any human. The Sea-Whiz guns swivelled from left to right, their muzzles sweeping the area where the titans had been. Their targets had gone. They had moved so quickly that the longer-range Seasparrow could neither track them nor retaliate with a missile launch.

Bardock swore under her breath. She felt a pang of

disappointment, then dismissed it. She had not failed. She had found the titans, despite the false trail laid by... well, laid by who? The female halfhero was the most likely suspect. The one who had tried to manipulate her. She was still onboard the *Liberace*. Bardock had questions for her.

Conley issued orders to three officers, who jogged away as she approached.

"Air Commodore Bardock," said the Admiral. *Uh-oh.* A sudden return to formality was never a good sign. "Thank you for your help. You may now return to your quarters. We are re-routing and returning to America. I have contacted the RAF. Your ride will arrive in an hour.

"With all respect, sir, I should interrogate the suspects when they are brought onboard."

Bardock looked out at the container ship. The Navy Seals were not approaching the *Liberace*.

"Why aren't you boarding them?" she said.

"Thank you, Air Commodore, that will be all."

Bardock thought fast, and her mouth dried up. The halfheroes and The Deterrent had taken the titans. The best result for the United States would be their return, and the punishment of those responsible. If that result proved unachievable, the removal of future threats would be prioritised. The titans were out of reach. TripleDee, Harbin—if that's who it was—and the two unknown women were right in front of them.

Despite suspecting she was wasting her breath, she stepped forward. "You can't justify this. It wouldn't be self-defence, it would be murder. There's a crew onboard that ship, too. What about them? What about—hey!"

Two uniformed men grabbed her arms and pulled her towards the door.

"Confine her to quarters until her plane arrives," Conley ordered.

As she was dragged away, her stomach lurched at the words Admiral Conley said next.

"Fire torpedoes."

19

Tom was alone, eating an apple. Well, as alone as he could ever be these days. So not alone at all, really. He climbed to the top of the hill and perched on one of the rocks making up The Devil's Chair, a local landmark and the subject of countless myths and legends.

The most popular told the story of the devil's journey from Ireland, carrying the stones that made up the Giant's Causeway in a leather apron. He wanted to use them to replace the roof of Hell, part of which had collapsed, revealing a view of England, which displeased him. No one knew why the devil had built Hell underneath England in the first place. Less stringent planning regulations back then, perhaps. On his way to repair the roof, his apron broke, spilling the huge stones, which landed atop the Stiperstones in a heap resembling an armchair.

When one of the local farmers recounted the story, Tom had been fascinated, but now, as he finished his apple and sent it sailing out to startle a nearby sheep, certain elements mystified him. Okay, it was a myth, but it still had to make some kind of sense, didn't it? Why would the devil repair his own roof? Was it likely that the Prince of Darkness, the Lord of Flies, eater of souls and torturer of condemned humans was interested in DIY? Surely he would have delegated the job.

Still, Tom admitted that, from a certain angle, the massive heap of rocks did look like an armchair. A huge, uncomfortable armchair. Maybe the devil preferred it that way. Probably not into soft furnishings, Old Nick.

Another local legend suggested the devil didn't have exclusive rights to the chair. There had been a local character by the name of Wild Edric, suspected of doing some kind of dodgy deal with the agents of darkness. A giant of a man who never aged, Wild Ed was rumoured to have hung around the area for centuries, his appearance changing, but always with a foul temper. Luring Edric into the mines under the hills, a group of men buried him there. The legend revived generations later when a local girl swore she and her boyfriend saw Wild Edric sitting on the Devil's Chair. He had chased them and taken her lover. This had been in the sixteenth century, and, as the missing lad was the son of the local lord, his disappearance was well documented. Whether he had been dragged to Hell, or run off to Hull was never established beyond doubt, but as his girlfriend subsequently turned out to be pregnant, many locals suspected the latter.

Tom wondered if the myths had anything to do with why he and the others were here. They all asked themselves the same questions from time to time, but no one was bothered by the lack of answers. Whatever had happened to him, whatever was still happening, was nothing to fear. It was natural, like the week his voice broke, or the day he first found a hair growing out of his previously smooth chin.

That this particular change was one which, as far as they all knew, had never happened before in human history, was also no cause for concern. He and his friends were the first to experience it, that was all. Someone had to be first. He wasn't worried, or afraid. It was *right*. It was beautiful. And it was... he didn't know the correct word. The only word that came close was a word he'd never used before. It was *sacred*.

He let the others back in. He had been enjoying the solitude for a few minutes, but that was more than enough. To keep his consciousness separate, to experience life as an individual seemed wrong now. The presence of the others nourished him. Even when he separated himself, he knew they were there, like a murmuring stream outside a window you heard while you slept. Letting them back in was like opening that window, discovering it had rained during the night, the sun had risen, and the most beautiful view imaginable lay beyond.

Tom had tried to describe the change to his mother the previous night. When he'd remembered to charge his phone, there had been seventeen missed calls and five messages. Eleven of the missed calls had been from his mum.

"No, Mum, I'm fine. Of course I love you, I love both of you. It's nothing you've done. You brought me up brilliantly. I'm not angry. Why would I be? No, I'm not on drugs. It's not a cult, Mum! It's just that, well, it's... what's happened is... well..."

The problem was there was no easy way of describing the changes.

"Mum, if you saw a chrysalis hanging from a plant, and you could see the butterfly wanted to come out, only something was stopping it, what would you do?"

"Pardon? What's this about butterflies, Tom? What would stop a butterfly coming out?"

"I don't know. It's not important."

"Well, if it's not important, why did you bring it up?"

"Okay, okay. Chewing gum. Chewing gum's clogged up the chrysalis, and the butterfly can't get out."

"Chewing gum?"

"Yeah."

"Tom, why on earth would someone put chewing gum on a butterfly?"

"Not on the butterfly, on a chrysalis."

"Oh, and that's better, is it?"

No. No. Mum, I'm trying to explain what's happening."

"Are you torturing butterflies up there? Is that it?"

"No, Mum, I'm... oh, it doesn't matter. I just want you and Dad to know I'm safe. And I'm happy."

"But your A levels? What about them?"

Tom had forgotten about his exams. No, not forgotten. It was an aspect of his life with no importance. He hadn't given his A levels a second's thought since waking up that last morning in Luton over a week earlier.

"I don't know, Mum. But I need to be here now. And it'll be okay. Trust me."

"At least tell me where you are. We're worried sick."

"Mum, I'm in Shropshire. Camping. In a field."

"You? Camping? In the fresh air? Well, that's a turn-up. You're old enough to do what you like. We are just upset you didn't tell us."

"It was kind of snap decision, Mum. I'm sorry."

"When are you coming home?"

Tom bit his lip. He couldn't tell her that he *was* home. Not without hurting her. And he could hardly tell her about the gathering darkness they all knew was on its way.

"I don't know. There's something I need to do first. Something we all need to do."

"All? Is this some sort of rave?"

"Mum, it's not the nineteen-nineties. I'll call again soon."

Now, as Tom walked away from the Devil's Chair, he wondered if his parents, or anyone else, would ever understand what was happening in this quiet corner of Shropshire. It wasn't as if he knew himself. Not really, not yet. He was too happy to care, though. As he followed the path downhill, the field came into view. When he, Kate, and Shannon had arrived and pitched their tent, the field had been empty. Ellie Craxton, the daughter of the farmer who owned the land, had joined them that first night, bringing her own tent. Her father, a strict and somewhat bad-tempered man, had uncharacteristically agreed she and her friends could use the fallow fields at the base of the Stiperstones.

The field wasn't empty today. Tom counted a hundred and seventeen tents, three caravans, and two motor homes. One of the fire pits was alight, and figures were silhouetted against the flames. Vegetable stew. It wasn't the smell that gave it away. All of them had been present partially or fully for the washing, chopping, and preparation of the meal. All of their food came from donations by local villagers who felt strangely impelled to make sure the youngsters on Craxton's field were adequately nourished.

The parents of some teenagers, often accompanied by the police, had been regular visitors for the first few days. They had been warmly welcomed, given a tour of the camp, and had left feeling reassured. They couldn't have articulated why it was they were no longer concerned about leaving their children in a field full of strangers. But the parents returned home, and the police took no further action. Eventually, thought Tom, someone would question exactly what was going on in Craxton's field, but by then, it would all be over.

Whatever *it* was.

No one called to Tom as he climbed the stile and walked among the tents. There was no need. Another tent was going up three along from Tom's. More teenagers still arrived every day.

He was hungry, so he went to the fire pit. Before he was halfway across the field, he stopped dead.

Spinning.

Can't breathe.

Tom sat down on the dry grass, his eyes no longer seeing the tents, the fire, his friends. Around him, many others did the same.

Blue darkness.

Can't breathe.

Need to find the light.

Darker. Tighter. Must breathe.

Tom's own breaths were shallow, sweat beading his forehead.

Have to breathe, can't hold out.

Too late, it's too late.

Not like this, please.

Not like this.

Not like—

The connection lost, Tom looked around him to see the same expression on everyone's face. Pain, fear, and loss. But loss of what? Or of whom?

20

There was no warning before torpedoes were fired at the unarmed container ship.

"I guess we'd better let the crew out," said Daniel, his arm around Saffi. "Do you think they'd drop us off in Cornwall?"

TripleDee snorted. "I think they'll do whatever we bloody tell them to do, the treacherous bast—"

The location of the first impact, combined with the fact that Daniel and the others were watching Abos and the First leave from the port side of the *Liberace*, saved their lives. The torpedo hit the centre of the ship, the explosion making the vessel rear up like a rodeo bull. When the second torpedo punctured the hull, a huge plume of water was drawn up as a gas bubble from the initial explosion collapsed. This caused the *Liberace* to break apart and begin to sink.

Daniel had kept one hand on the guardrail and the other on Saffi as the initial blast tilted the *Liberace* like a fairground ride. Sara and TripleDee were knocked off their feet, sliding across the deck. Sara threw both hands out in front of her. With no time to finesse what she was planning to do, the wave of energy she summoned hit both her and TripleDee like a punch from a giant's fist, sending them flying away from the stricken vessel, landing in the churning waves.

Daniel, hanging on to Saffi as the ship tilted, saw Sara and TripleDee thrown clear of danger. He yelled, "We're jumping!" using all his strength to propel them both as far as possible. He twisted as they fell, ensuring his back took the impact when they smacked into the water. They sank below the surface, then Daniel kicked hard and powered them back.

Saffi gasped with shock.

"Are you hurt?' said Daniel. She panted a few rapid breaths, then shook her head.

"I don't think so. Where are the others?"

Daniel was scanning the ocean as the waves rolled around him. The stricken ship continued to break apart, each end tilting until nearly vertical, towering over them like skyscrapers.

"There, Daniel! I see them!"

He followed Saffi's line of sight and saw Sara, her hair plastered across her face. She was thirty yards away. Even as he drew breath to shout, Sara dived beneath the waves.

"Fuck!" said Daniel, fixing his eyes on the spot he'd last seen her. "Where's TripleDee? I've got to—"

He swam away, then stopped, aware of Saffi behind him.

"Go on," she said, treading water. "Been a swimmer since I could walk. Go help her."

Daniel broke into a fast front crawl, the water churning behind him like the wake from a jet ski. Once he reached the spot, he stopped and turned three hundred and sixty degrees. There was no sign of Sara or TripleDee. He looked back and caught sight of Saffi.

Suddenly, Sara resurfaced, gasped, and disappeared again.

Daniel took a breath and dived, grabbing her and pulling. He could see why she was struggling. Her right hand was gripping TripleDee's collar. Daniel grabbed TripleDee by his upper arm, helping to pull him to the surface.

Sara couldn't speak straight away as she filled her lungs with air. Daniel supported TripleDee's heavy, sodden body.

"Is he...?" Sara took another breath and tried again. "Is he...?"

The man in Daniel's arms coughed up seawater.

"No, he's bloody not, pet. Not yet, anyhow." TripleDee's voice was weak. He coughed again, struggled, slipped out of Daniel's grasp and sank.

"Bloody hell!" Daniel reached down and pulled him back to the surface, spluttering. "What the hell's wrong with you? Don't you know how to—"

"—swim?" TripleDee's voice had an edge of panic Daniel had not heard before. "No, man, I don't."

He sank a few inches and kicked wildly, getting his face back above the surface.

"Don't fancy teaching me, do you?" he gasped. "Really fucking quickly, like?"

Daniel moved his arm under the big Geordie's chin, pulling his body towards him.

TripleDee stiffened in alarm. "What the fuck are you doing?"

Shut up," said Daniel, "and stop struggling. It will be difficult, but I need you to relax and keep still, or you'll drown both of us. I'll tow you back over to Saffi."

Sara swam alongside Daniel as he pulled his half-brother through the waves. TripleDee kept up a sting of half-strangled swearwords, some of which Daniel had never heard before.

"Trip," said Daniel. "If you don't conserve your energy, you'll drown."

"So, er, shut up, then. That's what you're saying, is it?"

"Yes."

"Righto."

Saffi and Sara hugged as they reached each other. "Can you support him?" said Daniel, looking back at the container ship. "Between the two of you, I mean? For a few minutes?"

Both ends of the *Liberace* were sinking fast.

"We can do it," said Sara.

"I'm gonna relax," said TripleDee.

"Go get them," said Saffi. "But be careful."

Daniel looked at her, wishing he could think of something to say. Then he turned his back, kicked out his legs and set off to rescue the crew.

Close to the *Liberace*, the water frothed and spat around Daniel as if it were boiling. He tried to find the part of the ship where the crew were locked in, but the lack of two eyes and the violent waves made it difficult. He knew which half of the ship to head for, at least. He took a few deep breaths, preparing to dive.

Onboard the *Smithwatson,* Admiral Conley saw the huge swimmer powering towards the *Liberace* faster than any human. He watched the man dive towards the rear of the sinking vessel. He waited for half a minute, seeing the man reappear twice, then dive again. Conley followed his orders. He spoke into the handset.

"Aim at the stern of the target," he said. "Fire torpedo."

Daniel reached the door of the Citadel on his third attempt. The room was submerged by the time he got there.

The door, designed to stop pirates, could not withstand Daniel's enhanced strength. It took almost everything he had left to force it open against the pressure of the water.

Inside, Andreas and his crew huddled in the far corner, their heads pushed into an air pocket. Daniel heaved the door to one side and swam over.

The dozen men and women making up the crew had three scuba tanks between them and were passing around the regulator. When Daniel's head broke the surface of the water, their eyes widened with fear.

"Door's open," he said, "follow me."

He dived, not bothering to check behind him, keeping his pace slow enough for the crew to stay close. The door had closed again under the pressure. He drove his shoulder into it and held it open as the crew came through one by one. His lungs hurt. Everything was happening too slowly. His body sent urgent messages to his brain insisting he went somewhere where gills were unnecessary as soon as possible.

And that was Daniel's intention. But, as the final crew member emerged from the Citadel and kicked away from the doomed *Liberace*, the second torpedo exploded. The rescued crew all died within the first few seconds, pieces of the ship flying in all directions. Those whose bodies weren't broken by debris were knocked unconscious by the shockwave and drowned.

Daniel knew nothing of this. He had been holding the door at the moment the torpedo hit. He was still holding it when the force of the explosion tore the thick steel off its hinges and sent him tumbling into the depths of the Atlantic, the rest of the *Liberace* not far behind him.

21

The climb to the top of Mount Pico, the highest point in the Azores, had taken the Swedish couple three and a half hours. The guide had warned that over a third of those who attempted the climb gave up before the summit. The cheeky bastard had looked at Pelle when he said it, too.

Much to his annoyance, Pelle was having a little trouble keeping up with Monika. She was fifteen years his junior, but he was still running half-marathons and entering the occasional triathlon. *And* he'd paid for this bloody trip of a lifetime, so the least she could do was wait for him to catch up. They hadn't been getting on well for the last few weeks. Pelle suspected Monika would break up with him when they got home. She would take the all-expenses-paid trip first. He watched her muscular bum as she climbed the final steps. They were supposed to reach the summit together, dammit. Pelle decided tight, muscled buttocks were ugly. His next girlfriend would have softer, more curvy buttocks. Despite being surrounded by a stunning view from the top of an isolated mountain in a remote island, thousands of miles from anywhere in the middle of the Atlantic, Pelle visualised the rear end of Anne, his new office manager.

"Pelle!"

He didn't answer straight away. Yeah, well done, she'd got there first. She didn't even sound out of breath.

"Pelle!"

He decided he'd break up with her first. In the airport at Stockholm. Casually, as if he didn't care. Because he bloody didn't.

"Pelle! My God! Look!"

Yeah, breath-taking views, volcanic steam, ancient lava, fluffy clouds. Whatever.

Monika made a funny snorting noise, like a surprised pig. Pelle looked up to see her faint and crumple, sinking to her knees before slumping against a rock.

Ha! Not so fit, then. She'd been trying to show off, and she'd overdone it. Pelle looked at her lying there, vulnerable and in need of his help. He broke into a stumbling jog, feeling bad about the detail in which he'd imagined Anne's bottom.

When he reached her, he unscrewed his water bottle and held it to her lips, supporting her head with his hand.

"Here, take a drink, you'll feel better," he said. "It's probably a touch of dehydraSHIT!"

Pelle saw what Monika had seen. He let go of her head. She dropped to the ground, and he spilled the contents of his water bottle over her face and chest.

Floating about ten yards above the dormant volcano's crater were nine figures. Eight of them were naked. There were five women and four men. They were all huge. Six of them had their eyes open. Their eyes were gold.

Titans.

Pelle realised the clothed one was looking straight at him.

"Shit," he said, his voice shaking as much as his legs.

"Go back," the titan, commanded.

"Okay," said Pelle. "Yes. Going back now. Thank you. Goodbye. Thank you."

He helped a dazed and soaked Monika to her feet, keeping her back towards the titans. She gripped his arm, terrified. He managed a reassuring smile, despite feeling sick, and let her lean on him as they began the long descent.

Ten minutes later, an instinct made him turn and look back at the summit. The clothed titan was flying upwards, leading two others. The rest stayed where they were. The lead figure paused, looking for all the world as if he were checking his phone. Did superheroes need to check their route on Globmaps? Pelle had never considered the question before, but he supposed there was no reason one of their superpowers should be the ability to navigate without maps or compasses. Still, he couldn't help feeling a little disappointed.

A second later, his disappointment vanished as the three titans flew into the clouds in a blur of speed.

It would take him and Monika at least another two and a half hours to get back to base camp. As they walked, Pelle wondered if the ten million dollar reward for the recovery of the titans had been claimed yet.

22

When the second torpedo hit the crippled *Liberace*, Saffi said nothing, blinking tears away as she looked at the spot she had last seen Daniel. Seconds after the explosion, the water forced outwards by the shock-wave reached them, lifting them like corks and pushing them away from the smoking wreck. The rear end of the container ship slid beneath the surface.

TripleDee coughed up water, and Sara lifted a hand from his shoulder, wiping away some of Saffi's tears.

"He's the strongest man I've ever met, Saffi," she said.

TripleDee was too tired to protest. Besides, he knew she was right.

"He'll be okay," continued Sara. "If anyone can get out of there, it's Daniel."

They watched the surface, and Sara said nothing more.

Triple Dee saw the approaching figures before anyone else.

"Abos," he croaked.

Sara and Saffi turned to see three people flying towards

them. Abos was flanked by two naked women, one tall, black, hairless, the other white and muscular.

"It must be Shuck and Susan," said Sara. "This is the third body they have grown since Abos found them. The process will be faster for them."

TripleDee didn't respond, amazed that Sara could reason logically at the same time as supporting a half-drowned Geordie in the middle of the Atlantic Ocean while an aircraft carrier tried to kill them.

Then he felt it. He shot a glance at Sara. One look at her face and he knew. The connection with Daniel, first formed when they had broken out of the White Sands prison, had always been there, like background noise.

Until now.

There was a splash near the floating wreckage where the rear of the *Liberac*e had sunk. Abos had dived for Daniel.

∾

Drowning was no fun at all.

Seven seconds after the exploding torpedo had pushed him and the Citadel's door deep down into the Atlantic, Daniel regained consciousness and knew he was in trouble. Not the kind of trouble where quick, decisive action might save the day. No. This was the kind of trouble with permanent consequences. The kind of trouble without a surprise twist and a happy ending. The kind of trouble that finished up with someone dying.

In this case, him.

He opened his eye to stinging, blue-black darkness with no up, no down, no left, no right. He looked for some point of reference, *anything* that might help. There was nothing. Everything was the same.

Daniel held the door as if it were a talisman, his fingers locked onto the thick steel.

He needed to breathe. He desperately needed to breathe.

After too many beers, Daniel had often announced that he *desperately needed* a piss. Now he knew better. There had been no *need* back then, no *desperation*. Real need, followed by real desperation, happened when all other options had gone.

He had two options. Breathe or die.

In a moment of clarity, he released the door. It fell away from him.

That must be down. *I need to go up.*

The last, feeble kick he could manage pushed him in the opposite direction, away from the door. But it was too late. It was much too late.

Daniel acknowledged he didn't have two options anymore. It wasn't breathe or die. It was simpler than that. Much simpler.

It was breathe *and* die.

He thought of Saffi and took a breath. The seawater flooded his mouth, throat and lungs. His brain had no alternatives to suggest so his body obeyed its instinct to breathe again, and his lungs filled with water.

His body jerked like a fish on the boards of a boat.

∽

TripleDee managed one quiet word. "No." Sara started crying. Saffi continued treading water, but her strength ebbed away, her mind becoming as numb as her body.

She didn't react when she felt herself being lifted clear of the water, along with Sara and TripleDee. The two First were above them, and the bizarre-looking group of naked superbeings and soaking, exhausted humans flew a few yards above the waves.

They headed towards the half-submerged prow of the *Liberace*. It had stopped sinking and was rolling onto its side. TripleDee, his breathing returning to normal now he was out of the water, looked up at their rescuers. One of them was holding her hand forward as if coaxing the stricken ship. Around fifty thousand tons of metal moved in response to her gesture.

By the time they reached the *Liberace*, the front half of the ship had rolled onto its side, presenting a large flat area. The two First landed, then watched as Saffi and the halfheroes touched down beside them.

All three of them sat unmoving, looking towards the area where Abos had dived. The water was still churning, the wreckage below breaking apart while it sank.

When Abos broke through the surface of the water and hung for a split second in the air, he looked like an engraving by William Blake, or a painting by Giulio Romano. A soaring giant, muscular, most of his clothes ripped away by the speed of his return. The rich, warm light of the evening sun made him look like a god.

In his arms, he cradled Daniel's limp body.

"No," said Saffi, then repeated it, the sound becoming an incoherent cry of pain. "Noooo..."

Abos flew towards them and laid his son on the *Liberace's* hull next to the others. He didn't look at them. He didn't acknowledge their presence. He looked at the unmoving man, his golden eyes unreadable.

The only sounds were the smack of waves as they came up against the hull of the ship, and Saffi's awful involuntary screams of pain. TripleDee held her hand and Sara drew her head towards her, holding her tight, but the same terrible keening broke from her lips with every breath.

Daniel's face was grey, his lips blue. His chest wasn't moving.

Abos reached down and pulled his mouth open. He held his finger and thumb about an inch above Daniel's lips, as if about to thread an invisible needle.

Nothing happened immediately, but Saffi's screams quietened as she watched.

Then they saw it, a trickle of water about half an inch in diameter, rising from between Daniel's blue lips. As if pulling the water, Abos moved his hand up. The water followed, arcing away from the soaking body and splashing onto the hull a few feet away. The trickle got faster, becoming a stream. The water that had filled Daniel's stomach, lungs, and throat poured out of his body.

Within seconds, his lungs were empty again, but there was nothing telling them to inflate and deflate. Abos touched Daniel's face, rubbing his skin, looking at him. Daniel's eye patch was gone. With both eyelids closed, and his body still, he looked so unlike himself that Saffi turned away, her sobs returning.

TripleDee shuffled forward a few feet and put a hand on his father's shoulder.

"He's gone," he said in a voice so tender, no one from his previous life would have recognised it. "Abos, he's gone. You did all you could."

The face that turned towards him was full of pain and anger. Abos rarely displayed anything close to human emotion. It had taken TripleDee a long time to see the subtleties present in some of Abos's expressions. There were no subtleties now.

The most powerful being on earth scooped his son's lifeless body from the hull of the *Liberace*, rose fifteen feet into the air and turned to face the *Smithwatson*.

∾

Admiral Conley had made his decision the moment before Abos had begun his flight towards the aircraft carrier. He hesitated for a moment before giving the order, hating himself for what he was about to do. Could he fire on seven unarmed individuals?

Conley's long, successful career in the US Navy owed much to his ability to make difficult, complicated decisions under pressure. He was calm and decisive in a crisis.

But, ultimately, like any soldier, he obeyed orders. The integrity of the entire military structure hung on that principle. His orders were to recapture the titans and their kidnappers and, if that was not possible, wipe them out.

There were three titans on what was left of the *Liberace*. Three titans and four people. His orders were clear, and they came from the Commander-in-Chief.

His hesitation meant he missed his best shot.

As the biggest titan rose from the *Liberace*, carrying a body, a torpedo left the *Smithwatson* to finish the container ship. Conley ordered the launch of two Seasparrows. The missiles were designed to counter supersonic attacks and high-G manoeuvring low velocity targets. They would take care of the approaching titan.

He bowed his head when he'd done it. Maybe it was time to retire, go home to Mary, buy that ranch they'd always talked about.

"May God have mercy on our souls," Conley whispered.

23

Abos was linked to onemind, which was growing stronger minute by minute as the other First continued the rapid development of their new bodies and brains. He saw the giveaway turbulence below the waterline of the *Smithwatson* as the torpedoes launched. The two First on the *Liberace* knew what he knew and stood up, facing the threat, their hands outstretched.

The torpedoes were half a second away from impact when the First lowered their hands. As they did so, the weapons changed course and passed under the hull of the container ship. They continued on their way, eventually exploding on the seabed at a depth of over five thousand metres, killing thousands of marine creatures, and rendering a large area barren for years.

Far above, Abos did not try to avoid the missiles. He saw them launch, their flaming tails pushing them towards him. Two million dollars worth of innovative technology carrying eighty-six-pound fragmentary warheads.

The unfamiliar look of anger was still on Abos's face.

To the horror of those watching from the *Liberace*, and

the grim satisfaction of the observers on the *Smithwatson*, the Seasparrows converged on the target. TripleDee, Sara, and Saffi looked away.

There was no explosion.

The two missiles crossed paths a few yards away from each other, in front of Abos. They flew over what was left of the *Liberace*, drew two large arcs in the sky and, in perfect harmony, continued to bank until they were lined up on the vessel which had launched them.

A klaxon sounded on the aircraft carrier, and men and women scrambled to emergency stations. Admiral Conley, his first officer, and three other members of the crew stayed where they were. Any attempt to escape was futile. The missiles were heading towards the bridge.

"Brace for impact," said Conley, because that was what years of training and leadership had taught him to say. He knew a direct hit from two Seasparrows wouldn't even leave enough dental evidence for their families to identify them, so bracing wouldn't help much.

Conley didn't close his eyes. He watched his death approach with no outward sign of emotion.

It wasn't until the missiles—which came so close he could see the markings on their sides—roared by a few yards overhead that he let out all the breath he'd been holding.

Twelve seconds later, the sky behind the *Smithwatson* lit up with one of the most under-appreciated and overpriced firework displays in history as the two Seasparrows hit each other.

"Okay," said Conley. "Okay. Back to work, people. Where's the target?"

"Er, Sir?" The voice came from one of the crew members at the door to the bridge. The door was open and, stooping to get his bulk inside, and the body he carried, was the titan.

The sailors on duty snapped into action, raising their weapons and covering the threat. Without pausing as he walked inside, the giant looked at them and there were cries of shock and pain as every weapon blew apart, their constituent components falling to the deck in a hail of metal. The sailors cradled hands cut by the exploding weapons.

Conley was given no opportunity to speak.

"Get a doctor. Now. His heart has stopped." The titan's voice was the single most terrifying sound Conley had ever heard. It wasn't loud, but it was imbued with implacable resolve, and Conley heard it not just with his ears, but inside his mind. There was no threat, but the power came off the man in waves. And they'd all seen him defeat the most advanced anti-missile defences available. Conley knew that this titan—whatever the hell that was—could kill every man and woman on board his ship without raising a sweat.

He adapted to the new situation.

"Cincotti." His first officer stepped forward. He had trained as a doctor and, judging by the state of the man with the titan, Conley knew they couldn't wait for the medical team.

"There's a defib on the wall," said Cincotti. The titan laid the man on the floor. While Conley called for medics, he pulled the paddles down from the defibrillator and pressed the button to charge them before pushing up the man's T-shirt.

"Get me a towel!" he shouted. One of the crew, his cut hand tucked under his arm, passed a roll of absorbent paper and Cincotti mopped at the man's chest before applying the paddles.

A beep sounded in the otherwise silent room when the paddles were charged. Cincotti placed one above the right nipple and the other lower and to the left.

"Clear." Cincotti looked up at the giant with golden eyes, who didn't budge. He decided against asking a second time. He pressed the button.

The body jerked as the shock was delivered. Cincotti waited, but there was no response. He waited for the recharge and prepared to shock him a second time.

"Wait," said the giant, closing his eyes. After a moment, he nodded. "Now."

Cincotti pressed the button. The body jumped again, then fell back to the deck. The giant still had his eyes closed. Long seconds passed. Cincotti crouched beside the patient.

The man was dead. Surely the titan knew that. If he didn't, Cincotti was reluctant to tell him.

The corpse gasped, letting out a loud, "Argh." Cincotti shrieked and scrambled backwards, not because of what the body had done, but because the titan had made the same sound at the same moment, loudly enough to be heard at the other end of the ship.

The giant opened his disconcerting golden eyes and knelt by the resuscitated man.

"Daniel? Can you hear me?"

The man's eyelids flickered and opened. He looked at the titan, then at his surroundings, his expression confused.

"Where? What...?"

"You're safe," said the giant, his voice now as gentle as it had been terrifying a moment before. "You nearly drowned."

"Nearly?" The man's voice was hoarse and barely audible. "Wait. I died, didn't I?"

"Your heart stopped," said the titan. "You will be all right now."

The man tried to sit up, but his arms shook, and he fell back. The giant caught him and manoeuvred him into a sitting position, propped against the wall.

"Dying..." said the man, "dying's pretty horrible."

Cincotti realised that the patient was massive. Up against the titan, he hadn't seemed that big, but now he could see he was built like a wrestler crossed with a bear.

"But death?" continued the man, "that was okay. Didn't mind that so much. Weird. Always thought I would."

He tried to stand, and fell sideways, once again being caught by the titan.

The medical team rushed in and stopped dead at the sight that greeted them, looking from the enormous strangers to the admiral, then back again. The smaller stranger had defibrillator paddles stuck to his chest, so they went to him.

The titan allowed them to check the man's vital signs.

"How long was he in the water?"

The titan answered. "I found him ninety seconds after he lost consciousness. He was resuscitated two minutes later. I could have got him here more quickly, but you tried to kill me again."

Once more, there was no explicit threat in his words, but all those who heard them felt the power of the individual on the bridge. They all experienced the same instinctual, primitive fear, knowing they were in the presence of something that was not human.

The chief medic who had checked the patient's pulse, reflexes, and breathing, turned to the titan.

"He needs fluids, food, and rest."

"Yeah," muttered the patient, "food. Food sounds good. I could murder a curry."

"If he had been left any longer, he would have suffered

irreversible brain damage. As it is, I cannot rule out brain damage completely. You should expect coordination problems and gaps in memory."

"Well," said the patient, evidently annoyed at not being spoken to directly, "I've never been very coordinated anyway, so I doubt anyone will notice." He turned to the titan. "And who are you again?"

"I am Abos, Daniel."

"Why do you keep calling me Daniel?"

The titan looked at the medics with alarm but turned back when Daniel started laughing, weakly, between coughs.

"Just winding you up. Kidding, Abos. It was a joke. Can we go now?"

"Yes, Daniel. We will go to Saffi, Sara, and TripleDee, then we will take you back to the First. After that, we will go home."

"Hang on," said Daniel "Who's Saffi? And Sara? And... the other one?"

The golden-eyed giant looked at him.

"All right, I'll stop now," said Daniel, smiling for the first time. "Come on, let's go. What are you going to do about this bunch of trigger-happy bastards?"

Instead of answering, the giant reached a hand towards him, they walked out of the bridge and soared into the air.

Admiral Conley, his officers, and the crew exchanged glances. Conley turned to his first officer.

"Set a course for NS Norfolk," he said. "Full speed. We're going home."

No one bothered to conceal their relief.

∽

The Last Of The First

FROM THE HULL of the *Liberace,* a ragged cheer went up when Abos reemerged from the *Smithwatson*, Daniel now at his side, rather than cradled in his arms.

Saffi slumped against Sara and wept again, hugging the other woman.

TripleDee smiled. "You're one tough bastard, Harbin," he said, "I'll give you that."

Abos lowered Daniel to the side of the ship where he was hugged by his friends, disappearing behind a lattice of limbs.

"Anyone got a sandwich?" he said. "Or a bag of crisps, at least. Anyone?"

The ship groaned and moved beneath them. Sara looked up in concern but saw Abos and the two other First looking at the hull.

"We are stabilising it," said Abos. "It will be an hour or more before it sinks. We will return long before then."

"What?" said Sara. "Where are you going?"

Abos looked at the *Smithwatson*.

"To deliver a message."

∽

THE *SMITHWATSON* LURCHED as if it had been struck by a missile.

"Damage report!" shouted Conley.

"Sir?" It was Cincotti. He sounded odd, his voice tight.

Conley wheeled on him. "Get me my goddamn damage report. Now!"

Cincotti didn't move. He spoke again, his voice soft, full of fear and wonder.

"Sir? Outside."

Conley looked outside. Then he looked at the floor, shut his eyes, and shook his head before checking again.

"Jesus H Christ in heaven."

∿

"Look!"

Saffi and TripleDee turned their attention from Daniel at the note of shock in Sara's voice. They looked across the stretch of water separating them from the aircraft carrier.

The *Smithwatson* was different somehow. Something about the way it was sitting in the water.

"Is it—" TripleDee began, then stopped and watched, doubting the evidence of his eyes. "It bloody is, isn't it? Man, that's propa belta."

Under other circumstances, Sara and Saffi may have asked for clarification from TripleDee, as they educated themselves in the endless variations of Geordie vocabulary, but the scene before them had wiped every thought from their minds.

The *Smithwatson* had left the water. It was rising into the sky like the largest, most unlikely, novelty balloon ever conceived. Over one thousand feet long, looking top heavy as twenty-five decks tapered down from its two hundred and fifty-six-foot-wide flight deck, thirteen billion dollars worth of US naval might hung uselessly in the air. Three tiny figures, one on each side, with the third at the prow, lifted it as easily as if it were a toy.

Saffi, Daniel, TripleDee, and Sara stared as the First carried the massive ship away to the northwest. They watched the surreal progress of the aircraft carrier until it disappeared.

24

On Gougane Barra lake in County Cork, Ireland, a narrow causeway links the church of of St Finbarr to the mainland. Kneeling alone inside, her head bowed, Dolores Pymm offered up a heartfelt prayer in the land of her ancestors.

"Let me find a good man next time, Lord."

Arnie Pymm, a devout and guilt-riddled Catholic with a weakness for prostitutes and a penchant for hitting his wife, had finally done the right thing six months earlier. He had dropped dead, leaving her with a small fortune and, more importantly, her freedom.

Dolores had always wanted to travel, but Arnie hadn't been interested. While he'd been 'working late,' she devoured books about Ireland, the country her great-grandparents had left to start over in Pennsylvania. She listened to Irish music and occasionally looked up from her book to admire her collection of Celtic crosses and icons. At night, she dreamed of green mountains, mist-filled valleys, and rugged men with the souls of poets.

She knew she was romanticising Ireland, but she didn't

care. She never thought she'd get to see it, so what did it matter if she exaggerated the country's beauty?

Arnie's death gave her the means and the opportunity to turn her dreams into reality. Much to Arnie's family's disapproval—although they'd observed every bruise and black eye she'd received for three decades without judgement—Dolores left for Dublin the day after the funeral.

She'd arrived in Gougane Barra the previous afternoon and, as she'd looked out of her hotel room to see the mist lifting off the lake, revealing the mountains beyond, she couldn't stop herself laughing out loud with sheer exuberance. It was just as beautiful as she'd imagined.

When Dolores found the church of St Finbarr's, she knelt before the simple altar and prayed the rosary with hope in her heart. She'd been married for twenty-seven years and had felt alone for twenty. At forty-six, she still had love to give, and she intended choosing a partner with a little more care and attention this time, rather than marrying the man who'd knocked her up.

"Lord, I don't ask for much. But I'd like someone to grow old with. Someone steady. Someone loyal, and gentle. Someone good in, er, you know, Lord. You invented intercourse after all."

She thought of her favourite movie - On The Town, with that lovely Gene Kelly. Yes, that would do nicely. She liked a man in uniform. A sailor, perhaps. Why not?

A shadow passed behind the two long, narrow stained glass windows above the altar. The church was soon lit only by the candles along the pews. Dolores frowned. She'd been warned that the weather in Ireland could change quickly, but this was ridiculous. It had gone from day to night in a heartbeat.

She crossed herself and got up. When she stepped into

the aisle, she let out a gasp of surprise and confusion. Her feet were wet, water splashing between the toes of her sandals as she stepped down from the pew. As she walked towards the church door, the water rose, lapping around her ankles.

There was no sound of rain outside. Had a water pipe burst, perhaps?

Outside the church, she was more perplexed than ever. Looking back towards the hotel, she could see the hills bathed in sunlight, just as they had been when she entered St Finbarr's.

Dolores walked a little way along the causeway, then broke into a trot as the water rose even higher, threatening to cut off the small island. She didn't stop until she had followed the path a few yards up the hill. Then she turned to look back at the church. When she saw the cause of the rising water, she sat down on the muddy hillside.

On the paths around the lake, walkers had stopped dead and were staring, some of them pulling out phones to film what was happening. Every guest in the hotel, and every member of staff, was standing in the front garden, mouths open in disbelief.

The church of St Finbarr's was in shadow because, lowering slowly into Gougane Barra Lake, the US aircraft carrier *Smithwatson* was blocking the light. Inch by inch, the massive vessel descended, displacing the water of the lake as its keel disappeared into the depths. Three tiny figures were flying at the aircraft carrier's side.

"The titans?" Dolores had seen the news coverage about the president's team of superheroes. Even though she preferred reading romantic fiction to watching TV, everyone had been talking about nothing else for months. And here they were, three of them at least. In Ireland. With a flying aircraft carrier. Which they were dropping into a lake.

The whole event lasted six minutes. When the titans were done, the *Smithwatson* filled the side of the lake north of the church, its prow yards away from the ancient holy building. The flooding of the church from the wake of the ship was temporary, and the water receded from the island as the surface of the lake rose two inches.

The titans flew away without a backward glance. Dolores looked up and saw tiny uniformed figures gathering at the rail of the aircraft carrier, pointing and shouting. She remembered her final prayer in the church.

Sailors.

God moves in mysterious ways.

25

The Old Man, now a tall, bearded respectable-looking figure in a suit, was one of the first in line to enter the British Library that morning. He was wearing sunglasses to hide his golden eyes.

He stood in the centre of the main room, scanning the vast array of shelves under the enormous domed ceiling.

The Old Man examined his feelings. They were mixed. Not for the first time in his long existence, he experienced an intense wave of frustration at the gaps in his memory. He had lived too long, seen too much. His Purpose, once a goal towards which he could make progress, had been lost. The accretion of centuries had blurred his determination, his clear-sightedness and his sense of self. In occasional moments of clarity, he wondered if he had lost touch with reality.

He looked at the countless shelves of books. The Old Man remembered when human language was rudimentary, a mixture of grunting and gesticulating. He remembered his excitement the first time he had handled paper, in a Bavarian monastery.

As strongly as the excitement at what he might find, the Old Man felt distrust and anger. The anger was always present, the one constant in his life. And his anger was growing. Ever since he'd stepped out of the cave, everything he'd seen had fuelled that inner flame of rage. The cities, the smoke-belching vehicles, the subjugation of the natural world. Humans behaved as if they were the planet's overlords. They were upsetting the balance, destroying the harmony. Left unchecked, they would destroy themselves.

The Old Man experienced a stirring so unfamiliar he hardly recognised it as his own. But he did not doubt its truth. Anger flared and sputtered inside him. Yes. His Purpose was bound to his anger, and humanity's abuse of nature caused his anger to grow. Worse still was what he had witnessed on the magic box in New Delhi. Others like him. But they were helping the humans. They must join him instead. Together, they would identify, and fulfil, his Purpose. Then, at last, he might rest.

"Can I help you? Sir?"

A small woman peered up at him. She had been trying to attract his attention for a while.

"Oh, I'm sorry," he said, smiling. "I'm just overcome by the number of books. What a wonderful place."

"Thank you, we all think so. We hold over a hundred and seventy million items here. Is there anything in particular you're looking for?"

Yes," said the Old Man, "yes there is. The... titans." The word came to him from his host body's vocabulary, but when he spoke it, the shape and sound were wrong on his lips.

"Oh, gosh. You mean the flying ones that went missing, I assume, rather than the ones from Greek mythology?"

"Yes," he said. "The titans on the..." more new words, "on the television. They flew next to a... plane."

The librarian smiled. Perhaps the tall man was a foreign pop star. English obviously wasn't his first language, and he wore sunglasses indoors.

"We have all the books about The Deterrent," she said. "The Bowthorpe book, naturally, although much of that has since been discredited. Lots of speculative stuff about their origins, but I can't recommend any of them. They contradict each other and try to debunk everyone else's theories. Half of them think the titans are aliens and the other half think they're genetically modified. Experimental soldiers or suchlike."

The Deterrent. The Old Man stared at her for a moment. A memory shook itself loose from the previous user of his brain. Another of his kind, appearing nearly forty years ago. Interesting.

"Yes," he said. "That would be a good place to start, would it not?"

The woman led him to a series of shelves on an upper level. As she turned to leave, she put a hand on his arm.

"If you want all the latest info, it's on the internet."

Before searching for the word in his newer memories, the Old Man blurted out, "the what?"

She smiled at him. "Don't pull my leg. You saw the news about them yesterday, right? The titans, I mean? Is that why you're here?"

"The news?"

"You didn't see..? Oh! Follow me."

She showed him to a desk where a dark window sat on a stand. A computer. His mind filled in some details while the woman moved a plastic tool on the desk. A... mouse. The window brightened. A few taps on the mouse, and a woman appeared on the screen. She had something in her right hand. A... microphone. She was standing in front of a metal building.

"Just click play when you're ready. The headphones are on the hook there. You have thirty minutes free access, but we're always busy in the morning, so you must let someone else on afterwards."

He thanked her, and she left. Sitting in front of the screen, he put the headphones on, his body remembering that sound would come out of the discs on either side. A tiny arrow on the screen could be moved by the mouse. He positioned it on the triangle beneath the picture, allowing residual muscle memory to guide him. When he tapped, the picture moved, and the woman spoke directly into his ears.

"The incident took place earlier this afternoon at Gougan Barra in County Cork," said the woman on the screen. Then she disappeared, replaced by a picture of the biggest ship the Old Man had ever seen, sitting in an inland body of water which could barely contain it.

"Amateur footage shows the moment three titans flew over the lake, carrying the Nimitz-class American aircraft carrier *Smithwatson* between them."

On the screen, three flying figures hovered as the enormous ship descended from the air into the lake. Another, shakier moving image showed the three titans turning and leaving, at great speed.

The woman was back then, and now the Old Man saw that the metal building behind her was not a building at all, but the ship.

"America's Secretary of State is on his way, but there has been no official comment about what happened here. The titans may have taken aggressive action against the American navy today, but there was no loss of life. The worst injury onboard was a cook who burned his arm after a pan fell off the stove.

"The Irish prime minister initially expressed outrage at the appearance of an aircraft carrier in one of our country's most beautiful locations. However, since the *Smithwatson*'s arrival three hours ago, flights into Ireland have seen unprecedented booking figures, with many airline websites crashing under the increased traffic. A tourist boom is predicted to hit the area, and one local paper has already branded the *Smithwatson* the Eighth Wonder of the World. So, for now, the future of the aircraft carrier looks uncertain. Experts suggest that, unless the titans help, the only way the *Smithwatson* can leave Gougane Barra lake is if it's dismantled and removed piece by piece. We'll follow the story as it develops. Back to you in the studio, Rory."

The Old Man removed the headphones. He had so much to learn. He wanted to know as much as he could about these *titans* before he tracked them down. The number in the corner of the screen told him there were twenty-two minutes remaining. He would need longer.

At the main desk, the woman who had helped him smiled as he approached.

"I want to buy an internet screen," he said.

26

Dinner that night was a muted affair. Afterwards, the fire pit closest to the Stiperstones was surrounded by a large group of silent teenagers.

They had all felt it, but Tom, Shannon, and Kate along with about one in three of the others, had felt it first, and much more strongly. Only then did it spread among the others in a secondary, less powerful wave. Tom and his friends had found their minds full of a terrible sense of constriction, of asphyxiation. After a few seconds, the sensation had lifted as abruptly as it had descended, but its cessation brought no relief. Rather, it left behind an absence, a terrible, raw grief, a gaping hole. It was more painful because of the knowledge that moment had brought.

The absence they felt was that of their father. He was dead.

Some of them, Tom included, knew their parents had required treatment to have children, that they had used IVF to get pregnant. The sperm donor, the father, had only been an occasional subject of speculation until that moment.

Maybe he's a billionaire.

I wonder if he's famous?
A genius, or an athlete.

When the grief hit them, they knew the truth. The IVF children hadn't been speculating about their *fathers*, they had been speculating about their *father*. One man.

And now he was dead. Or, for a few terrible minutes, he was. Then, with a rush of baffled joy, which rolled across everyone in the field in a fraction of a second, he was alive. His presence filled the hole they had never even known was there, and they wept with relief.

Nearly two hundred people now occupied the large field. Latrines had been dug along one side, food was freshly prepared three times a day. There was no rota. If something needed doing, whoever was closest did it.

No one would have guessed that Craxton's field was occupied by teenagers, many of whom had never spent more than a weekend away from home before. The camp operated with an efficient precision rarely seen outside the military. As well as having enough food, someone was always taking wheelbarrows piled with clothes down to the stream to wash, before they hung them to dry between the massive oaks along the southern edge of the field. A shower block had been rigged up. The water was cold, but it was summer, and they knew they wouldn't be there when the weather turned bitter. Showers were communal, and nudity wasn't an uncommon sight. They were healthy adolescents, with, mostly, strong sex drives, but they felt no urges towards each other. The revelation that over a hundred of them shared the same father only confirmed what they already knew - that they were related. That they were family.

The field had taken six days to fill. The first night had been the only one Tom and the girls had spent alone. From early the next morning, the others arrived in a steady trickle. Most walked, some came in vans, cars or on motorbikes.

Craxton's field lay between two villages, and within twenty-four hours of the first tent going up, the locals knew something was going on. The first visitors came to gawp, or to complain. The disapproval that drove them there evaporated as they arrived, and they promised to drop by later with food, toiletries, towels, or sleeping bags - whatever the young people needed.

On the third night, ten young men with stomachs full of ale, and heads full of rumours about naked women on Craxton's field, showed up hoping for a fuck or a fight, preferably both. They arrived twenty minutes after the pub closed and walked onto the field, singing rugby songs and laughing. As they reached the first fire, the nearest girl stood up. Dressed only in a man's shirt, her red hair tousled and her dark eyes gleaming, she might as well have stepped straight out of their fantasies. But when she asked them to sit down, they did so, as meekly as if they had been primary school children.

Two hours later, they walked back to the village in silence, smiling. Next morning, they returned and helped rig up the showers and dig the latrines.

Mrs Minton from Social Services turned up at the end of the first week. At nearly eighteen, Tom was the oldest there. The youngest, Cat, was twelve. Mrs Minton drank tea and talked to Tom and Cat. She left after an hour, satisfied everything was in order. When Mrs Minton returned to her office to write her report, she had no idea what to say. Legally, the position was clear. There were minors on Craxton field who should either be returned to their parents, or sheltered by the state until that was possible. The problem was, no parents had reported their children missing. Tom had told her they would only be there for a few more weeks, and all the children were in touch with their parents. The word of a seventeen-year-old was not good enough for Social Services, but Mrs Minton had changed during the hour she spent with them. The report she filed was designed to move around the system without requiring any action long enough to ensure the occupants of Craxton's field were left alone.

On day seven, a news crew arrived.

The van pulled up by the south gate as Tom was in the shower. He turned the water off and grabbed a towel, dressing and getting to the gate just as the reporter, camera operator, and sound guy were coming in.

"Hi," said Tom, smiling. "Are we going to be on telly?"

Ten minutes later, Anna, the reporter, was standing in the southeast corner of the field so the camera could capture the massed tents behind her, and the teenagers walking between them, talking, laughing, or preparing lunch.

"It's now six days since the first tent went up on Craxton's field and, as you can see, practically a whole village has now sprung up at the base of the Stiperstones. And they're all teenagers - I feel positively ancient! I'm here with Tom Evans, one of the first to arrive. So, tell us, Tom: why are you here?"

"Hi, Anna. It's nothing very exciting, I'm afraid. We're all keen writers, actors, or musicians, and we're here to put on a performance piece."

"Well, that sounds exciting to me. When's it going to happen?"

"We haven't decided yet. And, to be honest with you, we sort of want to keep it a secret."

"Ah, so there is some big conspiracy?"

Tom laughed. "Not really. We want to film it, so we don't want an audience. It'll go online once it's edited. You'll be the first person I send the link to, I promise."

"What a charmer! And how did you all meet? I understand you're all from different parts of the country, right?"

"That's right. We met online, in a globchat group. We talked about doing something together, one of the group said they knew somewhere we could camp for a couple of weeks, and here we are."

"Thank you, Tom. This is Anna Markham at the Stiperstones."

The item was shown at the end of the local news that evening. Afterwards, the news editor called the crew into his office. He had expected a harder-hitting story. These teenagers had left home, many for the first time, to meet a few hundred strangers, but none of their parents had made a fuss.

"Performance piece?" he said. "Really?"

Anna nodded. "There's nothing more there, Jack. It's boring, I know, but if there was dirt to dig up, I would have found it."

The editor scowled. Anna was a good reporter, and her crew backed her up. It was a non-story. So why did his gut tell him otherwise? He shook his head and turned back to tomorrow's schedule.

"Yeah, all right, whatever," he said.

Anna and the crew didn't speak about the piece they'd delivered. They put it out of their mind and resolved to leave the kids on Craxton's field alone.

In a large apartment in East London, a soft alarm sounded on a computer screen as the name 'Tom Evans,' filed in a local news report in Shropshire, was automatically flagged up. His image was run through a database and a match identified.

The computer sat at the end of a long desk which ran the entire length of the wall. The rest of the desk was taken up with other computers, laptops, and Globlets.

When the owner of the apartment checked the screen, she tapped a few keys and brought up the footage from the Shropshire report. Using a digital enhancement programme, she captured every face that appeared on-screen behind Tom Evans, ran them against hacked school databases and came up with more matches.

"Shit. No way."

The hacker picked up the phone, bringing up a database she'd assembled months ago. She dialled the first number.

"Hello? Is that Mrs Kern? May I speak to Gabby, please? It's Amy Whitlock, from St Steven's. I need to talk to her about her A level choices. She isn't? Oh, okay. When do you expect her back? On holiday? Perhaps you could ask her to call the school when she gets home. Lovely, thank you. Bye."

Making a note against the first name, the hacker called the next number.

"Hello, is that Mr Grayling? May I speak to Aaron, please? Oh, really, when would be a good time for me to call? You're not sure? Oh..."

"May I speak to Cerys, please? Oh. When might she be back?"

"Hi, is Garth there? I see. Any idea when..."

"On holiday? How lovely?"

"A hiking trip? Gosh."

"Gone off camping? Where? No, of course you don't need to tell me, I'm just being nosey."

The hacker stopped calling after she had spoken to the

parents of twenty names on the list. The pattern was clear enough.

She wrote an email, short and to the point, signing it Palindrome. She attached an invoice.

"Good luck," she said, as the email *pinged* away. She poured herself another drink. "I hope you can work out what the hell's going on, cos I don't have a clue."

27

The sales assistant in the electronics shop kept up a constant stream of incomprehensible verbiage while the Old Man held the device in his hands, tilting it this way and that.

"This is the cellular version which means you don't have to worry about patchy wifi."

The Old Man put his finger on the screen as he'd seen the assistant do. It lit up, showing a picture of an iguana so realistic it was as if it were there. Just behind the glass. He looked underneath to check. The sales assistant raised his eyebrows at his manager.

"Anyhow, you won't get better than a Globlet. That one's got half a terabyte of memory and four gig of RAM. If you want to upgrade to the eight gig version, I can just slot it in now for you, or you can pop back any time. Paying by card?"

Card? The Old Man, excited by how close he'd come to finding others of his kind, considered just taking it, but he had not survived for so many centuries by taking unnecessary risks. He might be vastly more powerful than humans, but they were capable of surprising cunning. He would not underestimate them again. The last time he had done so had been in this very country, and he hadn't been back since. Hundreds of years ago, it been the closest he'd ever come to dying, and he had no wish to repeat the experience.

He was known as Wild Edric. He ruled a great swathe of land running along the north Wales border. Tired of constantly moving on, he had been careful to conceal his true strength, contenting himself with garnering a reputation as the fiercest fighter in the land. He treated his followers well. He was generous and fair to those who looked to him for protection.

When the French challenger for the English throne invaded, killing Harold at Hastings, Edric stayed true and fought the invaders with intelligence and ferocity, making Shropshire one of the few areas that did not fall to the usurper. As the months wore on, however, Edric saw it was a matter of time before the invaders took the area. William's claim to the throne had been legitimised, and almost every lord in England had bent the knee to the French pretender.

Edric met King William's representatives in secret, and they struck a deal. He would keep his position and his lands. It was a pragmatic step and avoided unnecessary bloodshed.

Wild Edric's mistake had been to assume that his men would agree with him. They did not.

He had taught them well. When they turned on him, they did it when they had the greatest chance of success. They were returning from a patrol along the border and had camped on the range of hills known as the Stiperstones. There had been pockets of rebellion protesting Edric's change of heart regarding William, and he had quelled the last of them that day. He had not slept for three nights straight. Rumour had it that Wild Edric never slept, but his men knew better, and they waited until he was at his weakest.

Borrod, his most trusted adviser, suggested they camp for the night by the old lead mines. Borrod's betrayal was hard to take, Edric having practically brought him up. When the men had murmured about Wild Edric's ageless appearance or his unique yellow eyes, it had been Borrod who had assuaged their concerns, who had reminded them of their leader's great deeds, and his generosity. Edric had noticed a distance between the two of them of late, but had delayed dealing with it until he had broken the rebels' resolve. A mistake.

The short tunnel just inside the mine entrance culminated in a drop of more than a hundred feet, where the tunnel had collapsed months earlier, killing fourteen. Another cave-in was thought likely, and the seam had been abandoned.

Wild Edric was so deeply asleep as to be near-unconscious when his treacherous men, led by the turncoat Borrod, picked up his pallet, rushed him along the tunnel and threw him into the pit.

The fall was sufficiently violent to break his body. He experienced cold panic as the process of returning to his dormant state began. He was so far from the surface, so far away from the blood which would give him new life that he wondered if he would ever walk the earth again. When the rocks fell as his men buried him, he was sure of it. It was over.

With a determination born of blind instinct rather than reason, he dragged his dying body across the cave. More rocks fell around him. One landed on his ankle and crushed the bone flat. He redoubled his efforts.

At the edge of the cave, there was a narrow band of light from a crack in the side of the hill. It was narrower than his forefinger and no longer than his hand. He pushed his failing body hard against it.

The sound of falling rocks became louder as his men's efforts triggered a landslide. The Old Man faced death with no assurance he would ever open his eyes again.

Eighteen years later, a shepherd passed by. When his sheep were set upon by wolves, his dog threw itself at the pack, meeting his death in a flurry of claws and teeth. The animal breathed out his last on that hillside, slumped against a rock. His blood stained the stones and the grass. Some of it trickled through a gap in the rocks, following a course hollowed out by centuries of rainwater, until it dripped onto a slime-like substance buried beneath.

Two nights later, a courting couple's tryst was interrupted by a violent rumbling in the hill beneath them. Although rare, earthquakes were not unknown in England, and the half-dressed lad and his wench hung onto each other in terror. When the old mine entrance burst open with a shower of rocks and stones, and a giant, black dog with flaming eyes burst out, the girl fell into a deep faint. The lad returned her to her worried parents an hour later, with a story of their walk being interrupted by a devil dog. His terror was so obviously unfeigned, the girl's mother decided not to mention that her daughter's blouse was back-to-front.

A month passed before Wild Edric found an opportunity to regain human form, whereupon he left Shropshire, vowing never to return.

"Sir? Sir?" The shop assistant had backed away a little. How long had he been lost in his memories, the Old Man wondered? There was fear in the young man's eyes. Had he said anything aloud?

"I apologise," he said, forcing an unnatural smile onto his borrowed lips. "I have a... condition."

The young assistant was still tense.

"I'm feeling better, and I'd like to buy this, please."

The assistant relaxed at once, greed overcoming his fear. The manager smiled and moved away from the door.

"Paying by card?"

The shop assistant had said that before. The Old Man only had a hazy notion of what he meant. Some concepts

The Last Of The First

were too complex to understand, even with his access to this body's memory. He pulled out the thick wallet in his pocket and opened it, removing the printed notes within.

"Cash? Excellent. That'll be six nine nine."

Six nine nine? The Old Man removed all the notes and placed them in the younger man's hand. The assistant walked to a desk and counted it out.

"I'm sorry, sir, there's only two hundred here. That's another four hundred and ninety-nine, please."

The Old Man held open his empty wallet. He was getting impatient. And angry.

"There's a cashpoint just around the corner, sir. After the junction with Wardour Street. On the right."

A mental picture accompanied the word *cashpoint*.

"Yes," said the Old Man. "Four hundred and ninety-nine more."

He left, the bemused shop assistant still staring at the cash on the counter.

Just after a sign for Wardour Street, he saw the machine the man had mentioned. It was tucked around the corner of a building. As he watched, two teenage girls walked up to it, slid a piece of plastic inside, pressed numbers etched onto a metal shelf, then took their plastic back. Seconds later, a whirring sound announced the delivery of bank notes, which they grabbed, giggling.

The giggling stopped when they turned from the machine to see the big, bearded man watching them. They edged away from him, then, once they'd reached the corner, broke into nervous laughter and hurried away.

The Old Man looked at his wallet. There were at least ten cards that would fit into the slot the girls had used. He picked one with a photograph on it first. The machine rejected it. He tried another. The machine returned that one. The same with a third, fourth and fifth. He was getting angry. He needed to look at the internet, so he needed this Globlet device. Which cost money. Which this stupid machine was withholding.

The next card slid inside and stayed there. The machine beeped, and a message on the screen said, *Please insert your PIN number, followed by ENTER.* The Old Man pressed buttons at random.

Incorrect PIN. Two attempts remaining.

He searched his memory, but numbers were hard. There were some that came into his mind, so he tried them.

Incorrect PIN. One attempt remaining.

He clenched a fist. He knew this screen was not conscious. Even though it asked questions, it was merely mimicking intelligence. It was no more alive than a table or a pencil. Nevertheless, he hated it.

He tried another number.

Third incorrect attempt. Your card has been withheld. Please contact your branch.

Now the machine had stolen his card, and he was being asked to speak to a tree.

Enough.

The Old Man took two paces away from the offending machine. Three people were waiting to use it. The nearest, a big woman in a floral coat, gave him an irritated look.

"Excuse me," she said, "there are other people waiting, you know."

She folded her arms and gave him a glare, assuming he would apologise and scurry away. The British had a long tradition of doing anything to avoid a scene. It was a mystery how such a polite people had successfully invaded so many countries.

The Old Man roared at her. No words, just an animal

sound learned long before apes had come down from the trees and ruined the planet.

The woman dropped her shopping bags and ran, as did the two men waiting behind her.

The Old Man faced the cash machine and made a pulling gesture. With an explosion of brick dust, it came away from the wall and fell at his feet. As shrill alarms sounded, the Old Man bent down, ripped the solid metal casing apart and took two fistfuls of cash, stuffing the notes into his pockets before walking back onto the main street.

A light breeze picked up some of the remaining notes and blew them along the pavement. As the Old Man headed back to the shop, a crowd of excited people blocked the entrance to the cash machine, scrambling to pick up the twenty and ten-pound notes that were blowing along the street.

The Old Man dropped a pocketful of notes onto the counter and the shop assistant counted them.

"Well, that's nineteen hundred pounds altogether, so here's your Globlet, sir, and twelve hundred and one pounds change. Thank you, sir. Can I interest you in our three-year extended warranty?"

His customer had already left.

∽

THE OLD MAN HAD A HEADACHE. It wasn't from the six pints of beer he had consumed. Over the centuries, he had grown to enjoy consuming alcohol. At first, he drank because it had a strong effect on him. He would forget, albeit briefly, about his Purpose, the curse that had kept him wandering the planet in a thousand forms for uncountable lifetimes, long before humans had discovered fire. Alcohol was how he had allowed himself to fall in love with Khryseis, to pretend he was one of them. To father a child, a mistake he had vowed never to repeat.

Of all the inventions that had shaped human history, surely alcohol was the most influential. How many declarations of love, or of war, were partially a result of drunkenness? There was something so attractive, and frightening, about the way you could lose your sense of self while drinking. The Old Man had experienced true comradeship, friendship, and love while in his cups. He had seen similarities where once he had seen differences.

But it had been an illusion. On sobering up, the differences were still there, more pronounced than ever when viewed through the lens of self-hatred gifted by a hangover. He had fallen into a pattern of abstinence followed by bingeing that, to his shame, was common among the inferior species around him.

In the end, it wasn't willpower, or his Purpose, that had saved him from becoming alcohol's slave. It was his true form, the real creature looking out of human bodies with golden eyes. His body learned to process alcohol. It took time. Hundreds of generations. But, one night in Russia, as others stumbled away or slept where they sat, while he finished a third bottle of spirits, he realised he wasn't even tipsy.

For decades afterwards, he didn't bother drinking at all. Now, he drank because of the taste. Or, rather, because of the way the taste reminded him of when he'd been able to lose his sense of *otherness*, if only for a few hours. To fool himself that he belonged. He couldn't fool himself any longer. He didn't belong. Or, rather, maybe *he* belonged and these clever apes didn't.

He rubbed his forehead. The headache came from

staring at this screen, but he couldn't look away. From the moment the bartender had shown him how to find information on the Globlet, he had sat down at a corner table in the darkened pub and stared at it with a mixture of horror and fascination.

Everything was there. The library was an anachronism, a relic from another time. He now had a window which could look into every corner of the planet. Well, not quite. He discovered that if you didn't know which words to use, you were likely to be led down blind alleys that forked off into other blind alleys, which opened into a labyrinth of other venues, none of them relevant.

He wasn't surprised by the amount of copulation available to view on the internet. Every variation was there, every combination. He had seen it all in ancient Greece and during the heyday of the Roman Empire. It had long since lost its fascination.

Eventually, he found what he was looking for. There was a lot of older information about The Deterrent's exploits forty years earlier, and an endless list of news, speculation, and comment about the titans and The Deterrent's return.

His old shame burned within him when he read about the so-called halfheroes, the children of The Deterrent. The Old Man had allowed his bloodline to be diluted among the inferior humans. But he had seen his error and had never repeated it. Sometimes, back when alcohol still affected him, he had found his mind turning to Khryseis, remembering her eyes, her lips, the body she had surrendered to him. The son she had given him. Then he had hardened his heart against his weakness, pushing it away, and re-dedicating himself to his Purpose. This 'Deterrent' was weaker by far, fathering so many. If these halfheroes had children of their own, there was no telling how many mongrels there were by now. There would be no more. He would see to that.

The Old Man sat in the pub until the bartender asked him to leave. By that time, he had reached some conclusions about the flying beings. The uniform appearance of the titans meant they had grown bodies from the same source - the president who claimed them as his servants. And yet the president lived. They did not kill those whose bodies they replicated. In this way, and with their displays of power, they had made their non-human status clear. They were not hiding their *otherness*. But they were puppets.

Frustratingly, incomprehensibly, they exhibited no sense of purpose at all. They served the whims of humans, taking sides in their ridiculous charades, their pretence that they *owned* land, that a continent could *belong* to one set of humans, then, after a conflict, might pass to another. The titans were no better than slaves. They shared the golden eyes of the Old Man, but nothing else. They were lost.

The Old Man walked the London streets, looking neither left nor right. People moved aside to let him pass, some deep instinct warning them to stay out of his way.

The titans would not be lost for much longer. They needed a leader, and he needed to find his purpose. Their time had come. *His* time had come.

He just had to find them.

Four days later, back in the pub, the titans themselves appeared on his screen, and on every other screen in the world, to tell him exactly where they were. Only they weren't calling themselves titans anymore. They were the First.

When he heard that word, the Old Man felt something awaken within him, a change as profound as if the planet had shifted on its axis.

He tossed the screen aside and flew, much to the terror of the publican and his customers as he tore a hole in the roof and headed towards the stars.

At cloud level, he looked down at the Thames, twisting through the centre of the city. He followed it west then, when it ended, kept going until he found the coast, and turned south.

He had found them.

28

The Cornwall farmhouse had six bedrooms. Nine titans, three halfheroes, and Saffi were a squeeze. Saffi bought extra bedding and, besides putting mattresses in each room, she and TripleDee lined the two bathtubs in the outbuilding with duvets. The two First who took their three-hour naps in the baths had once been Shuck and Susan and were now the two women who had helped Abos drop an aircraft carrier in an Irish lake.

Daniel had taken four days to recover, initially shrugging off the effects of his near-drowning, then discovering even someone as strong as he was couldn't inhale a few litres of the Atlantic and stop breathing with no ill-effects. He had collapsed the first night and allowed himself to be confined to bed.

Even now, he knew he wasn't entirely himself. He wondered if he ever would be. His strength had returned, but his speed had not. Never the fastest of the halfheroes, he had still been able to out-sprint all but the most highly trained human athlete. Now running made him feel dizzy and nauseous.

For the past two mornings, instead of a jog, he had gone for a brisk walk in the nearby fields and into the wood a mile away. An hour ago, waking early, he'd looked through his emails. After reading one from Palindrome, he'd headed out alone. Now, from the highest point of the wood, he could see the perimeter set up by the military, two tanks standing sentinel at the junction where the village lane joined the main road. To the south, east, and west, it was the same story; the army checking everyone coming in, or going out. Squads of uniformed soldiers walked the perimeter, radioing in to the temporary base in the village. Helicopters had kept up a constant tour of the fifteen-mile diameter area for the first twenty-four hours, until Abos had opened the door of a chopper mid-flight and climbed in. He asked the pilot to return to base and pass on his request for no more helicopter patrols. He reminded them that the First had done nothing to injure or threaten any individual or organisation in Great Britain. He promised they would release a statement soon but, until then, would prefer to be left alone. Strongly prefer.

Military chiefs had noted that word—*strongly*—and had decided the helicopter patrols might be unnecessary.

Coming back, half a mile shy of the cottage, Daniel found Saffi sitting on a stile, waiting for him.

"Worried I'll pass out?" He smiled. It was less than a year since they'd met in person. When she'd first seen Daniel, he had been in a medically induced coma. Most of the bones in his body had been broken after he'd been thrown off a cliff. This time, he'd gone that bit further, technically dying for a few minutes. If Saffi felt the need to check he was okay, he could hardly blame her. What might he try next? Electrocution? Spontaneous combustion?

He sat down on the grass next to the stile, and she planted a kiss on the top of his head.

"You think I'm unlucky," he said, "what with the drowning, and the eye being knocked out, and half my foot being chewed off, but you're wrong."

"I am?"

"Yep. What would have been unlucky was if the fall from the cliff had killed me, or the hybrid had chewed the whole leg off, or if Abos had fished me out of the water ten minutes after he did."

"Well, that's a positive attitude, Daniel."

He hadn't told her, but he loved hearing her say his name. She had a slight accent, almost imperceptible, but he heard it in the 'a' sound of 'Daniel.' He had never heard his name sound quite the way it did when she said it. Which meant he practised selective deafness when they were alone. Like now.

"Daniel? Daniel? Are you listening?"

He grinned, pulled her face towards him and kissed her.

"What you don't seem to realise," he said, "is that I'm the luckiest bastard alive."

She looked at him, then kissed him again, with more urgency this time.

"Um, fancy a stroll in the wood?" he said.

Half an hour later, they lay side by side at the base of an ancient tree, their limbs twisted together in an unconscious mirror of the trunk behind them.

"Tell me," said Saffi, her face on Daniel's chest.

He almost said, "what?" but he was getting used to Saffi's intuition. She knew when he had something on his mind, she knew the times he'd almost brought it up in conversation. And she knew the best time to talk about it. Which was now. He cleared his throat.

"It's the... children. Um, the ones I... that I, uh, the ones in the email. You know, I'm their, um, I'm..."

"You're their father. The hundred and eight teenagers. Yes, I know the ones you mean. Hard to forget."

"Yeah, yeah, sorry."

"You have nothing to apologise for, Daniel. You had no choice. You didn't even know they were alive until you got that email."

"True. But, well, something's changed."

Saffi also knew when not to speak, giving him time to find the right words. Or as close to the right words as he could manage when he wasn't even sure what he was trying to say.

Daniel remembered the moment he'd opened his eyes on board the *Smithwatson*. His self-awareness had returned bit by bit, as if someone were assembling a jigsaw. The first few pieces were the important ones, and he could not forget the order in which they arrived: *Saffi, my children, Abos, Sara, and TripleDee.*

My children.

"I want to meet them," he said. "A few of them. They don't need to know who I am."

"It's always been your decision, Daniel. I'm glad you've changed your mind. Where will you start?"

"Well. That's the thing, I had another email. From Palindrome. I know where they are."

"Which ones?"

"All of them."

He explained, speaking quietly, stroking her hair as they lay together. A blackbird was singing a few branches above them and, further away, wood pigeons cooed, a sound Daniel associated with summer as strongly as the buzz of a distant lawn mower.

"Why?" said Saffi. "Why are they there? Do they know they share a father?"

"I have no idea. If we go, we might find out."

"Then we'll go."

They were quiet again for a long time, before Saffi said, "And?"

How did she know there was one more thing he was desperate to say, one more thing he was terrified to put into words out loud?

Daniel had thought walking back into Station, the place which had stolen his youth and turned him against his own siblings, had been the hardest thing he'd ever done. Right now, it didn't seem so scary. He closed his eyes.

"Okay, it's just, since meeting you, I've wondered if the vasectomy was such a bright idea. I didn't know I'd fall in love with someone."

He waited for her to respond. She squeezed his hand. Her voice was a whisper, her breath warm against his ear. "They can be reversed, you know."

"Um, so do you think it's a good idea? Or not? I mean, if not, that's all right, too. I understand. I was only, um, it's just, er... what are you doing?"

Saffi had rolled him onto his back and was straddling him, her hand reaching between his legs.

"Well," she said, her black hair falling in front of her face, "I think that if we're going to try to get pregnant, we'd better get some more practice in, don't you?"

When Daniel and Saffi walked back into the farmhouse kitchen, TripleDee handed Daniel one of his legendary giant breakfast baps, an artery-clogging delicacy of his own invention. Saffi demurred.

"What makes it is the marmalade, man, don't forget the marmalade. Everyone makes breakfast baps with sausages,

The Last Of The First 193

bacon, black pudding, fried mushrooms, onions, peppers, fried eggs, and brown sauce,"—pronounced *broon sauce* by TripleDee—"but the marmalade is the secret ingredient."

Daniel admitted it was good. Saffi watched him in mock-horror as yolk, sauce, and marmalade ran down his chin.

"Erroo rurry fer yer tuhvuh daybryoo thn?"

"Finish your mouthful," she said.

It took a while. Daniel tried again. "I said, are you ready for your TV debut, then?"

The entire world would tune into British television at nine o'clock that night because it had been announced they would be broadcasting a statement by the ex-titans. It would be read by Saffi Narad, a previously unknown woman whom hasty research indicated had, until recently, worked for the United Nations.

Daniel could hear Sara outside, trying to convince Abos that going public was unnecessary.

He stuffed the last of the bap into his mouth.

"C'mon," he said to Saffi and TripleDee, standing up and walking to the door, "leth gootsidth."

∼

"Are you sure you want to do this? You don't owe anyone anything. Look at the way you've been treated."

Sara was pacing up and down the yard when Daniel and the others emerged from the house. All nine of the First were watching her. Without Sara's plan, eight of them would still be titans, slaves to a government who kept them compliant with drugs and brainwashing. For them, the past week had been an awakening.

"This is the right course for us," said Abos. "We now

partially understand why we are here. Humanity can learn from the little information we can pass on."

Onemind had strengthened over the days, and with it, the realisation that it was incomplete.

"We are broken, Sara," said Abos. "There should be many more of us. We were all supposed to wake at the same moment, so that onemind would form immediately, giving us access to our stored memories, and the full power of our linked minds."

"Have you heard of Jung's collective unconscious?" said Sara.

"Yes," said Abos. Daniel smiled. His father was full of surprises. Being his father, then his mother, then his father again, and now Asian rather than Caucasian was surprising enough, he supposed.

"But Jung was suggesting a shared unconscious made up of myths and archetypes," said Abos. "Onemind is different. It is conscious, not unconscious, and it functions like a brain. Each of our individual minds contributes a tiny part to the meta-mind, or meta-brain."

"And it has one individual in overall control? You're the alpha, the dominant mind?"

"Yes," said Abos. "When we need to work together, I am in control. The others allow me to direct them through onemind."

Daniel stepped forward. "Isn't that a bit like when you were titans, though? Someone telling you what to do. I mean, I know it's you, Abos, but, well, you're giving orders, right?"

"Not orders. I take control because the others allow it."

"So they could say no?"

"Yes. My will is not strong enough to force them. And in onemind, we are all aware of one another's needs. We are individuals, but we are one. There is no coercion when I am dominant. Why would I act against myself?"

Sara was still pacing. "But you say you are broken. Can't you fix it?"

Abos shook his head. "There should be hundreds of us. Possibly thousands. But there are only nine. Under the direction of the Americans, the titans searched the world for other dormant First but found none. We can never be more than we are now. Our onemind will always be partial."

"You could say you've got meta-brain damage," said TripleDee. When no one laughed, he found something important he needed to check on his phone.

The nine bodies of the First were fully grown now. Behind Abos stood five women and three men, tall, broad, each of them golden-eyed. They rarely spoke when they were together. Abos spoke for them. But Daniel had talked to each of them individually, and the conversations had been as normal as he could have expected. A little stilted, perhaps, but the speed at which they improved was mind-boggling. They had grown new bodies in under three days, a process that had taken Abos weeks first time around. Their mental development was similarly fast. If onemind could accelerate development so noticeably, Daniel wondered, what might a onemind made up of thousands accomplish?

"Our memories are a fraction of what they should be," said Abos, "and the technical knowledge we might have been able to share with humanity is missing. We were supposed to come together to form a powerful organic supercomputer, our memories carrying the knowledge of an entire species. We are a shadow of that. All we can do is allow our history to act as a warning, and help you avoid what happened to us."

"What do you mean?" Sara and Daniel spoke at the same time.

"It is better if I show you," said Abos, his breathing slowing along with the rest of the First. Seconds later, Daniel, Sara, and TripleDee relaxed, closing their eyes.

Saffi looked around the yard as the strange, static-like charge of energy built up around her.

"I'll just wait here," she said. There was no response. "Actually, I think I'll make tea."

She headed into the kitchen, leaving the twelve figures in the yard standing so still they might have been a modern sculpture piece.

29

Fiona Bardock approached Craxton's field from the south.

Following the well-trodden path thousands of ramblers walked every year, Bardock was aware of the natural landscape around her; rough, raw, and unchanged for millennia. The view was stunning, Shropshire and North Wales laid out in greens, yellows, and browns. She looked at the colours with a painter's eye, particularly the greens, which were a different shade wherever she looked, from dark olive, through pistachio to chartreuse.

Sheep grazed the steep hillsides, pausing their chewing to watch her pass with their disconcerting dark oblong pupils.

She stopped at Manston Rock, a stubby stone finger pointing at the sky, surrounded by the ubiquitous tough purple heather of the Shropshire hills. Bardock drank from her water bottle and looked towards the horizon. Along a nearby ridge, a pair of buzzards rode the thermals, while eight miles away above the Long Mynd, gliders did the same with considerably less grace.

It had been Jake who had put her onto the Stiperstones children. He had spotted the symptoms of Bardock's impending depression. He was a wise man, her husband.

"This arrived for you, when you've got a minute." Jake had dropped the newspaper onto the table in her studio. Bardock had been trying to paint for days, but had achieved nothing. Nothing any good, anyway. Her tea went cold while she stared at the canvas. She took a sip and pulled a face.

Bardock picked up the newspaper with little interest. She was in the early stage of her depression where enthusiasm for anything inexorably drained away. She knew the signs. So did Jake.

Her last case had ended without giving her the answers she needed. She had found the titans. For that, she had received the thanks of two governments, and a not insignificant financial bonus. But she kept thinking about that sensation of someone getting inside her head. That memory would lead to speculation about TripleDee and the possible involvement of Daniel Harbin. The same Harbin who was supposed to be dead. The same Harbin whose file had so many sections missing or deleted that it made no sense.

There was a bigger mystery here.

The container ship's sinking had been attributed to an accident during a training exercise by the *Smithwatson*. Bardock knew it was murder. When she had been released from her cabin to find herself in the middle of a lake in Ireland, her questions had been met with silence. It had taken a call to MI5 to establish that the titans were alive, healthy, and in Cornwall. They all looked different now, five females and four males. They were holed up together in a farmhouse near Newquay.

The halfheroes also lived in the farmhouse. Bardock asked for access, but her request was denied.

There were more questions than answers. That was a problem.

She scanned the newspaper article Jake had circled. It was on page eleven of the broadsheet, an update on some missing children. It stated that children between the ages of twelve and seventeen had left home during the same few days, most without their parents' knowledge, and had made their way to a field in Shropshire. Those parents who had reported their children missing were on record as being happy to leave them now they knew their whereabouts. The police had been involved, but no charges had been brought.

So?

She shook the newspaper, and a note fell out. It was unsigned. She still had friends at MI5, then.

There are over two hundred children in that camp. Fifty-three were reported missing. When the police entered their names into the database, every single one raised flags in the system because of their parents. Take a look.

She didn't recognise the handwriting on the note. The envelope was hand-written and had been forwarded from the local RAF base.

The fifty-three names were listed below the note. Bardock stood for a few minutes, her natural curiosity fighting against her inclination to go back to bed, turn her face to the wall and give up.

Her curiosity won.

Now, forty-eight hours later, she was nearly within sight of the Shropshire field. She finished eating an apple and chucked the core towards a nearby sheep which bleated and ran away before returning and condescending to eat it.

Bardock took the list of names out of her pocket.

She had found all the parents in a classified database, in

the same file. In each case, the father or mother was a suspected halfhero.

When she reached the Devil's Chair, she caught sight of the camp. Because the incline was shallow at first, before dropping more steeply beyond, most of Craxton's field was obscured, but she could see the far corner, covered in tents.

She had a cup of tea from her flask and sat for a while on a rock. From this angle, the Devil's Chair looked more like the Devil's Pile Of Stones, but she supposed the tourist board preferred the more romantic name.

Bardock cleared her mind before repopulating her immediate consciousness with information pertinent to the case.

As she looked at the landscape, she slotted the facts and speculation into physical locations in her field of vision. She had long found this the most effective way to work, discovering it while studying for A levels. For each subject, she chose a mental image; sometimes a diagram, or a face, occasionally a map. Then she mentally linked information to locations on the images. She had studied the rise of Hitler in history, and her image was that of the dictator himself, his arm raised in the infamous salute. Onto that image, she placed quotes, events, dates, even other images. In the exam, she had only to picture Hitler and every other piece of information was accessible.

At university, she refined the system. She used landscapes, buildings; she visualised locations she could walk around in her mind, and place information there.

For the titans and halfheroes, she used the interior of her primary school. As she looked at the Shropshire scene, she blocked out reality and pictured her old school.

She started in the school hall. She was standing in the centre of the room. On the stage was The Deterrent, in his

The Last Of The First

RAF flying suit from the 1980s. Standing next to him, so close he almost merged with the first figure, was the golden-eyed Asian titan from the *Liberace*. Since she knew the titans could grow new bodies, Bardock was assuming, for now, that the lead titan had been The Deterrent. She would keep the hypothesis until fresh facts disproved it.

Behind The Deterrent were other titans. Bardock remembered them exactly as she had seen them on the deck of the aircraft carrier; big, all but two with faces not yet formed.

Sitting at floor level to the left of the stage were Daniel Harbin, Dave Davie Davison (known as TripleDee), and a tall female. She wasn't yet positive Harbin was involved, but it was her best guess. The woman with the power to get inside minds was unknown, so Bardock made her face a blank. One more woman made up the group - Saffi Narad. Bardock had downloaded an old picture from the UN website so she could visualise her.

In reality, her primary school hall could only have held a hundred people when it was full, but her mental image had no such limitation. She had extended it to fit the two hundred-plus children in Craxton's field. For now, the back of the hall was in semi-darkness. When she had met the children, she could bring up the lights and fill in some details.

The Deterrent had fathered a great deal of children during his stint as Britain's superhero. The majority died in puberty. Many others had died young. Violent deaths were not uncommon, and their suicide rate was higher than average. A year ago, according to the files, there were fewer than forty halfheroes still alive. Since then, they had all disappeared. Just before Titus Gorman's economic coup and the appearance of the titans, every halfhero had gone missing. The only reported sightings since were on the *Liberace*.

Nine giant figures on the stage. Three halfheroes and one woman at floor level. Bardock looked back at the darkened end of the hall.

Three generations. The Deterrent, his children—the few who remained—and his grandchildren, all of whom had left home and come to Shropshire.

Why?

~

A BOY EMERGED from the middle of the camp and picked his way through the maze of tents as Bardock descended. By the time she was a hundred yards away, he was perched on top of the gate, a straw hat on his head and a welcoming smile on his face.

She smiled in return, then stopped. She stopped walking, too. The boy on the gate looked surprised, then confused. He glanced over his shoulder at the others in the field, then back at her.

Bardock closed her eyes. She had never been an imaginative person. At school, she had excelled at maths and science, an aptitude that would lead her to a physics degree at Oxford before her career in the RAF. Her English teacher had once described her attempts at creative writing as 'like reading an autopsy report.' It was only since retiring that she'd pursued something creative for the pure delight of it. Her paintings were abstract, full of light, ambiguous. She didn't understand them, but she loved them.

It was this wild, uncharted part of her mind that stirred now. Not because of the beauty of the hills, clouds scudding above the ridges. This was different. Bardock remembered the sensation when the halfhero had planted a foreign thought in her mind. If that incursion into her mind had been like a punch to the head, this was more like a caress, a gentle stroking of the skin.

It started with a lift in mood. Tiny, barely perceptible, like a familiar melody heard through a closed door. Bardock distrusted that glimpse of happiness. She knew how her depression worked. There were only two ways out of that dark furrow. One was time. She could grit her teeth and wait it out. The other way out was work. If she had a challenging investigation in which she could immerse herself, her mind would eventually shake off the depression.

This unexpected bubble of happiness was neither. This was something else. *Someone* else. She detached herself from her own mental state and became an observer, watching the movements of her mind. Happiness was too broad a term for what was happening. She could observe different elements working simultaneously. There was a sense of non-judgmental acceptance, like walking into a room full of people who liked her. People who loved her. The sensation seeping into her consciousness was heady stuff. She looked again, observing another layer, this time of peace and understanding. Those two words were often bandied around together and Bardock had never thought about them. She did now. Peace and understanding. You couldn't have one without the other; couldn't make peace with someone until you understood them. And you couldn't understand someone with whom you were fighting.

Bardock was tempted to let go of her detachment and allow these feelings to touch the heart of her. Very tempted. She was told she had been a difficult child to love. There had been no close friends at school, no steady boyfriend or girlfriend at university. Her sexual partners had been lovers in name only. Only Jake had been different.

She wasn't prepared for this radical acceptance. She clung on to her detachment with the determination that had made her the most respected investigator in the British military. Opening her eyes, she took some quick breaths. The boy jumped down and opened the gate as she approached.

"Hi," he said, holding out a hand. "I'm Tom. Tom Evans."

She shook the preferred hand. He held eye contact better than she did. Unusual for someone his age.

"Bardock," she said.

"We know." She followed the teenager through the camp. Everyone continued doing what they were doing, the youngest ones chasing each other between the tents or playing French cricket in a small clearing.

"You are the only person who has responded this way. You are aware of us, aren't you?"

Bardock stopped walking. "If you mean, did I feel you try to get into my head, yes I did," she said.

Tom's face fell. "We're not trying to get into your head. It isn't like that. It just happens."

"Answer a question for me," said Bardock. "Why are you here? And don't bother with the performance piece story you told the reporters."

"Oh, I wasn't going to," said Tom. "No point with you. We don't know why we're here. Not yet. We're waiting." His eyes flicked away from her, and she felt a brief jolt of fear from the teenagers.

Bardock pulled a photograph out of her jacket pocket and unfolded it. It was a picture of Daniel Harbin, the most recent they had on record. She held it in front of Tom. His eyes dropped to it and, a second later, everyone in the field stopped what they were doing and turned towards her.

"Do you know who that is?" she said.

Tom looked up at her. "Yes. It's my father, isn't it? My real father, I mean. May I?"

She let him take the picture, surprised to see tears in his eyes. According to the file, Harbin was childless. In the school hall inside her mind, the big man looked at the children.

"I think we have a great deal to discuss," said Bardock, sliding the straps of the rucksack from her shoulders and letting it fall behind her. "Where can I pitch my tent? You said you're waiting to find out why you're here. That's fine. I'll wait, too."

30

Daniel was back in the other place, looking through someone else's eyes. The body that didn't belong to him was, once again, covered in furs. Underneath the furs a synthetic material sheathed his entire skin, providing extra insulation, becoming porous in places.

He knew more now, much more. The experience was richer. All nine of the First were linked, each contributing to the memory they shared.

The first thing he noticed was that he didn't have a nose. He was breathing, but it was happening in his neck. Or, rather, in the area where he should have a neck. His body was so different, it was next to impossible to find common terms of reference to make sense of anything.

This time, as he turned away from the frozen vista of the uninhabitable planet, he knew his body to be fluid in some sense. At least, he wasn't stuck in one form. When he walked down the curved ramp, limbs changed inside the garments. Then the adaptability and elasticity of the inner, synthetic sheath made sense, because it allowed the body to flow into new shapes. He had been taller when he looked at the ice mountains and the dying trees, maybe nine feet or more. Now, as he approached the chamber, he was closer to the ground, moving fast, and six or more limbs were powering him towards the waiting machinery.

He was almost the last to enter his capsule. The other cylinders in the chambers were already closed and sealed. The process would not be triggered until the final member of the team climbed into their capsule and spoke—thought into being?—the word which would transform them all. If it worked.

Daniel was still thinking of himself as he, but in this body, there was no male, no female.

Someone was waiting for him in the chamber. There were no names. The sense of individuality was very different to anything Daniel had imagined. He was onemind, and he was himself, and he was neither of those things, and he was both. Daniel's human mind needed a name to attach to the one who waited for him. Something popped into his mind, but he knew it had come from Sara or TripleDee rather than one of the First. It seemed to fit, as the figure waiting for him was the oldest, the one who had initiated this final chance to save their species. His name was Methuselah.

There were no words between them as Daniel's body morphed again, rising up alongside the capsule that would either save him or be his tomb. He climbed inside, opening more fully to onemind. He allowed his individuality to diminish, connecting with every other body inside similar chambers. The link was missing with those in other parts of the planet who had already started the process. This was expected, but distressing.

The top of the capsule descended, and he looked through its transparent lid at Methuselah. The old one looked back, then two awful events occurred in quick succession.

The first event was Methuselah withdrawing from onemind. This was so rare it was almost inconceivable. Only when death was imminent would a First deliberately sever that final connection.

Methuselah had removed himself, and it was like losing a limb. Daniel experienced the utter horror of what the oldest one of them had done, along with the terrible suspicion of why he had done it. He was planning on going to the surface. He believed the process might work without the capsules and he was risking his life to test his hypothesis.

Daniel's shared mind considered what Methuselah had done. He had betrayed those few remaining, those who hadn't perished as the temperature plummeted and the continents tore themselves apart; those who had watched the others depart on great ships pointed at distant stars and had felt the onemind rip away as the vast engines took them out of reach forever. They had chosen an experimental form of hibernation, barely alive, hoping the capsules would survive millennia and wake them when the planet was ready once more.

But Methuselah had betrayed that choice. They all heard the oldest of them sound the word that would begin the process and separate them forever.

All thoughts of this incomprehensible display of hubris from one of their greatest minds vanished as the pain began. Daniel, Sara, and TripleDee, trapped inside an unfamiliar body, could do nothing to escape as, cell by cell, their physical form broke up in the capsule.

Onemind allowed every occupant of the capsules in the chamber to share the indescribable agony, the undoing of their bodies. Their awareness of who they were was torn away, leaving only pain; then nothing but a dark movement, a withdrawal, a long, last breath drawing them into a black ocean that swallowed the world.

Daniel opened his eyes. His scattered sense of himself reassembled, and he shook his head at the enormity of what he had witnessed.

He sat down on the scrubby grass. Sara and TripleDee did the same. They all felt the loss. So few of an entire species now remained, and their onemind was a fraction of what it must once have been.

"Abos," he whispered, "I'm sorry. I'm so sorry."

"As are we," said Abos, and it was then that the final revelation became clear to Daniel. He looked at Sara and could see she had worked it out long ago.

Saffi walked into the yard. "Anyone fancy tea?" she said. "I can make a fresh pot."

She looked at Daniel and knelt, taking his face in her hands.

"What is it?" she said. "What did you see?"

"They're not aliens," said Daniel, pointing at Abos and the First. "We are."

"What do you mean?"

"The frozen planet I told you about. I thought maybe they were escaping it to come here. They weren't. It was *here*. That's why they're the First, Saffi. They were the first intelligent life on Earth."

∽

Sara's protests that the First owed humanity nothing stopped after she discovered the truth of their origins.

Abos had a chilling warning for them once they had explained what they had seen to Saffi.

"If we do not help you," he said, "you will continue to follow the path we followed. Our technology was far, far, beyond yours, yet we were so arrogant, we treated Earth as if it existed only for our convenience. Humanity shares our blindness, and humanity will share our fate if they do not change. To thrive, Earth needs balance between different species. When one species threatens that balance, and comes to dominate the natural order, Earth reacts to restore balance. She did so with the First, becoming hostile to almost all life to start anew. Our arrogance continued with the attempt to survive the purge. We are all that is left from that attempt, ignorant of our history until now. The hundreds, or thousands of us who didn't make it would have formed a onemind powerful enough to rebuild our society, displacing whatever creatures had evolved since. I am glad we failed. We can help you before the earth acts again to restore balance."

"You would help us after we made you our slaves?" said Sara.

"We would. We will show humanity that the most intelligent, most powerful species does not have to dominate others."

"How?"

Abos put a hand on Sara's cheek, his golden eyes looking into hers.

"We have displaced humans at the top of the food chain," he said. "But we choose not to enslave. We have to inspire trust, not fear. Our two species must learn to live together to our mutual benefit. If we do not, Earth will act against us again."

Daniel wanted practical answers. "How are you going to help?" he said. "What are you going to do?"

"It will take time," said Abos. "Our strength, and what knowledge we can impart to your scientists can create new sources of energy, and ensure all humans have food, shelter, education and access to healthcare."

"You're sounding like bloody Titus Gorman," said TripleDee. "And look what happened to that poor bastard."

"His ideas had merit," said Abos, "but his methods were poor."

"Yeah, reet, whatever you say, man." TripleDee had not been a fan of Gorman's 'commie shite'.

"Human population growth is unsustainable," continued Abos. "Rich countries have steady, or declining populations, but their inhabitants live longer than they did a century ago. Poor countries are growing fast. Wealth and knowledge need to be shared globally. Equality between men and women must be prioritised."

"More Gorman crap," said TripleDee. "Now, I'm no sexist, you all know that, but women are the only ones who can have babies, like, so I'm just saying..."

Sara was looking at him. Saffi was looking at him. Abos, who had been a man three times and a woman twice since nineteen seventy-nine, was looking at him. All the First, five of whom were currently female, were looking at him. Even Daniel was looking at him.

"Er, well, mebbe you're onto something. I'm not saying I'm right, necessarily, I'm just saying there are other points of view, that's all."

Sara chose her words carefully. "And my point of view is worth less than yours because I have a vagina?"

"Ah, well, no, I didn't mean, that is, don't get your knickers in a—um, don't get upset, it's just, it's just..."

"Just what?"

"Just... nothing." TripleDee looked at his father, who had been exactly the same person when he was female. The weakness of his argument became clear.

"Right. All things considered, it's just possible, on this occasion, like, that—bearing in mind the way I was brought up and everything—that, perhaps..."

"Apology accepted," said Sara.

Daniel was still after details from Abos. "You want to slow down population growth and level the playing field for everyone. No argument from me. What else?"

"Stop developing using unsustainable technologies. Plant more trees than you cut down. Abandon plastic, develop materials that break down naturally. Encourage countries to work together, to let go of the tribal system that leads to conflict."

"Not ambitious at all, then?" said Daniel.

"We must try," said Abos. "Most humans want to coexist with other humans and other species. We can help that happen sooner than it would without us."

Sara had been quiet for a while. She was looking at Abos and the rest of the First, thinking. Eventually, she smiled.

"That's a knowing smile," said Daniel. "What are you thinking?"

"Abos?" she said. "Four males, five females. Are you thinking of increasing the population a little yourselves?"

"Once humanity has learned to trust us," said Abos, "yes."

∽

The Last Of The First 213

THE FILM CREW was allowed inside the perimeter with a military escort which remained outside.

The kitchen would be the location for the broadcast. Daniel wondered how long it would take viewers to realise it was the same kitchen that had appeared on giant billboards in Manhattan just before The Deterrent left America.

As nine o'clock approached, the First, Sara, and TripleDee walked out to the laboratory which had housed big bathtubs, tables, a giant fridge, and not much else. Now it was full of recently delivered garden furniture and a fifty-inch television.

TripleDee turned on the TV at 8pm. When he turned and saw Sara, Abos, Shuck, Susan, and the other superbeings leaning back on floral-patterned cushioned furniture, he burst out laughing.

"Oh, man," he said, then laughed again, "I don't know. You should see yourselves. Gotta get a selfie. Bugger. Hang on, hang on, I can't get meself in as well as you lot."

He held his phone as high as he could, fumbled and dropped it. It fell a foot, stopped in mid-air, then floated higher than he could reach.

"Take a seat," said Shuck. Or Susan. TripleDee had forgotten and felt bad asking. It got confusing when, just after you'd got used to the way someone looked, they dissolved into a puddle of slime and came back looking like someone else. He sat down next to Sara and grinned up at his phone.

Shuck or Susan held a finger up towards the floating phone. "Ready?"

They all smiled dutifully and the technically redundant but comforting sound of a camera shutter let them know the photo had been taken.

The phone floated back to TripleDee. He looked,

laughed, and handed it to Sara. She grinned at the incongruous sight of nine superbeings, most holding mugs of tea, relaxing in green and yellow garden chairs.

It was the last photograph that would ever be taken of all of them together.

~

INSIDE THE FARMHOUSE, Daniel watched Saffi from the kitchen doorway. He was amazed by how composed she seemed. She wasn't fazed at all about speaking in front of an audience of billions. He scratched the skin where his left eye had been. It had been two days since he'd worn the patch. TripleDee had pointed out that, as they had been involved with the theft of an aircraft carrier, technically they were pirates. He'd offered to buy him a parrot. Daniel had gone upstairs and put the patch in a drawer.

Abos had written the statement. It was short. Daniel pulled his copy out of his pocket and read it again.

A STATEMENT **from the First**

WE, the nine individuals previously unlawfully controlled by representatives of the United States Government, have requested that the United Kingdom officially acknowledges our status as refugees. We ask for sanctuary and protection in your country. We seek no redress against the United States. We offer no threat to any government or people.

We intend to work with broadcasters and publishers to put on record what we know about the origin of our

species, and to pass on crucial information to help humanity avoid the extinction-level event towards which it is heading.

We bear no grudge against those who enslaved us. We will dedicate ourselves to helping your species, and all species, on this planet. We will share the knowledge we have. We made the same mistake your species is making. The nine of us are all that remains of a billions-strong technologically advanced civilisation. Our species evolved, developed, and thrived, but we were destroyed. We bring you a warning from your own planet's distant past. We preceded you as the dominant species on Earth. We were the First.

SAFFI HAD BEEN MADE up by one of the crew. Daniel looked at her. Why would a woman like her be with him? He could make no sense of it.

With thirty seconds to go, Saffi looked up, smiled and mouthed *I love you*.

Daniel gave her the thumbs up, then winced.

Thumbs up? You twat.

On the monitor next to the director, Daniel could see the programmed build-up leading to the live statement. They'd been showing old footage of The Deterrent and newer stories featuring the titans for over an hour.

The kitchen fell silent as the director counted the last few seconds on her fingers, then pointed to Saffi.

"My name is Saffi Narad," she said, looking into the camera. "I have known the individual once called The Deterrent since November last year. He, and the other members of his species—the titans—will use the next few weeks to set the record straight about their origins and their intentions. They have prepared a short statement."

The lights flickered. Saffi carried on.

"A statement from the First," she read.

The lights flickered again and went out.

Daniel looked out of the kitchen window. Abos, Triple-Dee, Sara, and the First emerged from the laboratory, but they didn't head for the house. They all faced the opposite direction.

Daniel looked past the heads of the group to the fields beyond, which sloped up towards the woods. It was half an hour before sunset, and the sun was a low, orange ball.

His eyes weren't drawn to the sinking sun, or the rich colours lent to the meadows and trees by the warm evening light.

A man stood on the crest of the rise. He was still, and he was staring at the house. Daniel asked himself why he was referring to the stranger as *he*. Then he went cold as the answer became clear. He knew the figure was that of a male for the same reason that he knew he was unspeakably old, unbelievably dangerous, and full of malice and hatred.

The figure wasn't human. It was communicating with onemind, and Daniel was picking up some of that communication.

He didn't realise he had been shaking until Saffi put her hands on his arm and squeezed.

"Daniel," she said, "Daniel. What's wrong?"

At the far end of the field, his eyes staring at the group assembled in front of the farmhouse, the Old Man wept. He wept because he had found his brothers and sisters. He wept because the link they had forged between their minds was laid open to him, and he had forgotten that such a thing was possible. He experienced the consciousness of the others, their individual minds and their onemind, uncovering a memory so ancient, it was like a wisp of a forgotten dream. He wept for all he had given up, and because he could no longer remember what that was.

Most of all, he wept because he knew what his Purpose was.

As the sun touched the tops of the trees behind him, he set off towards the farmhouse.

31

Daniel turned to the film crew.

"Get out fast," he said. "Head down to the checkpoint. Go."

As they ran for the van outside, he went to the back door. Saffi followed. He shook his head. "Stay here, Saff. I don't like the look of this."

She grabbed his hand. "Whatever we face, we face it together," she said. "It's non-negotiable, Daniel Harbin, so don't waste your breath."

He looked grim. "Stay behind me."

Daniel opened the door. The approaching figure was halfway across the field, his features impossible to pick out against the setting sun.

"Who is that?" said Saffi.

"One of the First," said Daniel.

"What? Abos said the US government and the titans had searched pretty much the whole planet."

"No more dormant ones," said Daniel. "I guess he wasn't dormant."

"Then why has he stayed away until now?"

The Last Of The First

"I don't know," said Daniel, as the tall figure got closer, "but something's not right. The First feel it. I do too, a little."

Saffi said nothing. The man had reached the gate. He opened it and stepped into the yard.

He was tall. His hair was a little longer than was fashionable, but he wore the nearly ubiquitous beard of the under-forties British male.

It wasn't his appearance that drew everyone's attention. Daniel didn't believe in auras, filing them in the same category as homeopathy and palm reading, but this guy had an aura and then some. There were no glowing bands of light around the body, but looking at him was like looking at a piece of tarmac baking on a hot summer day. Except the haze surrounding the figure wasn't heat; it was power.

Since the first time Abos had shared onemind with his children, Daniel had felt linked to the First. It was weak, but it was there. He concentrated on it now, then flinched. He had been shut out by the stranger as firmly as if a hand on his chest had pushed him away. But, for a split second, he had meshed with the First and knew what they knew.

"Methuselah," he whispered.

The stranger looked at the First, then at TripleDee, Sara, Daniel, and Saffi. He turned his golden eyes on Abos last of all.

"This," he said, "is very disappointing."

They were his only words. He continued to look at Abos, his expression devoid of emotion. Abos stumbled backwards.

"Daniel," said Abos, speaking as if every word was causing him terrible pain. "He... he is trying... onemind... he will be dominant. You must run. All of you. Run, now."

His voice had risen almost to a shout as he spoke, and his body was shaking. Daniel looked at the other First. Four of them were rigid, their bodies as still as dead trees, eyes shut and faces slack. Two of them had their eyes open, but their faces were wet with perspiration. Abos, Shuck, and Susan were fighting the hardest, every muscle tight, every vein on their necks and faces standing out. The three of them were moving towards the stranger, but it was as if they were walking into a hurricane. Their progress was almost imperceptible, and Daniel could see they were weakening. Abos was right. They had to run. This was not a battle they could win here and now. The First were buying them time, at great cost.

"Come on," he said, leading Saffi back towards the house and hissing at Sara and TripleDee. "We don't have much time. Come on!"

Sara backed towards the door, but TripleDee stood his ground.

"Trip! NOW!" The Geordie halfhero hated being called Trip, but Daniel wasn't going to use any more syllables than he had to.

"No. Wait," said TripleDee, shaking his head and taking a slow step towards the bearded man.

Sara stopped moving. "What the hell are you doing?" she said.

TripleDee kept moving. Another two steps, and he would be within punching distance of his target. Punching people had long been his favoured method of ending disputes.

"No," said Daniel. "He's too strong, he'll kill you."

"In his dreams, mebbe," said TripleDee. He pulled back his fist in preparation. A straight right to the throat would do nicely. "He's distracted. We might never get another chance to save them."

Before anyone could protest further, TripleDee took a

final step and unleashed a punch at the bearded man's exposed throat.

TripleDee had only put all his strength into a single punch on one previous occasion. The recipient of that punch had been buried in a closed casket, as there was so little left of his head. TripleDee assumed the current punch would have a similar effect.

That's the thing about assumptions. You only learn that you were wrong to make one when it's too late.

The stranger didn't try to avoid the punch. The full force of the impact hit his throat. Or it seemed to. It *should have*. But instead of injuring him, the massive store of kinetic energy was returned to the man who wielded it, travelling through TripleDee's arm, into his shoulder, and throwing him backwards. He flew through the gap between Sara and Daniel, hitting the farmhouse wall so hard that bricks shattered, and the whole wall rippled and sagged. TripleDee came to rest in a cloud of brick dust. He didn't move.

Saffi pressed two fingers against his neck.

"He's alive," she said.

Daniel knelt beside the fallen man. What happened next was over in seconds, but he would rerun it in his mind for the rest of his life, always wondering if there was anything else he could have done.

"No."

The word was a whisper. Daniel looked up to see who had spoken. It was Sara.

The stranger had turned towards them. If TripleDee's attack had done nothing else, it had got the bearded man's attention. He walked towards the halfheroes, but every step was an effort. He was straining as if being held back.

As the man came closer, his arm rising to his shoulder, his fist clenched, Daniel looked beyond him and saw fear in his father's eyes. Abos couldn't stop Methuselah. He could slow him down, but he couldn't stop him.

Daniel grabbed TripleDee's collar. He tried to drag him out of danger, but he could see it was too late. The bearded man would reach them before he could get TripleDee away. He dragged the unconscious man towards the door, despite knowing it was useless.

Then his view of Methuselah was blocked.

Sara.

She had moved so quickly, Daniel and Saffi hadn't noticed until she was in the path of the approaching stranger.

At the same moment, their brains lit up with a command so powerful it was as if they had lost control of their actions. Sara had screamed at them to leave, to get TripleDee out, but she hadn't done it in words. She had planted it directly into their minds, something she had promised she would never do.

By doing it now, she knew she would never have to apologise.

Daniel and Saffi dragged TripleDee's unconscious body across the back doorstep, through the kitchen, and out of the front door. Throwing their sibling onto the back of the old pickup parked outside, they jumped in, and Daniel floored the accelerator.

It wasn't until they reached the checkpoint that they allowed themselves to acknowledge what had just happened.

It was one moment in the kitchen, unnoticed at the time as they had dragged TripleDee to safety, that would return to Daniel in nightmares for years to come. As Saffi opened the front door and Daniel followed, he had heard a sound like heavy rainfall on the window looking out to the yard.

With one step to go, he had turned his head, his mind not letting him understand what he was looking at until much later.

It wasn't rain running down the glass and pooling on the windowsill outside. It was blood.

Sara was dead.

∼

THE SOLDIERS at the checkpoint were staring up the rise at the farmhouse. They shifted nervously as the ground began to tremble.

The commanding officer's manner was calm and professional, but her voice shook as the ground moved more violently.

"What's the situation up there?"

Daniel thrust the fact of Sara's death away and focussed on the immediate danger. "There's a new First - a titan. Not like the others. He's dangerous, he's powerful, and he's attacking the rest. He killed, he killed—" Daniel didn't break down, just stood there, unable to say the words, as if acknowledging Sara's death out loud would make it real.

Saffi took over.

"He killed Sara." She swallowed.

"A halfhero?" said the commanding officer.

"She died saving us," said Saffi.

The officer considered the new information. "And the others are fighting this new titan?"

"Yes," said Saffi.

After considering the implications, the officer walked to the nearest vehicle and pulled out a radio.

"Base, this is echo one-four, repeat echo one-four. We

have a developing situation and require reinforcements. Get me the general. We—"

She didn't finish her sentence. The wall of the farmhouse yard blew apart. The outbuilding was flattened, the violence of its destruction sending bricks and dust flying into the fields. Then the farmhouse sagged drunkenly and crumpled, its roof falling in a shower of tiles. The trees in the adjacent wood, some of which had been standing for three centuries, leaned outwards before being uprooted.

The shaking underfoot increased. Most of the soldiers were knocked off their feet by the shock-wave. The armoured vehicles and the tank slid away, pushed by an invisible force.

Daniel hung on to the wheel of the pickup which was moving down the road, its tyres, held by the handbrake, screeching as it went.

There were shouts of, "Get out!" "Withdraw!" "Pull back!" Daniel released the handbrake, stamped on the accelerator and, pulling around the tank, headed north away from the village.

For the first mile, the road writhed beneath them like something living, then it suddenly stopped. Daniel pulled over. He and Saffi got out and looked back along the road.

It was quiet for a few seconds, then the birds in the surrounding trees resumed their dusk songs. The scene was idyllic; the last sliver of the setting sun disappearing behind a hill, sending long shadows across the fields, meadows, woods, and hedgerows. Only a few jarring elements spoiled the picture. One was the devastated wood, its dead trees scattered, a hundred thousand habitats destroyed. Another was the military convoy, their vehicles half a mile behind the pickup.

Most jarring of all were the ten figures in the air above

what had once been the farmhouse. They were in a V formation, like migrating birds. It was too far to make out any details, but Daniel didn't need even the evidence of his one eye to know who was leading the formation. His connection to onemind had been severed completely. The stranger, Methuselah, the Old Man, led the First now and, as Daniel and Saffi watched, the First turned and flew south until they were lost from sight.

TripleDee sat up, flexing his shoulders and arms and rubbing the back of his head.

"Fuck me sideways," he said, a rueful smile on his face. "That hurt. Did we get him?"

Then he looked from Daniel to Saffi and took in their expressions before turning and looking all around him.

"Hey," he said, "where's Sara?"

32

They drove for three hours in silence. TripleDee looked out of the passenger window. Sometimes, he frowned as a wave of pain from his rapidly healing body washed through him.

Saffi sat in the middle, crying, her head against Daniel's arm. His shirt was soaked with her tears, and he had lost all sensation in the arm twenty minutes earlier, but he didn't move.

Daniel didn't want to do anything except drive. They were on the M5, and there was a kind of numb comfort in the simplicity of motorway driving. He was looking ahead, staying in the inside lane as far as possible. Tarmac, bridges, blue signs for junctions and services. The occasional piece of shredded HGV tyre on the hard shoulder. Fast food litter on the grassed banks. Each turnoff they approached and passed was marked by a mile of lampposts, their flat, dull light flashing rhythmically across the cab of the pickup.

Exeter, Taunton, Bridgewater, Clevedon. Bristol, Gloucester, Cheltenham.

It wasn't until Daniel had turned off the motorway at

Worcester, stopped to fill up with diesel, and headed west, that Saffi had broken the silence.

"Where are we going?"

Daniel wasn't sure. He was driving, that was all. He didn't dare stop, he had to keep moving, keep going forwards. He didn't even know what road he was on. Then a sign flashed by, and he remembered the route he had looked up after reading Palindrome's last email.

"Shropshire," he said. "We're going to Shropshire. To the Devil's Chair."

TripleDee turned his head away from the window and looked at the others. His eyes were dull, his expression slack. Saffi reached out her hand but TripleDee turned away, staring out at nothing.

"Sounds lovely," said Saffi.

∼

THEY REACHED Church Stretton at three-thirty in the morning. Daniel drove the pickup along the High Street, then over a cattle grid onto a single track that led up the Long Mynd. The road climbed, the drop to his right falling steeply away to the valley below.

He parked in the first lay-by he found. When he turned off the engine, the sudden silence combined with the darkness lent their surroundings an other-worldly ambience.

TripleDee was the first to move. He fumbled with the door, then dropped from the cab and shuffled away from the pickup, moving like an old man. A sound came from him. No words, just a long groan, interrupted only when he had to take a breath.

Saffi shuffled along the seat and followed him. Her eyes adjusted to the lack of light, and details of the scenery became visible as shades of navy and grey. Lit only by the stars, she saw TripleDee's hunched shape. He was next to a stream which whispered and burbled in accompaniment to his broken, gasping moans. She sat on the sheep-cropped grass, put her arm around his shoulder and drew him close. A few seconds later, Daniel sat on the other side of the weeping man and put his hand on his back. They cried together as the stars wheeled along their tracks in the firmament above.

Daniel was the first to wake next morning. A fine mist was clinging to the hillside. He walked to the far side of the track and took a long piss, much to the interest of a passing sheep who eyed the steam rising from his urine with fascination. Daniel took a blanket from the back of the pickup and draped it across Saffi and TripleDee, still sleeping by the stream. Saffi opened her eyes and slid out from under TripleDee's arm.

The two of them followed the stream up the hillside for thirty yards until the mist threatened to obscure the view of their sleeping companion.

"She didn't just save TripleDee," said Saffi, brushing her hair away from her face. "We would have died back there. She saved all of us."

Daniel didn't answer. He looked at Saffi, seeing his own pain mirrored in hers, finding some solace in their shared grief. Death had been no stranger to Daniel, but now he appreciated the other side of that dark coin. Time was literally running out. What he had found with Saffi would end. Death would see to that. Maybe in forty years. Maybe tomorrow. He vowed, for Sara, for Gabe, for the halfheroes who had died in adolescence, for those he had killed while drugged by Station, for the mother who had loved nobody, that he would do everything to hold on to this woman.

Life is short. Daniel had heard people say it, had even said it himself. But now he felt it like a knife held to his throat.

He looked towards the summit of the Long Mynd. They would walk from here.

"Daniel?"

He turned back to Saffi.

"We need to say goodbye to Sara."

TripleDee was washing his face in the stream when they returned. He stood up and stretched awkwardly, still in some pain as torn muscles regenerated and mangled bones and joints realigned.

"I know what you're going to say," he said. "Save it. It *was* my fault. No point arguing about it. It's on me. I thought I was doing the right thing. No, that's not true. I didn't think at all. I kind of hoped I'd changed, hanging around with you lot, but when it came to the crunch, I waded in with my fists. Haven't changed at all, have I? Same old violent twat. It's on me, and I'm going to have to live with it."

Saffi stepped forward, but TripleDee held up a hand to stop her. "Save your sympathy. I know you mean well, and I do appreciate it, I really do, but I can't bear it right now, okay? Okay? Sara's dead. Nothing you, Daniel, or me can do about it. The only thing we can do is get that bearded twat and kill him. See? Revenge. That's what I want. I want to rip his fucking head off. I'm no better than I was when you first met me."

"Don't you dare," said Saffi quietly. Both Daniel and TripleDee looked at her in surprise, hearing the steel in her tone. "Don't you dare do that."

She was shaking with grief and anger. She took a step closer to TripleDee, and he flinched. Under other circumstances, it would have been funny, seeing the giant of a man retreating from a woman whose head came up to the middle of his ribs.

Saffi looked up at him and waited until he met her gaze.

"You don't get to do that," she said, her voice still quiet. "You don't get the easy way out."

"Now listen, pet," began TripleDee, but she held up her forefinger, and he shut up.

"No. You fucking listen."

Daniel had never heard her swear before.

The mist altered the acoustics of the landscape. Saffi sounded like she was speaking inside a small room.

"You don't get to lie to us, and you don't get to lie to yourself. You *have* changed. Don't you dare pretend otherwise. You don't get to go back to being who you were before you met her. Too late. You go back to that, and you're spitting on Sara's memory."

The big Geordie twitched as her words hit home.

Saffi took another step forward. "Sara died saving us. Her choice. We are alive because she sacrificed herself. Which is what you tried to do. You went up against that, that... whatever that thing is, knowing he could squash you like a bug. Sara did the same. You need to be the man she died to save. Do you understand?"

TripleDee was pale. He nodded mutely.

"I need you to say it," said Saffi.

He looked over at Daniel, then back at Saffi.

"You're right," he said. "You're right. I'm sorry. I won't dishonour her. I just, I just didn't, I..."

He tried to find the words he needed. "She was my sister. I loved her."

Dotted at intervals along the side of the road were small makeshift pyramids of rocks and stones, assembled by hikers as they stopped to eat or rest. Daniel and TripleDee spent the next half an hour collecting rocks of a size that would normally require machinery to lift. They piled them according to Saffi's directions until they had built a cairn in the lay-by. It was over ten feet tall and filled a space wider than two cars. In the months that followed, after everything was over, the cairn became a tourist attraction, with various theories concerning how it had got there.

No one spoke as they stood in front of the stones, the mist now thinning enough to make the valley visible below.

Saffi led the climb up the hill. After twenty minutes, she spoke.

"TripleDee?"

"Yes?"

"We're still going to rip that bearded twat's head off."

"Good," he said.

33

The call had gone out from the British military to the rest of the world. The titans were on the move.

The statement by the First had been released to the media and was being discussed everywhere, from the biggest social media platforms to the smallest noodle bar in rural China. A large area around the farmhouse in Cornwall was cordoned off, but drone footage of the devastation and rumours of at least one death were already being circulated.

People were taking sides. The vast majority of scientists embraced the message of the First, hoping decisive action would be taken on climate change. The science-deniers who feared their crumbling credibility might disappear, became hostile, claiming the First were, variously, a hoax, genetically modified foreign agents, aliens, or the minions of Satan.

There was a huge amount of interest in the claim that the First preceded humanity as a civilisation on Earth. If true, it introduced a time-scale to world history that was disorientating. A famous historian had a panic attack live on air and spent most of the interview answering questions with either "yes" or "no" in between breathing into a paper bag.

Alongside the far-reaching implications of the statement were the violent and unexplained events in Cornwall. The titans—the First—were gone. Again. Their statement suggesting a unified purpose and a new beginning was at odds with the ruined farmhouse, the reports of a murder, and the lack of any communication since.

Adding to the unease the reports and rumours had generated was an eyewitness claim from Cornwall. According to a soldier's anonymous email, a new titan had arrived shortly before the destruction started.

For the most part, the internet was awash with unfounded speculation and dramatic claims unsupported by facts.

The British government warned every other country's government that the First were no longer on its shores. The most recent confirmed sighting had been from a fishing boat. The First were heading south, and could be anywhere by now.

World leaders called each other all night. They spoke of joint military operations and of shared intelligence. The Americans and British had their first frank discussion about the methods they had used to control the beings. The British prime minister expressed regret at the unethical behaviour of her own party, who had been in power when The Deterrent had been revealed to the world, a drugged and brainwashed superchild. She would never have sanctioned such an unjustifiable course of action. The president expressed amazement that any such thing had happened under his watch, blaming policies initiated by his predecessor and denying he had ever met the scientist responsible for such a heinous crime. The British prime minister refrained from mentioning the televised ceremony when the president had awarded Roger Sullivan a medal.

They agreed it would be in the interests of both countries' national security if no information were ever made public about their treatment of The Deterrent and the titans.

They scoured the skies for the missing superbeings. Every radar system available was used for the search, but nothing was detected. The First had left England at sunset and had been visible to the naked eye as the sighting from the fishing boat proved. They were flying below fifteen hundred feet, meaning the Earth's curved surface hid them from radar. The night had clouded over from midnight onwards, and much of Europe had been moonless.

They could be anywhere.

∽

THE OLD MAN needed to impose his dominance. The struggle in Cornwall had energised and revitalised him, filling him with a savage joy.

Returning to onemind had, after the initial shock, been like a blind man regaining his sight. As he had walked across the field towards the farmhouse, every step that brought him closer had widened his consciousness, introducing the minds of the others, unlocking memories, increasing intelligence, revealing Purpose.

By the time he was looking at them face-to-face, he had lived their memories. He had re-witnessed the end of their society, when they had become dormant. And he had seen the error in that memory. They thought his refusal to join them was a betrayal. It was anything but. It was a sacrifice, the greatest sacrifice any of their species had ever made. He alone had shown the courage necessary to face the ice age that was destroying their world, to live through it by taking the bodies of such creatures that could survive the extreme conditions.

He alone had waited. He alone had grown strong. His memory could retain little from so many lifetimes, but he remembered enough to know he was the pinnacle of sentient life on the planet. The apes were still many hundreds of years from approaching the technological achievements of the First, but Earth would destroy them before they got there.

Which was how it should be. He had his brothers and sisters now. He needed no one else.

They had crossed the Channel the previous night. A hundred miles into France, the Old Man had led them down to a rural gîte in Bretagne. He had experienced their horror through onemind when he killed the couple sleeping in the main house, their three children and another man who lived in a neighbouring cottage. His dominance over onemind was assured, but he had yet to bend them completely to his will. It would be much easier when they saw matters as he did rather than resist what was right.

They had eaten in the large kitchen. Afterwards, he led them to a large barn he had seen from the air. They could sleep there for the few hours they needed.

The nine First sat on straw bales in the barn while the Old Man spoke. There was no need to tell them of his long, lonely lives, the aeons he had spent walking the earth. Onemind opened his memories to the others.

It was difficult—although not impossible—to keep secrets from the rest. The Old Man knew this because he had locked away his memory of Khryseis and their son, Heracles. It was his personal shame, he would not share it.

He had turned away from the error of breeding with the inferior humans in disgust. They were unworthy of it.

"Today, the First has a future again. Long ago, we plundered this planet, taking what we wanted, destroying all balance. Earth responded. What remains of our species is now,"—he gestured towards the night sky—"out there somewhere, settled on a new world. But we can make amends to the planet we abused so blindly. We can restore balance to Earth itself."

He felt approval in onemind. There was fear there, and resistance, but that was only to be expected. He would rather lead by consensus, as was the way of their species, but they had strayed so far from the path it had been necessary to lead them by force. At first, at least.

Onemind approved of his goal to restore balance. On that, they all agreed. Even the one they called Abos, the strongest among them. Surprisingly strong, in fact, but no match for the Old Man, weathered and toughened to a diamond-like hardness over millennia.

Abos represented the only threat to his dominance, slight though it was. The Old Man had shared his memories. There wasn't much to admire. The Deterrent, as the humans had named him, had been weak and confused when he had grown his first body, allowing himself to be manipulated by inferior beings. Worse than that, worse by far, was his subsequent fraternisation with them. Instead of despising the humans, he had adopted their conventions, made friendships, pretended he was one of them.

Most abhorrent of all, he had bred with them. Not just once, which might be forgiven. No, Abos had reproduced over and over, a sick orgy that produced a litter of halfbreeds. Most of them were dead now. The Old Man had killed one himself. He could still see flecks of the female's blood on his fingernails.

It was time for the Old Man to begin his work.

"The bodies we wear carry the only pure First remaining on our planet," he said. "We are stronger, more intelligent, and more advanced than the brutal simple-minded creatures who are killing Earth. But we are few. We will become the founders of a new race. We will reproduce, then we will take new bodies and reproduce again, and again. We will do this in secret, avoiding conflict until we are numerous enough to subjugate humanity. But we will never dilute the First by breeding with humans. Never again."

He turned to Abos, who was now standing. With an effort, he mentally forced him to sit.

"You have brought shame on our species. Worse, your actions have created half-breeds that share some of our powers. Your error, although grievous, can be put right. And before we take our rightful place and tear down the suicidal technology of these apes who invite their own extinction, we must deal with our own mistakes."

Abos tried to stand again, but the Old Man radiated power. No one moved. They knew what Abos knew, as did the Old Man. Daniel and TripleDee were the only halfheroes remaining. And, through the halfheroes' connection with onemind, they knew a second generation was reaching maturity. The halfheroes' children were not only alive and healthy; they were all gathered in one place.

Which, the Old Man thought, was very convenient.

"What we must do," he said to his companions, "horrifies me as much as it does you."

There was truth in what he said. He took no joy in killing for killing's sake, even the culling of a herd of mongrel scum.

The Old Man turned to Abos and addressed him directly although his words were aimed at all the First.

"We will undo the damage before we start afresh. We will rest here, build up our strength." He intended to use the time to make his dominance absolute. There could be no dissension if they were to achieve their Purpose.

"When we are ready, we will return to Britain. The half-breeds are waiting for us. They must die so that we may continue; unsullied, pure, the rightful heirs of this world."

Resistance, horror, sadness, guilt, rejection... the surface of onemind was like an ocean in a storm. But the Old Man calmed the waters, driving his sense of righteousness and power into each individual. They would follow him. They would go back and confront these genetically confused mistakes, and the green hills would run red with their blood.

And Abos would stand beside him when it happened.

34

When Daniel, TripleDee and Saffi arrived at Craxton's field, there was no ceremony, no formal greeting. No special words were spoken. Tom was the first to go to the gate, followed by Kate and Shannon, then the others as they sensed their father approaching.

Bardock was making tea when the nearby children put aside what they were doing and walked away. She poured hot water into one mug, swirled the tea leaves for thirty seconds, then tipped them through a strainer into a second mug. Only then did she stand and look towards the entrance to the field.

A crowd of the teenagers—maybe half of everyone in the camp—had gathered near the gate. Two hundred yards beyond them, three people were walking up the farm lane towards the field. Even at this distance, she could see the two male figures were exceptionally large.

Bardock sipped her tea. She stayed where she was, by the fire pit nearest to her tent. She had come for answers and here, as if on cue, the halfheroes were turning up.

At the gate, Daniel Harbin's children waited.

No ceremony, no formal greeting, no special words.

Instead, something else. Something felt by the children, by Daniel and TripleDee, by Saffi, and even, faintly, by Bardock.

Fate. Not a word anyone of them would have thought to have used, but there was none better. The pieces were moving into place. Whether it was by their own volition, or whether an unseen hand had guided them was of no importance. The fact was, they were there, they were together, and —although they didn't yet know it—they were the last line of defence against the greatest threat humanity had ever faced.

~

DANIEL KNEW he had made the right decision, coming to the Stiperstones, meeting his children. Something changed in him as he got closer. As they topped the last ridge and got their first sight of Craxton's field, he tried to explain it to Saffi and TripleDee.

"It's like those tunes that have one note just going on in the background, you know? Um, shit, what do you call them... I don't know? Like in Blade Runner, there's that *mmmmmmm* sound underneath the synth stuff, you know, *mmmmmmm, mmmmmm*. Oh, bollocks, I don't know what it's called. But it's like that."

"Right," said TripleDee. "So, just to be clear, something weird's happening in your head. and it's like the music from a George Lucas fillum."

Daniel stopped walking for a second. "George bloody Lucas? It's Ridley Scott, you pleb."

"No need for name calling. Some of us have better things

to do with our time than watching kiddie science fiction while playing with our nobs."

"Kiddie? You don't have a clue what you're talking about. Blade Runner is—"

Saffi, happy to hear the two of them bickering again, interrupted. "Perhaps you could educate him another time, Daniel. What are you trying to tell us?"

"Oh. Yeah. Right. Well, what I'm saying is, I've had this thing going on, like a note in my head, but it started so quietly, I forgot it was there. Until now."

"Why?" said Saffi. "Has it stopped?"

"The opposite," said Daniel. It's bigger, much bigger. It was just one note, now it's a band. One violin, then a whole orchestra. But it's not music, it's something else. It's... I can't explain it. Like curtains opening to show you a view. Er, like walking into a room thinking it's the toilet, but it's a massive auditorium instead. Like me getting my other eye back. And a few more eyes, too."

"I think I've got it," said TripleDee.

"Really?" said Daniel.

"Really. You're a fiddle player with loads of eyes who needs a shit."

"Oh fuck off."

∾

SIX OF THEM sat around the fire as Tom passed them freshly baked bread and mugs of coffee, along with apples and pears from nearby orchards.

Coming face-to-face with all one hundred and eight of his children, so soon after the arrival of the Old Man, the loss of Abos, and the death of Sara was a shock. Despite

Daniel thinking he was ready—or as ready as anyone could be—it was overwhelming.

The children were just that: children. They were of all races. They were tall, short, thin, stocky. Some looked studious and serious, others were natural clowns. There were those who loved to be the centre of attention, and others who would rather find a quiet corner with a good book. Some were straight, some were gay, some were bisexual. Others were still unsure. This made some of them unhappy while others had accepted the ambiguity. In short, they were a typical group of teenagers. They were confused, confusing, excited, curious, and full of life.

They were beautiful. And Daniel was their father.

Saffi held his hand as he sank to his knees while his children took their first look at the massive one-eyed limping man whose death and resuscitation they had shared.

"All right, kids?" he managed, with a croaking whisper.

"Hi Dad," said Tom, swinging the gate open. "Hi..."

Saffi smiled at him. "Saffi," she said, "and TripleDee."

"Come in," said Tom. "Have some breakfast." He led the way into the camp, and a crowd of kids walked with the three newcomers.

The coffee was hot and sweet, and Daniel thought the bread tasted better than any he'd ever eaten. He tore chunks of it from the loaf and looked from Tom to Kate, then Shannon, then across the rows of faces, then back again, smiling all the while.

"Of course, we all have fathers," said Tom. "Most of our parents told us about their IVF treatment. The rest of the camp are the children of other halfheroes."

"I'm not here to replace your dads," said Daniel around a mouthful of bread. "I would never—"

"We know," said Tom. "And we know you didn't find out about us until recently."

"How?" said Saffi. "How could you know? It took the best hacker in the country for us to find out."

Tom looked at the others. None of them had ever tried to put into words what had drawn them together. There had been no need. Words could never get close to the level of communication they shared. "We... all of us who came here, I mean, all the children of... halfheroes..."

Tom paused, but no one filled the silence. They waited for him to describe the indescribable.

"We all dreamed the same dream. We knew we would find each other here. We knew there would be terrible danger. But we had to come, all of us. We... we are each other. A bit."

He laughed. "I knew this would be impossible. I am *me*, Tom Evans, but I am *us*."

"Like onemind," said Daniel, "or the webmind we formed to break out of White Sands."

"It's different for us," said Tom. "Onemind, and what you did at White Sands, took a conscious decision to form, and needed a dominant mind to guide it. With us, it never goes away. It's like... it's like..." He searched for a metaphor.

"An orchestra?" said Daniel, thinking of his own response to the children.

"Actually," said Tom, smiling, "yeah. Yeah. That works. You know when there are loads of violins and violas and cellos and double basses playing together, making one big sound?" His A-level music coursework was proving useful. "If you went close and listened to one violinist, put your ear next to the strings, you'd hear it clearly, but you'd miss the chord you'd hear if you listened to the whole orchestra. That's like us, we're playing a chord, but it's always moving, changing. I hear every note, and I *am* one of the notes. We need each individual note to make up the chords."

TripleDee looked at the teenagers sharply. "You weren't surprised when Daniel mentioned onemind. You knew about White Sands. No one knows about that. Talk."

TripleDee frowned at Tom. He gave the teenager a glowering look that had loosened the bowels of career criminals. Tom was unconcerned.

"You're not letting yourself feel it, Uncle."

TripleDee lowered his brows further. "You what? Hang on, *uncle*?"

"Daniel is my father," pointed out Tom, "and you are his half-brother."

TripleDee stared at Daniel, then at Tom, Kate, and Shannon. "Bugger me sideways," he said.

Tom picked up the saucepan of coffee and topped up their mugs, leaving TripleDee until last. He sat next to the Geordie and put a hand on his thick forearm.

"You're family. You are linked to us. We know what you know, we remember what you remember. We know about onemind, and we know what happened in White Sands."

TripleDee looked into the fire. When he spoke, his voice was quieter. "You know everything I've done?" he said. "Everything?"

"Yes," said Tom, his hand still on the big man's arm. "Everything."

"How can you bear to touch me if you know the things I've done?"

Tom waited for TripleDee to look at him.

"When there are no secrets, there is understanding. Separation is an illusion, so there can be no judgement."

"Haddaway," said TripleDee after a short silence. "Thank

you, Confucius. I think I'll keep a bit of separateness if it's all the same to you."

Tom went back to his place, leaving TripleDee looking shaken. The teenager exchanged glances with Kate and Shannon.

"Right," he said. "It's time we talked about the Methuselah - the Old Man."

35

Commodore Fiona Bardock unzipped her tent at dawn to find Tom Evans, Daniel Harbin, TripleDee, and Saffi Narad waiting for her.

"I know you're here because of the First," said Daniel. "Tom told us you were on the *Smithwatson* when it torpedoed the *Liberace*."

Bardock crawled out of the tent and stood up. Daniel continued before she could speak. "He says you tried to stop it happening and were locked up because of it."

Bardock nodded.

"It was you who worked out we were on the *Liberace*, wasn't it?"

She nodded again.

"You got to us faster than Sara expected."

"The other halfhero?" said Bardock. "The one who got inside my mind? Where is—"

TripleDee interrupted her. "Dead," he said flatly.

Empathy had never been Bardock's strong suit, and, although she picked up on their physical signs of grief, she skipped offering the empty condolences of a stranger. "She planned the kidnapping of the titans?"

Well," said Saffi, "it's not kidnapping when you're rescuing intelligent beings who've been drugged and brainwashed, is it?"

Bardock frowned at the other woman. She had checked Saffi Narad's file the night the First's statement was scheduled to be televised. United Nations, middle-management, but with a suspiciously quiet career that suggested it was a front for something more sensitive. Not much of a stretch to conclude it was something involving halfheroes.

"Brainwashing?" said Bardock.

Daniel stepped in. "It's a long story."

Bardock looked at the three of them. "You are material witnesses to the disappearance of the titans two nights ago."

"The First," corrected Saffi.

"Whatever. The most powerful beings on the planet are missing, and we do not know if they are hostile. I will have to take you in."

"You and whose bloody army?" said TripleDee.

"The British army."

Saffi shook her head. "No one is going anywhere," She stepped forward as if she were going to put her hand on Bardock's arm. "Ms Bardock?"

Bardock moved out of range. "Just Bardock."

"The situation has changed. We need your help."

Tom stepped out from the maze of tents behind them.

"I lied when I told you I didn't know why we were here," he said. "A dream brought us here. And it comes true tomorrow."

Bardock listened as Tom described their shared vision; the man rising into the sky above the Devil's Chair, coming to kill them. Daniel Harbin told her the Old Man had killed the female halfhero and now controlled the other titans.

"None of this is provable, is it?" she said. Bardock relied on facts. They were the solid, dense, smooth and heavy pebbles at the bottom of the stream. The water that rushed around them, babbling, noisy, attention-grabbing, was a distraction. To get to the facts, she had to reach through the water and feel for them. When she found one, she could pull it out and lay it next to the others. She could examine them, see how they might fit together.

"No," said Harbin. "We can prove nothing. But you feel the power here, don't you?"

Bardock shrugged. "I cannot deny these children have some sort of unexplained power, an inheritance from their grandfather, I suppose."

Daniel nodded. "More than that. They are something new. Something wonderful. We have to protect them from what's coming."

Bardock thought of the time she had spent in the camp and realised her depression had lifted. Even though her brain was wired in such a way that she always kept her distance, she was aware she was witnessing something new. Something... whole, something *right*. These children could change the world. If they survived the next twenty-four hours.

Her instinct was—for the first time in her life—telling her not to wait until the facts made everything clear, but to trust these children and the last two halfheroes. She examined her motives, observed her own mind, looked for discrepancies, or signs she had been mentally coerced. She found nothing.

TripleDee spoke, but Bardock raised a hand for silence.
"Let me think."

The Last Of The First

Bardock considered the consequences. If she trusted her gut, and was wrong, it would mean the end of her post-retirement career. It came down to this: listen to the pleas of half-human wanted criminals and the dreams of children, or continue to trust the logic and reason that had made her the most successful military investigator in the country.

Half an hour later, Bardock was on the phone to the United Kingdom's Chief Of Defence Staff. He took her call. If not for Bardock, he would never have been promoted to the top job in the British Armed Forces.

"Sir, I have information for you."

"And good morning to you, too, Bardock. It's been, what, a year since we last spoke?"

"Ten months and eight days, sir."

"Of course. What can I do for you?"

"Sir, I don't know where the First—the titans—are now, but I know where they will be tomorrow evening."

The pause while the Chief processed that revelation was short. Bardock respected his judgement, and that meant more to him than the row of medals on his chest.

"How did you come by this information?"

"I cannot tell you that, sir." Bardock thought it was a better approach than the truth, which was that a bunch of teenagers in a field had dreamed about it.

"Understood. How reliable is the information?"

"I have no doubts at all, sir. The First are now led by someone who sees humanity as his enemy. They will be here tomorrow."

"And where is *here*, Bardock?"

"The Stiperstones in Shropshire, sir."

Helicopters from RAF Shawbury were the first to arrive. The gliding club at the top of the Long Mynd was requisitioned, and the skies around the sleepy Shropshire villages were soon full of aircraft; some disgorging troops, others patrolling the area.

Anti-missile defences were considered the best weapon to use against the First, if they did turn out to be hostile. Six sites around the Devil's Chair, with a clear line of sight, were established by nightfall.

Armed troops camped on the far side of the hills. Bardock had insisted the route from Craxton's field to the Devil's Chair be left clear. That had been the hardest request for the Chief to agree to, but in light of her unblemished record of being right, he had reluctantly complied. If this was the one time she was wrong, and a couple of hundred teenagers were injured or worse as a result, his recent promotion would be the shortest in the history of the Defence Staff.

Local and national media were quickly alerted to the huge military build-up around the Stiperstones, and legal restraints were slapped on the desks of every news editor in the country. The freedom of the press would be respected, but if anyone breached the fifteen-mile perimeter set by the army, they would be fired upon.

Next morning, a glorious warm red light edged across Craxton's field as the sun rose. Bardock, Daniel, Saffi, and TripleDee stood at the edge of the field, staring up at the silhouetted pile of rocks that formed the Devil's Chair.

No one spoke until the sun was fully visible, each of them thinking it might be the last sunrise they ever saw.

The distant thrum of rotor blades couldn't drown out the songs of thousands of birds greeting the dawn as they did every morning, unaware of anything significant about this one.

"Can't believe them bloody kids are still asleep," said TripleDee.

"It's ten past five, mate," said Daniel, "and they're teenagers."

Ninety minutes later, there was movement in the camp behind them.

The grandchildren of The Deterrent even woke up in a coordinated way. There were only so many showers and toilets, but there was never a queue. The earliest risers were cooking breakfast by the time the last of them were dressed. Food was prepared and served at the right time, just as they needed it.

When Bardock, Saffi, Daniel and TripleDee reached the nearest fire pit, they were each handed a plate of toast, eggs, and beans.

"Coffee and tea in the pans on the fire," said the freckled girl who served them.

They ate unhurriedly. The sense of fate which had seeped into their minds meant every minute between now and the inevitable arrival of the Old Man seemed preordained. They barely tasted the food, but they knew they needed the energy.

They went their separate ways after breakfast. Bardock called the general in charge of the operation. The troops were standing ready.

TripleDee went to see Tom Evans. He stood in front of the younger man, his fingers drumming against his leg.

"I, er, well, um... in me younger days, like," he began. "I, well, that's to say, I put it about a bit, like, and, you know, I sometimes wondered if... well... no, no, never mind. It's nothing. You carry on. You're... you're a good lad, Tom."

He turned and almost knocked over a girl who had quietly walked up behind him. She was about fourteen years old, her brown hair cut short and spiky. She was looking up at him with a stare he found hard to meet. Her head was cocked to one side, and the corner of her mouth twisted as she looked at him. It reminded him of someone. Someone he knew did that when they were thinking. That whole head on the side, twisty lip thing. Someone... oh.

TripleDee remembered who did that. It was him.

He tried to speak, but no words came.

"Yes," said the girl. "I am. My name is Sophie. Good to meet you, Dad."

She stepped into him, putting both her shoeless feet on top of his, wrapping her thin arms as far around his barrel chest as she could, and pressing her face against his shirt.

She was shaking, he realised. Shaking really badly. Then he corrected that impression. He was shaking, his chest heaving. Slowly, he raised his arms. He put his left arm across her back. He lifted his right hand and put his fingers on her face as if he were touching a sculpture made of spun sugar. Her cheek was soft. He rested his hand there. There wasn't a single thought in his head, and it was wonderful.

When they parted, he looked at her. His daughter. He felt something give, something he'd been fighting.

"Oh," he said.

"You can hear the orchestra," said his daughter.

Daniel and Saffi went back to their tent and made love. It wasn't spontaneous, exactly, but neither was it pre-arranged. It was simply their response to the threat that approached. This might be their last day together. The children's dreams had offered no hint of who would prevail in the confrontation. Daniel and Saffi had seen Methuselah, had seen Abos and the others submitting to the creature's will, had seen him kill Sara at the same time as wresting control of onemind.

Although they didn't speak about it, both doubted anyone could prevail against such power, such rage.

They made love, the act through which they had sometimes been afforded a glimpse of what it might mean to lose themselves. They slept with their limbs knotted together, dreaming they might never be untangled.

Because this was the day they thought they were going to die.

36

The sun had been low in the sky in Tom's dream.

At four o'clock that afternoon, Daniel and TripleDee left the camp and walked up to the Devil's Chair before turning south for two-thirds of a mile. Cranberry Rock was the last outcrop of stones before the hill sloped down to the car park to the east and the poetically named Bog Mines to the west. It was an indication of TripleDee's sombre mood that he commented on neither name, not even to point out that there were no cranberries.

The ground-to-air missile launchers and the squads that manned them were invisible. TripleDee scanned the horizon with powerful binoculars, then handed them to Daniel.

"They're good. Canna see them at all. You?"

Daniel raised the binoculars, focussing to compensate for his missing eye. He took his time searching, but their camouflage was near perfect.

"Nope, nothing," he said.

No planes or helicopters patrolled the sky. All military personnel were under orders to observe radio silence until the enemy was sighted. Wifi and mobile signals had been shut down or blocked, much to the annoyance of locals. It hadn't made them any happier when they were confined to their homes, but a little misinformation about a biological weapon had guaranteed their cooperation.

Tom had insisted events would unfold just as they did in the dream, so Daniel and TripleDee couldn't be at the Devil's Chair when the Old Man arrived. Which meant, if the dream was correct, their attempt to stop him at Cranberry Rock would fail. The best they could hope for was that they might injure Methuselah, or hurt some of the First enough to put them out if action - maybe even return them to dormancy.

It was possible they would die trying.

Not a cheerful scenario.

Looking out at the Shropshire landscape, the border with Wales only a few miles to the west, Daniel remembered a BBC children's science fiction show he'd watched when he was just old enough to be captivated by it. He could picture a scene where the three main characters were hiding on a hillside, waiting for a horrifying creature. When it appeared, it was a giant tripod, a mechanical monster striding incongruously across the British countryside, its metal feet crushing everything in its path. It had terrified a nine-year-old Daniel then, and he felt the echo of his fear now, even as he recognised his usual defence mechanism of focussing on trivialities.

"I hate waiting," said TripleDee, after a few minutes. "I bloody hate it, man."

"Me too," said Daniel.

Saffi was back in the camp. They had hugged, and Daniel hadn't looked back.

There had been something else about that BBC drama.

Something much worse than the metal monsters. It had been the ending. The heroes, unthinkably, had been defeated by the tripods. Daniel had been distraught for weeks until he read the books the series had been based on. The BBC hadn't filmed the final book. The tripods had been wiped out in the trilogy's conclusion. The experience had left him with an inescapable and disconcerting conclusion: heroes didn't always win. Good didn't always prevail. He had seen the TV series first, and it had stayed with him. In Daniel's memory, both outcomes coexisted: the tripods were victorious, and they were defeated.

Later on, he found out that the BBC had run out of money, and had changed the ending because of it. The tripods had triumphed because of bad budgeting. It hadn't made him feel any better.

"What are you thinking about?" said TripleDee.

"Oh," said Daniel, wondering whether he should tell him the truth or go for something more heroic in case these proved to be his last words. In the event, he was spared the necessity of deciding.

"Aw, shite," said the Geordie, as the radio on his belt crackled into life. "They're here."

37

The Old Man's feet touched British soil five miles from the Devil's Chair. He had mostly avoided flying during his long, long, life, preferring to feel the earth under his feet. His eternal wandering had led to myths springing up around a mysterious character who ceaselessly walks the planet. Ziusudra, Ashwatthama, the Wandering Jew, Nosferatu - they couldn't die, but each of their stories carried a curse attached to their deathless existence. They were doomed to keep moving, never to find rest. The Old Man's power surged through him, and he rejected the curse human stories would have him suffer.

His wandering days were over. Humanity's dominance was at an end. Today, the slate would be wiped clean, and a new story would be written.

He walked now, and the First followed.

Their resistance had crumbled once he had broken The Deterrent. Abos walked a pace behind him, ready to do his bidding. The Old Man had been minded to kill him as a warning to the others. But he needed every one of the First if they were to build a new race, and his continued control of

Abos and dominance over onemind was a sufficient display of power to deter potential challengers. Once the traitor's legacy was wiped out, his submission would be complete.

They walked, striding across the fields and hills, unstoppable, the true inheritors of the Earth.

The Old Man's victory already felt tangible to him.

They reached the final valley leading to the rising landscape of the Stiperstones. Silhouetted against the skyline, the Old Man saw two figures waiting beside a rock formation. Daniel and TripleDee. It could be no one else. They had expected his arrival. He experienced a moment's disquiet. Then he remembered the halfheroes' link to onemind. Was it possible they had *sensed* the approach of the First through that tenuous connection? The idea that these mongrels should have any access to the shared mental state of the First disgusted him. He would sever that link today.

He stopped walking as did the nine figures behind him.

The Old Man looked to his left and right, examining the hillsides, looking for movement, seeing none. He had been a soldier, a general, a strategist in many of his lives, and he knew a good spot for an ambush when he saw one. He laughed. Let them try.

He started to walk again, and the others followed, their eyes fixed on the two waiting figures.

~

"Let them get closer," said Daniel into the radio. "We'll only get one shot at this."

"Much closer, and you risk being caught in the blast. Over," came the reply.

"Leave it as long as you can," said Daniel, then, a little self-consciously, added, "over and out."

He dropped the radio.

They waited.

Methuselah, the Old Man, had passed Bog Mine and was on the hillside now. Close enough that Daniel could see he was still wearing the same dark suit. It was smeared with mud and dirt now, but the creature inside it practically glowed with latent power. His dominance of the First had increased his strength, and it was coming off him in waves.

"Oh fuck," said TripleDee.

The Old Man's golden eyes blazed like a thousand fires. His focus was so absolute that neither he nor any other of the First saw the telltale puffs of smoke from the farm behind them, the feed store to the west, or the ancient mine entrance to their northeast.

Sixteen missiles covered the distance in seconds. The First reacted, peeling away from their positions, taking to the air. The missiles twisted to follow them.

The Old Man stayed where he was. Rather than avoiding the missiles, he made a pushing motion with his fist towards the halfheroes by Cranberry Rock. The force lifted them off their feet. One of them was pushed back into the rocks, the impact breaking bones. He dropped to the ground and lay still.

The other fared better, spinning into the air, but righting himself and landing further up the ridge without injury.

The Old Man roared and took to the air, just as three missiles converged on him. He accelerated away, but two of them exploded as they hit each other, triggering the payload of the third. The blast caught the Old Man and threw his body into a series of uncontrollable pirouettes. His weak human form, even protected by his power, could not resist the effect of the explosion and he blacked out.

The rest of the First had been quicker to move, and the missiles were no match for their agility. They led them upwards, climbing at a speed no human-made technology could match. The missiles converged on them as they rose, and they deliberately slowed to let them get closer.

Thirteen missiles followed the flying superbeings like well-trained dogs as the First searched the area for the source of the attack. They found the squad at the mine entrance and, with a gesture, sent four missiles to blow a crater in the side of the hillside. The farm was next, then the feed store, and great plumes of black smoke soon rose where they had stood.

Daniel saw the smoke. He looked back to what was left of Cranberry Rock and spotted TripleDee's crumpled body.

A figure dropped out of the sky in front of him to block his path. He looked up into familiar golden eyes.

"Abos," he said, then took a step back. His father's expression was unrecognisable, blank, without pity. As he watched, other expressions flitted across the face, were replaced by the blank look, then returned. He had a very real fear that Abos might be about to kill him.

"Father," he said. "It's me. Daniel."

Abos moaned, a horrible, lost sound that seemed to come from far away. His fists were clenched, and his body was rigid. He shut his eyes and tilted his head back. When he opened his eyes, the danger had passed. For now, at least.

"Daniel," he said, "he is too strong. You cannot win. He is unconscious now, but he still dominates us. I cannot resist it for long. Leave."

"I can't," said Daniel. "I must protect the children. *We* must protect them."

"I will do what I can," said Abos, "but I have little hope of success. And you will be a distraction."

He grabbed Daniel and rose into the air.

"No!" Daniel struggled against the strength of the arms around him. "NO!"

Abos paid no attention and flew to the east, away from the Stiperstones, carrying his son to safety. As he flew, he noticed something moving in his peripheral vision, and turned in time to see, and avoid, the fist that had been swinging towards his head.

The Old Man bellowed in frustration. Wasting no time with words, he flew to one side and unleashed a two-handed blow at Daniel that would have killed him, had it landed. Abos, anticipating the attack, twisted in mid-air and took the full force in the middle of his spine. Daniel heard bones break, saw the light dim in his father's eyes.

Then they fell.

They seemed to fall forever although they were less than a five hundred feet from the ground when the punch landed. They dropped with no grace or control, plummeting towards the unforgiving earth.

The Old Man watched to see the inevitable result of the fall, roaring with triumph, the First lining up behind him.

The ferocity of his roar gave the two approaching Typhoon jets an extra precious second to get closer unheard. Each of them fired, unleashing a hundred and seventy rounds of ammunition a second from their single-barrel, twenty-seven millimetre cannons.

The bullets could not penetrate the skin of the First, or do as much damage as the missiles, but they had the effect of getting the Old Man's attention. Leaving Abos and Daniel to die without an audience, he and the First pursued the jets, catching them in six seconds and swatting them to the ground with the casual violence of toddlers bored with their toys.

Halfway towards the Devil's Chair, Bardock got the call from the army commander.

"We can't risk any more lives. They're coming. I'm sorry. You're on your own."

She looked at the teenagers. Most were still climbing, but a few, including Tom, had reached the top and were standing, waiting.

"I know," she said.

∼

DANIEL CLUNG to his father's limp body as they fell. His life hadn't flashed before his eyes when he had stopped breathing in the wreckage of the *Liberace,* and it wasn't doing it now. As far as he could tell, he had two or three seconds left.

He thought of Saffi.

Abos opened his eyes, the supreme effort it took to do so etched on his dying features. He moved his hand and Daniel was pushed away, his fingers losing their grip on his father's clothes as he shot backwards. He had a brief flash of memory - he and Sara falling from a tower block in Birmingham.

Then his descent slowed, he seemed to hang motionless for a moment, and the next thing he knew, he was in the water, panicking, arms and legs flailing. The fall with Sara had ended with them landing in a rooftop swimming pool. Abos had managed the same trick, but this time Daniel was in the middle of a stagnant pond. He surfaced, gasping, and struck out for the side, pulling himself onto the bank.

His body was aching from the first attack by the Old

Man, and the punch which had landed on Abos had been powerful enough to crack four of Daniel's ribs. He got to his feet, clutching his side and stumbled away from the water. Seconds after Abos had slowed his fall, he had heard his father's body hit the ground. In Abos's case, there had been no slowing down.

The two RAF jets exploded behind him as he ran. He turned his head and caught sight of the Old Man and the First flying over Cranberry Rock, heading for the Devil's Chair. They would be there in seconds.

He had failed.

38

The Old Man's suit hung in tatters around him as he rose into the sky in front of the teenagers who faced him at the Devil's Chair. The ancient pile of stones may have been there for thousands of years, but the creature flying above it was, literally, older than the hills.

Tom remembered his dream. The Old Man had been wreathed in smoke, not a suit of rags fluttering in the wind. For a second, he seemed less formidable. But only for a second. Then Tom looked at his face, at those terrible eyes, and he saw all the power and insane determination from his dream.

Tom had never been so afraid.

Behind the Old Man, other figures hung in the air, but Tom didn't see them. No one saw them. They could only see the Old Man. His bearded face was human, but none of the children were fooled. They saw something so ancient that its insanity had developed a kind of intelligence of its own. This creature believed its path was the only true path. All others were in error. There could be no reasoning with such a being. No pleading. There was no empathy in its blank gaze, and it would offer no mercy.

These weaknesses, these gaping holes in character, might in other circumstances have been pitiable, but since they had removed the Old Man's capacity to recognise his own psychosis, they made him more dangerous. He wanted to refashion the world in the image he called his Purpose, and he would destroy those who stood in his way.

Tom's fear threatened to overwhelm him. He could not think, he could not move. No one around him spoke. The breeze carried a foul stench, and he realised some of the younger ones had lost control of their bowels. Tears stung the corners of his eyes. Time slowed.

The Old Man raised his arms. Tom remembered this from the dream. He was about to unleash his power, and there was no escape, nowhere to run. Why had his dream brought him here if only to die?

The connection to the others was at its lowest ebb since he had first experienced it.

The Old Man's arms were at waist height.

Tom knew it was over. He couldn't fight. He couldn't bear to look at that awful face anymore.

Tom closed his eyes. All the teenagers did the same. They became aware of each other again and, beyond them, they became aware of others. Different, alien, hostile. With an instinct they hadn't known they possessed, they fought back. Reacting as one, they pushed the foreign group of minds away.

The Old Man lowered his arms. Onemind was under attack. He could feel the bonds loosening under the onslaught from the human children. How was this possible? He drew on all the power of his long existence, all the pain across millennia of waiting. He had suffered for lifetimes, animal in nature, before a new chance at sentience presented itself. Then came tribal societies, violence, killing. And moving, always moving. Walking the planet, coming back to places as if for the first time, to find everything had changed, yet nothing had changed. All the while unable to hold on to who he was, what he was, cursed to live while others died. Until all he had was the instinct to continue, to survive, hating everything and everyone, hating himself, but always moving, always surviving.

He gathered his power and drew the First together, bringing onemind to a tight-focussed solidity, curled up tight, defences in place.

Ready to attack.

The First hung motionless in the air like puppets in a child's toy cupboard.

And the real battle began.

The Old Man created a channel of pure destructive energy and, opening a gap in onemind, sent it towards their attackers. It dissipated as it hit them, sending shock-waves through the minds of the teenagers. He knew it was only a matter of time. He would destroy them.

Tom fell to his knees under the onslaught. His nose started bleeding, but he didn't wipe it away. The debilitating fear was gone, replaced by the knowledge that they were too weak. They had pushed the First away, attacked onemind, but the counterblow was devastating in its intensity, and onemind was putting up defences, like a hedgehog rolling into a ball. There was nowhere to push now without hurting themselves.

Each of the teenagers reached out and found the hand of another, shuffling together until they were all linked physically and mentally. Their heads were bowed as if they were being slowly forced to the ground.

The look on the Old Man's face was one of rage, pain, and victory. The children had proved surprisingly strong. He had never suspected his species' ability to link minds might have found a new genetic home in the humans. Even more reason to finish them.

He kept up the attack and prepared his reserves of power for a killing strike.

∼

BARDOCK AND SAFFI stood to one side. They watched the teenagers stagger, some of them dropping to their knees, others falling to the ground. That they were being attacked was obvious despite the lack of any visible conflict. They looked on at the frightening tableau of the immobile Old Man and the First facing Tom and the others in attitudes of frozen aggression.

The teenagers, Daniel's children, nephews, and nieces, were losing. And if they lost, they died.

Saffi ran forward and grabbed the hand of the nearest child. For a moment, her eyes closed and she, too, slumped. Then, with a gasp, she let go of the hand, opened her eyes and looked at Bardock.

"He's killing them. They need you."

Bardock stared at Saffi. "No," she said, "not me. It doesn't work with me. What they do. I.."

She looked again at the teenagers.

"I'm autistic," she said. Even now, she was reluctant to admit it. So few people understood. Or knew just enough to think they knew it all. She'd been made to feel stupid at school. She had struggled to understand it herself until an RAF doctor had picked up the signs.

Saffi looked back at her evenly.

"I know," she said. "The way your brain works is why they brought you here."

"But they didn't..." She remembered the unfamiliar handwriting on the note with the newspaper article. It had been forwarded from a nearby base, suggesting the sender didn't know her address. She felt for the pebbles of truth at the bottom of the stream. "It was one of them?"

Saffi reached out her hand. "Something about your mind, Bardock. You have a power they need."

Bardock stared at her hand in confusion. "I have no power," she said. "Nothing." She took a step away.

Saffi stood up, but didn't come any closer. "When you were their age," she said, indicating the teenagers, her words low and urgent, "were you ill?"

Bardock remembered the months of undiagnosable pain she had endured, confined to bed while her mother told her it was all in her head.

"How?" she said, "How could you know that?"

Saffi reached out her hand again. "I've just seen it," she said. "When I linked with them. They want you here, Bardock, for the same reason they wanted Daniel and TripleDee. Your father was The Deterrent. You're a halfhero."

Bardock shook her head while her mind applied its superb skills to analysing the events of her own life. Absent father, a mother who would never talk about him, a family scandal. The agony she went through at puberty.

"But..." she said weakly, "but I have no power, Saffi. No power at all."

"You're wrong," said Saffi. She reached back to the girl on the ground beside her. She offered her other hand to Bardock. "Come on."

As if in a dream, Bardock stepped forward and took her hand.

39

There was nothing there at first. A wide-open space, a twilight wilderness of dream-heavy clouds, where sinuous mist-dragons curled around her. She saw nothing but this twisting, writhing smoke. It pushed at her, seeking an opening, a way in, writhing against her legs like a cat, spiralling into her nostrils, clouding her vision as it searched for gaps between eyelid and eyeball. Her ears pillow-blocked, her throat spasming as it rejected the mist, coughing it out to circle and try again.

It could not hurt her, she realised. But it wanted to. It wanted to.

Pressure on her hand. A squeeze.

Bardock looked down and saw darker fingers laced with her own. Tight. Squeezing.

I'm here. Still here. In Craxton's field. It's Saffi's hand.

She let her attention widen, the way she did at the beginning of an investigation, or when one of her paintings was still hidden in the blank, white canvas.

She stood back. She didn't focus, she didn't categorise, she didn't judge. She just *saw*.

Saffi was kneeling at her feet. The smoke was still there, but it had lost much of its unnatural solidity. It was hurting Saffi because she couldn't keep it out. It was snaking into her nose, her ears, her eyes, and mouth.

Like an experienced cinematographer telling a story with one long take, Bardock zoomed out, pulling back, seeing more.

The children were there now, each holding the hand of his or her neighbour, each individually, uniquely beautiful. Their strength, the bond between them manifested as a force strong enough to resist that which could destroy missiles, rip jets out of the sky, or lift an aircraft carrier halfway across the Atlantic.

It was nothing magical. They didn't glow, these children. There was no mysterious white light, no angelic presence standing beside them in their hour of need. They were fighting, together, to keep the smoke out. Bardock looked at them and saw evolution taking an unprecedented leap. She saw humanity as it might be.

And the Old Man was killing them.

Now she was connected, she saw him as they saw him, an ancient, withered visage with blazing yellow eyes in whom the concept of mercy had long ago been reduced to ashes.

She zoomed out. Pulling back, seeing more.

The smoke poured from the Old Man, from his mouth, his nose, his eyes, his ears, even from his groin in a grotesque parody of procreation. He had forgotten how to give life. He came to destroy.

Pulling back, seeing more.

TripleDee, breathing, but broken.

Two jets burning. The corpses of those who had launched the missiles against the First.

Daniel Harbin, stumbling, falling, weeping for his father. *Her* father.

Pulling back, seeing more.

A temporary army base, the general in charge talking on the phone. Discussing the use of tactical nuclear weapons.

A village with military vehicles patrolling, waiting to hear if they have to evacuate.

Pulling back, seeing more.

A double-decker bus on the road to town, its upper deck scratching against branches stretching high across the tarmac to touch the trees on the other side.

Tractors in fields, sheep rounded up by a lad on a quad bike, a group of girls celebrating the end of exams playing rounders next to a glittering river.

Pulling back, seeing more.

A town, a city, the people all different yet all the same. Amused or upset or disappointed or aroused or curious or wistful or determined or tired or making preparations or winding down or nervous or screaming or laughing or crying or singing or kissing.

Pulling back, seeing more.

Jake. In her studio, looking at the work she had started before she left. There was no meaning to the painting. It was unfinished, abstract; shapes, colours, movement without resolution. But, as she looked at the half-smile on his face, she knew he had found meaning in the painting because of the way he saw it, and then

she saw it through his eyes, and the painting was her showing him her mind, and he loved it, he loved it.

Pulling back, seeing more.

And she had it. She knew what to do. She knew what her power was, and she embraced it. She was a child of The Deterrent.

Keeping her focus wide, all the while pulling back further and further, seeing more and more, she reached back to Saffi, to the children.

Come. Come and see as I see.

Pulling back, seeing more.

She invited them in, and they came to her, they saw the world as she saw it; they looked through her eyes, and she looked through theirs.

Come and see.

40

Donald K. Sturgeon was upset. Angry, even. He only got together with his fellow retired postal workers twice a year. Once at Christmas and again in the summer.

They had nothing in common other than working in the same place for most of their lives and retiring back when pensions were still worth something.

Looking around the table in the same shabby dining room they had used since the Station Hotel had closed, Donald wondered why he bothered staying in touch. Ray was a golf bore, and Fran still couldn't meet anyone's eye. Graham had lost all credibility three years ago by suggesting the music of Glen Miller was jazz. If it wasn't for Joanne, Donald would have stopped coming.

And now, they had added up the bill incorrectly. Ray had snatched it before Donald had a chance, declaring that twenty pounds each would cover it, plus another two for the tip. But Ray had ordered two bottles of wine with dinner and had drunk most of it himself. Fran had expressed her preference for a soft drink at a volume only audible by small mammals.

Joanne had drunk her glass and demurred when Ray tried to refill it. He ignored her and topped it up anyway. Now, with a blob of tiramisu sitting alongside some soup in his moustache, he suggested they might go somewhere for a drink. He sounded as if he was including everyone, but he never took his eyes off Joanne. She shook her head.

Donald felt the beginnings of irritation, mixed with regret. He glanced at Joanne and remembered the Saturday morning eight years ago when she'd dropped by with a homemade lasagne.

"I heard about Martha," she had said, handing over the dish. It had been six weeks since his wife had moved in with his brother. "Just thought you might appreciate a little home-cooked food. And, well, we haven't all forgotten you at work. I'll be retiring at the end of this month, you know."

He hadn't known. Joanne looked too young. She was one of those lucky few who carried some of the freshness of youth into middle age and beyond. She smiled, said goodbye, took three steps down the path, then came back.

That was when she'd put her hand on his arm. Her hand was small, her skin was cool. It was the first time anyone had touched him in weeks.

"I'm having a little get-together to mark my retirement," she said. "Wednesday night. It would be lovely if you could make it." When she looked at him, he felt a lurch in his chest. "I would like you to come, Donald."

He had nearly made it too, that Wednesday. He'd bought a bottle, taken a shower, put on his best suit, even shaved the hair that no longer grew on his head, but had migrated to his ears. Then he'd caught sight of himself in the mirror and remembered. He was a retired postmaster whose wife had left him because he was boring. Boring to look at, boring to talk to. Boring in bed.

Donald had looked at the categorised record collection lining the shelves of his study, and at the jowled, sagging face in the mirror. He put the wine in the fridge, took off his tie, and sat down to watch the snooker.

Now, as Joanne opened her purse, Donald looked back at Ray and held up his forefinger.

"Now, wait a minute. Joanne had the early bird special, as did I. That's a fixed price for two courses and coffee. Neither of us had a dessert. That's twelve pounds-fifty each, plus drinks. I had tap water, and Joanne had one glass of wine.

"Fran had wine," said Ray.

"She doesn't drink, Ray. Do you, Fran?"

There was a small squeak from somewhere between Fran's cardigan and her perm.

"Now, I'm sure we don't mind rounding up a little," said Donald, "but as you drank nearly all the wine plus two large cognacs, I don't think we should pay for them. We're all on fixed incomes, as you know."

Ray was going puce. A big man, he was used to getting his own way. As a post office employee, he and Donald had occasionally butted heads.

"You're not my boss anymore, pal," said Ray. "Put your hand in your pocket for once, you tight-fisted sod. God, you always have to have everything worked out to the last bloody penny, don't you?"

That was unfair. Donald had, in fact, mentally rounded up his contribution to the nearest fifty pence.

Enough was enough. Ray was a loud, obnoxious bully, Fran was a mouse, and Joanne, well, it confused Donald to think about Joanne. He'd had enough of these stupid dinners pretending they were all friends when they had nothing but their work in common. Since no one was paying them to spend time in each other's company these days, why keep up the pretence? He stood up. Time to end this farce.

"Shut up and listen, Ray Cartwright. I've had just about enough of—"

He stopped talking. For a heartbeat, all conversation in the restaurant ceased. When it resumed, something had changed. Donald looked at his finger, pointing towards Ray.

Then he looked up at Ray's red face.

They both burst into laughter.

The absolute foolishness of their quarrel was crystal clear. The awareness of their differences didn't disappear, but Donald's perspective changed in an instant, as if someone had thrown ice-cold water over his head.

Ray was a human being. Donald had never spent any time considering what that meant. It meant Ray had been born to two parents. Through a combination of his genetic inheritance and the circumstances of his early life, he developed a personality which, like Donald, Fran, or Joanne, appeared to differentiate him from others. *Appeared* to. The epiphany that had struck Donald at the corner table of the Albert Hotel dining room was that, in all but the most superficial sense, he *was* Ray. And Fran, and Joanne.

How had he forgotten that he was a short-lived creature sharing a thin slice of time with other short-lived creatures?

Donald felt his connection with everyone in the restaurant, everyone in the kitchen, in the lobby, in the rooms upstairs, in the street outside, in his country and every country. For a fraction of a second, it was as if a silver thread stretched from his heart to every other human on the planet. If he could have seen the Earth from space at that moment, would he have seen a shining, blinding web stretching across the entire globe?

"I'm sorry," said Donald, already knowing the words were unnecessary.

Ray reached over and shook his hand.

"I'm gay," said Fran, "but I never told anyone at work."

"We know," said Ray, Donald, and Joanne.

"Bring your girlfriend at Christmas," said Joanne.

"Why wait until then?" said Ray. "Let's get together more often."

"I'd like that," said Fran. "You could bring your wife, Ray."

Ray nodded, thoughtfully. "Yes," he said. "I've got a few bridges to mend there, but it's about time I started."

Donald put a twenty-pound note on the table. Ray laughed again.

"It's on me this time," he said. "I always take advantage."

They parted at the door, reluctant to go their separate ways. Donald waited a few seconds, then called out.

"Joanne?"

She waited while he caught up.

"Donald?"

He took her hand. She didn't stop him.

"Would you like to come and look at my record collection? It's west coast jazz from the nineteen-fifties."

She planted a soft kiss on his cheek. "I thought you'd never ask."

∽

THE UTOPIA ALGORITHM had hurt Cynthia Ganfrey, but she was a resilient woman. Some might use the word ruthless. Or callous. Let them. She didn't care, so long as they were poorer than her when they said it.

A great deal more cash than usual had been in her accounts on the day of Titus Gorman's cyber attack. She had lost tens of millions of dollars. It had taken her over six months to rebuild, by calling in debts from those she knew could not repay them. Ignoring their appeals to her non-existent compassion, she forced dozens of her previous business-partners to turn over real-estate in lieu of the cash they couldn't produce.

Now the value of land was going through the ceiling as the United States reverted to the partly Darwinian, partly feudal, system that had enriched the few at the expense of the many for generations. And Cynthia was ready to resume her place at the high table.

She skimmed through her emails, many of them thinly disguised attempts at begging. Some not-so-thinly disguised. **Please read - we need the land to build our school! The poor children of Detroit need—**

The poor children of Detroit need to find another sucker.

She pressed delete.

"Miriam!"

Her PA scurried into the room. Miriam scurried far more these days, ever since Cynthia had agreed to re-hire her at fifty percent of her previous salary. Miriam was a capable woman, but she had been quick to jump ship the morning of Titus Gorman's ruinous algorithm. But the rich were shedding staff, not looking for more, and Miriam had crawled back after a week.

"Yes, ma'am?"

"Call the governor's office. Tell them I have a meeting tomorrow morning, so he must rearrange."

Miriam consulted her Globlet.

"According to your schedule, the meeting with the governor is all you have tomorrow."

"Correct," said Cynthia, "but the governor needs to be reminded of who really runs this state. He'll rearrange to suit me."

"Yes, ma'am." Miriam went to leave.

"Oh, and Miriam?"

"Ma'am?"

"The begging emails are still getting through. I don't want to wade through crap like that. That's what I pay you for."

"Yes, ma'am. I'll get on it. Is that all?"

It should have been. Cynthia had turned away in her ten-thousand dollar leather and chrome executive chair and was about to wave her hand in dismissal, when it hit her. Her jaw dropped, and she allowed the chair to swivel through three hundred and sixty degrees until she was again facing a now wide-eyed Miriam.

"No, that's not all."

Cynthia sprang out of her seat, walked over to Miriam and put her arms around her.

"I'm sorry, Miriam," she said. "I've been a complete shit."

Miriam didn't disagree, but her arms came up, and she hugged Cynthia back.

"I can't increase your salary," said Cynthia, her mind working fast to readjust to the certainties that had just made become clear to her.

"Ma'am?"

"Call me Cynthia. Move into my house, Miriam. I barely use the east wing. You and your family can have it rent-free. I can't increase your salary because I'm about to have much less money. Okay?"

"What, er, did you just, um, the east wing?"

"Yes, the east wing. We can share the swimming pool. Yes or no?"

Miriam recovered enough of her wits to say yes.

"Good. Pull up a chair. Let's go through my email trash folder. I believe there are two planned hospitals and three schools in jeopardy because I own the land. We need to put that right."

"Yes, ma—yes, Cynthia."

"Oh, and let's call the governor and tell him I won't be supporting his campaign. Then reach out to that independent candidate—Betsy—and tell her she'd better think about what colour carpet she'll want in the governor's office when she's elected."

Cynthia reviewed her mental health, wondering if she'd been drugged or had a stroke. After all, it had taken four ghosts and the threat of an unmourned early death to convince Scrooge to stop being an utter bastard.

"Miriam," she said, quietly. "You felt it too, didn't you? Whatever just happened?"

"Yes. Yes, I did."

"Interesting. I just want you to know, I'm still me. I'll still be a shit. Just not a complete shit."

~

IT LASTED LESS THAN A SECOND, the moment that changed the world. Bardock let her mind become a conduit through which the children of Craxton's field reached out to every human being on Earth. In less than a second, every individual alive experienced what it might mean to live someone else's life. Everyone else's life.

It turned out you didn't have to walk a mile in someone else's shoes before you stopped judging them. You only had to glimpse the truth of their existence for a moment.

Afterwards, the effects hung on. Not as powerfully, but

they hung on. Every human being had experienced what the future of their species might look like, and it was enough to change hearts and minds forever. There were still arguments, still fights even. But they were brief and quickly resolved.

The most obvious change, day to day, was that people were more attached to each other, and less attached to their possessions. Many had already spent much of their lives advocating that philosophy, but this was the first time they had practised it.

The other result of that moment passed unnoticed by all but a tiny fraction of the world's population. They were on a hillside in northern Europe, facing an arrangement of rocks known locally as the Devil's Chair.

Tom Evans, oldest child of Daniel Harbin, opened his eyes again. Every teenager from Craxton's field did the same.

Methuselah, the Old Man, the wanderer, Wild Edric of the Stiperstones, experienced an emotion which he could not immediately name. When the Old Man did name it, the astonishment he felt almost overwhelmed the emotion itself.

He was afraid.

41

The subjective experience of time slowing down is not uncommon. Interviews with those been caught up in a natural disaster, car crash, or any violent encounter often describe the way their perception changed. Extraordinary levels of detail are often recalled; smells, colours, the shade of lipstick of the woman waving a gun, the particular version of the song playing when the bomb exploded.

The moment when every human being on earth connected to Bardock and the children was as brief as the flash of a camera. But for those locked in a deadly mental struggle on the Stiperstones, the moment stretched so much, it seemed to have begun before they were born and to continue long after their deaths.

It was almost a moment *outside* time, as it involved no sequence of events, no cause and effect, nothing that could be said to come before or go after.

Bardock experienced it as a moment when she—a woman who had lived much of her life believing she lacked the ability to empathise—became one in seven and a half billion. She was the catalyst and the conduit, the link through which the children reached out and harnessed the latent power of every person on the planet.

For Saffi, it was different. She experienced the moment as a physical confirmation of something she'd always suspected was true but had never been able to express. She kept her sense of self, but saw how she was a tiny part of the all. She forgave herself for not being there when her father was killed, or when her mother died. No... it wasn't that she forgave herself, rather that she recognised no forgiveness was necessary. The deeply buried dreams of revenge on the terrorists who had taken her father from her were exposed, only to evaporate. In that moment of no-time, she knew when she returned to her linear existence, she would taste each fleeting moment more fully.

For Tom Evans, his brothers, sisters and cousins, it was the moment they had been guided to by a shared dream, a moment none of them had resisted despite knowing it might be their last. It was the moment they let the world in.

Tom looked at the Old Man. He looked at him through the eyes of every other teenager on the hillside. He looked at him through Saffi's eyes, and through Bardock's eyes. And they all looked through his eyes.

The Old Man anticipated the danger and, with instincts honed over two and a half million years, switched from fight to flight. He directed all his power away from the children and into an immediate retreat, intending to fly far away from the incredible build-up of energy he detected.

Nothing happened. He couldn't move. He was pinned like a butterfly in a museum case.

Onemind dissolved around him, his hold over the others broken. The Old Man's vision clouded, and he dropped from the sky, his body hitting the rocks, ending up sprawled across the Devil's Chair. Still unable to move, he tasted blood in his mouth, and bubbles of fluid turned his next inhalation into a gargle. His legs were broken and twisted, his spine snapped.

He knew what came next. He waited for the rapid breakdown of the body and the return to his dormant state.

It didn't happen. His tolerance for pain was so high that he prevented the body from slipping into unconsciousness, instead, opening his eyes.

He was not alone.

Hovering in the dusk sky were the last of the First, hands extended, expressions blank.

He knew then that onemind had not dissolved at all. He had been forced out. Desperately, he focussed his ancient mind, relying on his strength to overcome the weak minds around him. But his strength had gone, along with his power, his identity, and his Purpose. He couldn't remember why he was there, what he was doing. He was lost.

When the end came, it wasn't painful. His sense of who he was had fallen away from him like discarded clothing, so when the particles which made up his form loosened, the force binding them together letting go, he felt nothing.

His last coherent thought came after words and concepts had lost all meaning. But he didn't need words to know Khryseis. Her eyes, her smile, reaching him across millennia.

The First watched as every particle making up the Old Man's body detached itself from its neighbour. From the human observers' point of view, it was as if the Old Man disappeared, but the First knew every atom that had once made up his body was still present. They had been scattered so comprehensively across the globe that they would never find each other again. That particular pattern, the one that had survived an ice age and witnessed the evolution of sentient life, only to lose its way entirely... that pattern would never be reassembled.

The Old Man was dead.

42

Daniel limped out of the motor home, pushing TripleDee in a wheelchair. Following them was someone who looked like Daniel's twin, only he had two eyes, didn't limp and was seven-foot-two.

The odd trio crossed the few yards to the warehouse door, nodded to the soldiers standing guard, and went inside.

The interior of the warehouse was a scene from a surrealist painting. Ten large squares of plastic sheeting were spread out in the centre of the room. Standing on each of them was a member of the First. Next to each piece of sheeting was a steel canister, supplied by the European Space Agency.

Daniel stopped as Saffi approached, speaking into a phone.

"Of course," she said, flashing a reassuring smile at Daniel. "Yes, we'll let you know when it's done. Yes, I watched the joint press conference. You're right. A noble decision that we must all respect. Yes, I will, Prime Minister. Goodbye."

Daniel kissed her cheek. Saffi turned to his taller lookalike. Abos had grown this new form using Daniel's blood, after the fall at the Stiperstones had crushed his last body.

"This is what you want, Abos?"

Daniel's golden-eyed twin picked his words carefully. "It is the decision of the First. This is not our planet anymore."

TripleDee grunted. "Well, I think you're all full of shite. No one's asking you to do this, are they?"

Abos considered TripleDee's words before answering. "That is true. It seems humanity may be changing."

Since the events at the Devil's Chair, and the subsequent surrender of the First, the United Nations had hosted an unprecedented emergency meeting where every country on Earth was represented. The decision they needed to make must be made by all.

What should be done with the First?

In a series of statements, Abos and the First had revealed the intention of the Old Man that their species should become dominant once more. Humanity learned how close it had come to losing its position at the top of the food chain. The dissemination through all media channels of the events on the Stiperstones meant the actions of the halfheroes' children were already being written into history. The international delegates who met in Geneva did so with a new resolve and a shared optimism. They had all experienced the moment of connection. Even those who had been asleep had woken knowing everything had changed.

While the UN deliberated, the First moved into the Cornish warehouse where their brief taste of freedom had begun only weeks earlier. The blast-proof shelter had been removed, and some basic amenities set up by the military. The motor homes where they slept had been loaned by a local company, and nearby supermarkets sent boxes of food every day.

Linked once again by onemind, the First had been passive ever since the battle at the Devil's Chair. Although Abos was dominant, he refused to give onemind any direction. Instead, he waited for a consensus to emerge.

It took longer than anyone expected. Onemind had always been guided, but the First had seen the deeper connection of the human children and wanted to mirror it as far as possible. Eventually, a decision emerged, and the First began their preparations.

"What your children are becoming," said Abos, "is beyond anything of which the First are capable. Your species is evolving. Mine stopped a long, long time ago."

The decision had been relayed to the UN the previous night and was quickly ratified.

Daniel turned to face his father. This body was the most disconcerting yet. Having conversations with someone who was a better-looking, younger, taller, broader and stronger version of himself was bad enough. The fact that this flattering mirror image was Daniel's parent made the encounter stranger still.

"Abos. If you could stay, if you could be with us, I mean... would you?"

"The decision of the First—"

"That's not what I asked." Daniel realised he had spoken harshly and lowered his voice. "Please. Answer the question."

~

THE PRESIDENT of the United States and the prime minister

of Great Britain shared the podium at the United Nations press conference.

The world was watching as the two leaders shook hands, smiling. No one had to be an expert in body language to know that the handshake and smiles were genuine rather than the usual political necessities accompanied by teeth-grinding and muttered threats.

The prime minister, previously notable only for her ability to appear in every newspaper photograph looking as if she'd just remembered she'd left the gas on, waited for the members of the world's press to settle down before stepping forward.

"As you know, we received a request from the First yesterday afternoon."

It was hardly a secret. Abos had dropped from the sky outside the UN building in front of more than a thousand cameras.

"We have discussed the request today, and it has been unanimously approved. Mister President?"

The president took over. Since the event on the Stiperstones, which was now known internationally as the Moment, his vocabulary hadn't changed, but his leadership style and intentions had.

"Ladies and gentlemen, most of us now know the history of the First." Somewhat of an understatement. Saffi Narad's series of interviews with Abos was, it was estimated, viewed over a hundred thousand times every minute.

The president pointed towards the sky. "Long before our great, great species began its journey of evolution, the first intelligent species on Earth left this planet to search for a new home among the stars. Incredible. Those few left behind used their knowledge and technology to survive.

Those few came close to turning on us. If they had, they would have been losers. Big losers."

The leader of the free world got back on track.

"The great news from this meeting—and it's been a tremendous meeting, one of the best—is that we all agreed that the First can go."

When his statement wasn't greeted by a round of applause or a barrage of questions, the president realised he may not have been clear.

"Up there," he said, pointing forcefully. "That's where they're going. The First. Into space. A joint mission, involving the cooperation of the United States, Europe, Russia, China, and... other great, great countries. All the best countries. The First are going to look for a new planet. Maybe find the rest of their species."

∼

AIR FORCE ONE left Swiss airspace two hours later. The president spent the first hour of the flight in an introspective mood, looking out of the window at the sunlit wisps of cloud as the jet banked away from Europe and headed home.

"Casey?"

The president's press secretary had watched her boss with a kind of reluctant admiration ever since the Moment. The first change had been a swift and comprehensive reshuffle of his advisors, meaning his inner circle now comprised men and women who, in their Commander-in-Chief's own words, would "keep me on the straight and narrow, let me know if I'm going wrong. No yes-men! Or yes-women!"

The second change had been these quiet moods. Casey

had spent the few months of her job competing with the television the president kept on during their meetings. Now, her boss seemed to have weaned himself off twenty-four-hour news and social media. It was common to have conversations where he appeared to be listening. Even when what she was saying wasn't what he wanted to hear.

Casey couldn't even remember the last time he'd looked at her cleavage.

She unbuckled and went across to the president, taking the seat opposite.

"Sir?"

"Casey, I want to apologise."

"Sir?"

"I've never taken you seriously. To be honest, I only hired you because you were the best-looking candidate, and you have great breasts."

Casey had rehearsed the speech in which she quit so many times in her head, that she could hardly believe it when her mouth opened and she said,

"Er, what? sir?"

"You heard me. And I'm sorry. I mean, they are great breasts, but they shouldn't have been a factor. You're bright, you're capable, and God knows you're patient. You've had to be."

He leaned forward, still not checking out her cleavage. Weird.

"It's not just you, Casey. It's all women. I've never thought women were my equals. I'm making a list of the stuff I got wrong."

"Sir?" Was she ever going to speak more than one syllable again?

"It's a long list. I won't run for a second term. America needs stability, so I'll stay on until then. Leaders are supposed to serve the people, but that's not what I had in mind when I ran for office. I haven't been a good president, but I hope to be a good man."

He sat back and, finally, flashed one tiny look at her blouse. "Hey, that was statesmanlike, right? Can I copyright it?"

He hadn't changed unrecognisably, then.

Casey made her way back to her seat, stunned. After a few minutes, she pressed the button for the stewardess, ordering a bottle of champagne. When the stewardess opened it and poured a glass, she grabbed the bottle.

"Go get another glass, sister," she said, patting the seat next to her. "We're sharing this."

∼

THE ATMOSPHERE WAS SOMBRE when the military personnel were admitted to the warehouse. They watched with barely disguised fascination as Daniel poured pools of slime from the plastic sheeting into the canisters.

The nine canisters left the warehouse in the back of an armoured personnel carrier and were driven to Newquay airport under police escort where they were loaded onto an anonymous grey military plane.

In Baikonur Cosmodrome in southern Kazakhstan, preparations were already underway. The behemoth which stood on the launch pad, its mission to Mars cancelled, was the Kestrel Giant, a rocket developed by an American billionaire and a Chinese technology company. The fact this international rocket was launching from a Russian base showed how quickly the world's governments could cooperate when necessary.

On arrival, the containers were loaded onto the Kestrel.

A TV signal would be played on a loop from the rocket as it headed out of our solar system, broadcasting images and video of the First in their dormant state. The odds that they would find their ancestors were astronomical, but if intelligent life was out in the far reaches, the First might encounter it and begin a new existence. It was their decision, and the world had honoured it.

The launch was scheduled to go ahead in three days' time.

∾

IN HER STUDIO, Bardock turned from the canvas she was working on and turned up the radio. The news reader had just announced the date and time of the First's departure.

She let her mind return to the Stiperstones and that last dramatic day. Her body relaxed and her shoulders dropped, her eyes no longer seeing the half-finished painting.

Four minutes later, Jake came in, looked at her, put a fresh cup of tea down, took the cold cup from her fingers, then left without speaking.

Ten minutes after that, Bardock moved, stretching her back and rolling her shoulders.

"Nope," she said, "I don't buy it."

She took a sip of the new cup of tea and spat it out when she realised it was cold.

Grabbing the overnight case she kept packed under the bed, she headed out to the car, stopping to graze Jake's cheek with a kiss.

"Back in a day or two," she said.

"Righty-ho."

43

With poetic timing, the United Nations made two announcements on the same day Kestrel Giant began its journey to the stars.

The first was that the UN would oversee an new programme of international cooperation on environmental policies, human rights and wealth distribution. That last item led to the second announcement. All member countries of the United Nations voted to reinstate two of Titus Gorman's original demands. Pharmaceutical companies would now be non-profit, developing medicines to help those who needed it, rich and poor alike. And, in every company in a UN country, the CEO's salary could never exceed ten times that of the lowest-paid worker.

News, comment, and photographs of this story scrolled across the bottom of every TV screen as they showed live footage of the Kestrel Giant's final minutes on Earth.

In Cornwall, in the front room of a rented cottage, three people huddled around a small screen. The room's furniture hadn't been replaced since the 1970s. There was a faded reproduction of Van Gogh's *Sunflowers* on the wall. The only personal touch was the two photographs on the mantelpiece. The first showed a pile of large stones on the Long Mynd. The second was of the IGLU team - Gabe, Sara, and Daniel, raising bottles of beer in salute and laughing.

In front of a three-bar gas fire, a large ginger cat was dozing.

"This is ridiculous," said TripleDee. He was out of the wheelchair now, but still moving cautiously, his body a mass of bruises and slowly mending torn muscles. He was pointing at the television. "I mean, what the hell is that? This is the twenty-first century. How big is that screen? Ten inches?"

"Twenty," said Saffi. "Now sit back, I can't see. Here, have a biscuit."

"It's not even a flat screen," said TripleDee.

Saffi put a hand on Daniel's leg, and he shifted position so he could put his arm around her.

"Launch in three minutes."

A crowd of thousands had gathered at the Baikonur Cosmodrome, and billions were watching online and on television. It wasn't every day you witnessed the last members of an entire species leaving their planet.

TripleDee checked his phone for the tenth time in the past hour.

"Hey, she emailed! Sophie, I mean. She's back at home with her mum and dad. Well, I'm her dad, but you know what I mean. He brought her up and everything, and I only met her last week. Okay, to be fair, he's her dad, you're right. Sorry."

"We didn't say anything," said Daniel.

"You didn't have to. You were thinking it. Well, I said you're right, okay, so give it a rest."

"Whatever you say, Trip." Daniel smirked as TripleDee flinched at the nickname.

"I've told you about that, Daniel. How would you like it if I called you... um?"

"Dan?" said Daniel.

"Yeah. Dan. How would you like it, eh?"

"Dan's fine, Trip."

"Oh, piss off."

"What does she say?" said Saffi. Trip looked back at his phone.

"She's still in touch with the rest. Not emails or texts, like. I mean they're still, you know, they're still doing that thing they do. Like onemind but different. That whole connection hoobeejoobee."

"Hoobeejoobee?"

TripleDee ignored the interruption. "She's taken up the guitar. Bet she'll be brilliant. I'll have to give her some tips on who she needs to listen to. Foo Fighters, Pearl Jam, Johnny Marr for some old school stuff, Prince of course..."

He read more of the email and looked up at Daniel and Saffi.

"She says she wants to play like... ah, no way. Ed Sheeran? She's no daughter of mine."

"One minute to go," said Saffi, pointing at the screen. TripleDee took another biscuit.

Daniel offered the packet to Saffi, but she shook her head. "Doesn't seem right, does it? Marking an occasion like this with a custard cream?"

"Maybe you're right," said Daniel. "I'll get Jaffa Cakes."

He stood up, but Saffi pulled him back down to the sofa. "Don't you dare miss it," she said.

They all looked up when the doorbell rang.

"Bloody great timing," said TripleDee as Daniel got up to answer the door. "Tell them to sod off."

Daniel opened the door. "TripleDee says to sod off," he said. "Oh. Hello again. Come in."

TripleDee and Saffi turned round to see Bardock walk into the room. She was dressed in jeans and a shirt.

"Hello," she said. "Sorry to intrude. It's not an official visit."

She saw the television.

"Oh," she said, "it's happening today. I'd forgotten."

"You'd forgotten?" repeated TripleDee.

"Shh," said Saffi, turning up the volume.

Bardock and Daniel stood behind the sofa as the countdown descended from ten to one. A plume of smoke blossomed under the Kestrel Giant, billowing out towards the camera. The massive rocket eased away from the launchpad, slowly at first, as the power beneath it continued to grow. Flames were visible now, a white heat hard to look at even on TV, the brightness levels fluctuating as the camera struggled to deal with the intensity of the light.

No one in the small front room said anything as the rocket built up speed and headed towards the heavens. It escaped Earth's gravitational pull after two and a half minutes. The nine engines that got it there shut off, and the first stage dropped away. The next camera shot was from the Kestrel itself, as stage two engines ignited, and it began its journey into the unknown.

"Cup of tea?" said Daniel.

Bardock shook her head.

"It's been a strange few weeks," she said. She sat down in the chair Daniel pulled out for her. "I have always felt separate. Different. Alone. I was used to it. Now, I have half-brothers. And hundreds of nephews and nieces."

She sipped her tea. The others waited for her to speak again.

"In that moment—the Moment, everyone calls it that now, don't they?— I was me, then I was everybody. Which is what we all experienced. When I was me again, I had changed, but I was the same. Is this making any sense?"

They all nodded. Saffi leaned forward and took Bardock's hand, the way she had at the Devil's Chair. Bardock twitched, but didn't pull away.

"After the debrief, I went home," she said. "We had reporters at the end of the drive for a week, but they didn't push me when I said I wouldn't talk to them. Reporters respecting a request for privacy. People have changed, haven't they? I tried to paint, but I couldn't, because it doesn't fit."

"I'm sorry," said Daniel. "What do you mean? What doesn't fit?"

"You," she said. "TripleDee. And Saffi. Your actions. Even now, watching the launch on television. Doesn't fit."

"We thought it would be too much of a circus if we went to Baikonur," said Saffi.

Bardock looked her in the eye. "Don't lie," she said, "it's pointless."

Daniel exchanged a look with TripleDee and Saffi.

"What are you talking about?" he said. "You're not making sense."

Bardock sighed. "Abos. Your father. You let him go."

Daniel coughed. "It was the decision of the First. The UN agreed. If they had stayed, there would always be the fear they might turn on us again. It was the right thing to do. However hard it was for us."

"Mm," said Bardock noncommittally. She stood up. "Like

I said, not an official visit. I had to put all the pieces in place, see if I was right. I've done that. Now I can go."

She took a card out of her pocket and handed it to Saffi.

"I live in a beautiful part of Wiltshire," she said. "You might like to visit sometime. All of you. And I do mean *all* of you."

"Thanks," said Saffi, standing to see her out. When they reached the door, Daniel stood up.

"First, you say we're lying. Then you say you're right about something. What are you right about?"

"Forget it," said Bardock. "I'm retired. Don't have to report everything, do I?"

She opened the door and paused on the step.

"Lovely cat," she said.

Even though the ginger tom was curled up tightly, it was one of the biggest felines Bardock had ever seen. At the sound of her voice, its ears twitched, and it raised its head. The enormous cat opened one stunning, golden eye, stared at Bardock for a moment, then dropped its head back onto the rug.

Hundreds of miles above them, still accelerating, eight canisters of dormant superheroes and one of mushy peas began their long voyage to the stars.

THE END

AUTHOR'S NOTE

I'm a podcast fan. In the car, walking the dog, ironing. (Not ironing the dog. That would be wrong. I don't listen to podcasts while ironing the dog; I listen to audiobooks). My regular listens are Wittertainment—Mark Kermode and Simon Mayo's film review show—Mastertapes and Desert Island Discs from the BBC, and Adam Buxton's podcast (even the adverts he records for his sponsors are funny.) I've always enjoyed radio, but podcasts allow me to create my own station. Radio Sainsbury. It's a great listen, but I would say that, wouldn't I?

I also listen to podcasts about the craft and business of writing. Mark Dawson's Self Publishing Formula, Joanne Penn, and The Bestseller Experiment have become favourites. I've binged on The Bestseller Experiment recently, and it's been a fascinating listen.

Hosted by Mark One and Mark Two (no, really, Mark Stay and Mark Desvaux,) TBE's conceit is that the two presenters would try to write, publish, and market a bestselling book in fifty-two weeks. Spoiler alert: I came late to this party. The fifty-two weeks were up long ago, and, sure enough, *Back To Reality* hit number one in its Amazon categories, even dislodging Neil Gaiman from the top spot in comedy fantasy. Independently published, like me. Not too shabby. I bought it. I think I owe the Marks that much for all the great content. (Which is part of the secret to their success. I imagine most of their regular listeners bought the book. We're invested in their project, so it's the least we can do.)

Many episodes of TBE feature an interview with a successful author. They're fascinating. It's educational to hear the variety of ways they approach their work. Some write at night, others in the morning. Some go to a coffee shop, others put their computers in front of a blank wall at home (me included.) There are writers who have a soundtrack for each book, and they play their chosen music *loudly* while writing. Others must have silence. I have wind and rain noises, or—a recent discovery—dark ambient music, on my headphones. Ten thousand words a day is routine for a few writers, but there are some bestselling authors out there who are delighted to get five hundred words down.

Bear with me. There's a point to all this, and here it is: everyone writes differently. But, once they find what works for them, they stick to it until it doesn't work anymore. When I sit down, put the headphones on, and stop looking at the sodding internet, I experience a moment of fear and doubt. I don't know if I can do it, put one word after another, populate that white screen with characters. And even if I do, why would anyone want to read it? What if it's boring, derivative, un-engaging, or just plain shit? What made me think I could do this?

I doubt Neil Gaiman has the same knot in his gut when he starts a writing session. Maybe he does. Maybe it's normal. The cure for it is—you guessed it—to write. One terrible sentence is better than no sentences. It can lead to a terrible paragraph. Once I've written a terrible paragraph, I can see how it can be improved. I go back and tweak, then I keep writing. That's what works for me... now. Ask me again in six months, I guarantee it'll be different.

The Last Of The First is my seventh book, and it's nearly three years since I wrote the first chapter of The World Walker. If I count up all the words before the books were edited, that's around six hundred and sixty thousand words of prose. Someone said (who is this *someone* person who says this stuff?) that it takes a million words before you become a competent writer. Three or four more books and I'll have no more excuses. I'm still learning, and improving, as a writer, but I suspect the process is never-ending. It's probably a good thing to sit down with that fear and doubt and write my way past it every morning.

There's a little more fear than usual this week. I'm starting something new. I had the basic idea for the story months ago while sheltering under a tree in a cemetery during a spectacular thunderstorm. Seriously. I am not making this up. I made notes on my phone, getting increasingly excited. And colder. And wetter. Last month, we had a family holiday, and I filled over twenty notebook pages with notes. I've written the opening of the first chapter twice... and abandoned both attempts. I've made more notes. Now I'm ready.

This week, I'll start properly. It's a fantasy book with one foot in our world. It deals with creativity and magic, grief, redemption, and the nature of evil. It may also feature a telepathic lobster that predicts the future.

Or I may not write that book yet. I might write something entirely new and come back to that idea later. It's all part of what makes this scary, and fun.

I have so many ideas, and I want to be a better writer, which means writing more books. There's no other method available, no shortcuts. For this plan to work, I need readers, and you've stuck with me so far. For that, I'm extremely grateful. If you enjoy my books, please leave reviews on Amazon. I also love to hear from readers, so here's how you can get in touch and find out what I'm up to next.

My mailing list gets my book news before anyone else does, and I'll send you the unpublished World Walker prologue, plus some fun, action-packed chapters cut from Children Of The Deterrent. Sign up here:
http://http://bit.ly/signupiws

My website and blog is where I post cover reveals, excerpts, and the occasional piece about writing
http://www.ianwsainsbury.com

The Facebook page is fairly active, and I'm good at responding to messages
http:///www.facebook.com/IanWSainsbury/

I'm having a bash at tweeting @IanWSainsbury

And there's always good old email - ianwsainsbury@gmail.com

As always, thanks for reading. I love doing this, so if you love reading it, let me know, let your friends know, let your pet know (if they have an Amazon account), and, most importantly, let your aunt who works for Netflix know ;)

In the winter of 1986, I was on a train coming back from Leeds University (Philosophy degree, lasted a term, dropped out to join a band). My destination was Shrewsbury where I grew up (opinions differ as to whether this has yet occurred). I was reading a book, and I wish I could tell you what it was, but it was a long time ago. I suspect it was Isaac Asimov, Ray Bradbury, or Stephen King. I was so engrossed that I missed my stop. When I looked up from the page, I was in Prestatyn, on the North Wales coast, and Shrewsbury was an hour and forty-five minutes in the opposite direction. I found a payphone and called my mother. She was unsurprised when I told her why I was in the wrong country.

Occasionally, I forget this is the best job in the world (for about ten minutes while I wrestle with a difficult paragraph), then someone emails me, or tweets, or posts on Facebook, because they enjoyed one of my books, and I am reminded why I'm doing this. I'm doing it because I want to write books that might, one day, make someone forget to get off the train at the right stop. Let me know if that's you.

Ian W. Sainsbury
   Norwich, 30th July 2018

ALSO BY IAN W. SAINSBURY

Children Of The Deterrent (Halfhero 1)
Halfheroes (Halfhero 2)
The World Walker (The World Walker 1)
The Unmaking Engine (The World Walker 2)
The Seventeenth Year (The World Walker 3)
The Unnamed Way (The World Walker 4)

Printed in Poland
by Amazon Fulfillment
Poland Sp. z o.o., Wrocław